D1603147

THE
BLACKMAIL

M. RAVENEL

CHIKARA PRESS

The Blackmail
(The Plainclothes Tootsie Mysteries — book 2)

Copyright © 2022 by M. Ravenel
All Rights Reserved.

All rights reserved, including the right to reproduce, distribute, or transmit this book or portions thereof in any form whatsoever.

This book is a work of fiction. Any references to historical events, real people, or real places are used fictitiously. Other names, characters, places, and events are products of the author's imagination, and any resemblance to actual events or places or persons, living or dead, is entirely coincidental.

In accordance with the U.S. Copyright Act of 1976, the scanning, uploading, and electronic sharing of any part of this book without the permission of the publisher is unlawful piracy and theft of the author's intellectual property. If you would like to use material from the book (other than for review purposes), prior written permission must be obtained by contacting the publisher. Thank you for your support of the author's rights.

The publisher and author acknowledge the trademark status and trademark ownership of all trademarks, service marks, and word marks mentioned in this book.

Printed in the United States of America

ISBN: 978-1-7364913-4-8 (hardcover)

10 9 8 7 6 5 4 3 2 1

THE
BLACKMAIL

CHAPTER 1

Bronx, New York, 1975

Today was turning out to be one of those rare slow days. No phone calls, no clients, no paperwork. Just one of those days when I could relax in my office apartment and catch up on the latest news. The latter ended up being a wasted effort resulting in more of the same: Watergate hearings, skyrocketing inflation, more gas shortages, New York City edging closer to bankruptcy, murders, Mafia wars, pollution... oh, and rumors that the sanitation workers were threatening to go on strike again. Lovely. I didn't know why I bothered reading or watching the news anymore.

A series of heavy thumps echoed outside my front door, jolting me out of reading the *Dick Tracy* strip in the newspaper. I straightened in my desk chair and looked toward the door. Behind the slats of the half-opened blinds, a large shadowy figure was slinking around in the hallway. Frowning, I set aside the newspaper and got up from my desk. *If this is another attempted robbery, I swear…* It wasn't even noon yet. Criminals were getting bolder each day. The previous week had set a new record for my building—seven attempted break-ins, two in the same day. The head shop next door, owned by my neighbor, Beth Turner, had been the latest target. Beth blamed it on the fact that she'd run out of her magical "evil eye repellent." She was a special one, that Beth.

The thumps echoed again, louder, sounding like the person was using their foot to knock rather than their knuckles. I clenched my jaw. *Looks like I have to chase away another annoying punk.* At least I wouldn't have to pay rent this month, thanks to my swell deal with the landlord. Oh, the perks of being an ex-cop.

I opened my bottom desk drawer, grabbed my snub-nosed Colt .38 from its holster, and crept toward the door. The stranger was still in the hallway, pacing in front of the door of my other neighbor, Crazy Bob, the weird guy who never left his apartment. Not sure how he got that name—or if Bob was even his name at all—but the neighbors around here called him that, and it sorta stuck. No one had ever seen Crazy Bob, and when I'd first moved into the building, I didn't think anyone lived next door at all. Then, one night, I was awakened by the sounds of clackity typewriter keys, bells, and the occasional violent crumpling of paper from his apartment. Since then, those typewriter sounds were my only indication that someone was still alive over there.

Crazy Bob's visitor was a tall man who appeared to be in his late thirties. He had a broad build, sported a wavy blond mop top that covered his ears, and wore a pair of aviator sunglasses. He looked important, dressed sharply in a grey, three-piece Wall Street–quality suit, but I knew he was up to no good when he whipped out something from his coat pocket and huddled close to the door.

I rolled my tongue in my cheek. *Does he really think he's being discreet?* Robbers were as stupid as they were bold.

I flung my door open and aimed my gun at him. "Freeze, sucker."

The man paused, and his head snapped toward me, his eyebrows rising from behind the sunglasses. "H-Hey! Don't shoot!" he pleaded, his face paling as his shaky hands bolted up in surrender. A fat ballpoint pen dropped out of one hand, and a paper-filled manila folder flew out of the other.

I glanced at the paper-strewn mess on the floor then looked back at him and scowled. "You have three seconds to explain yourself," I demanded, keeping the gun aimed.

The man's Adam's apple bobbed. "I... I'm, uh... the tax collector. Yeah, that's right. I'm here on official business."

Hearing the hesitation in his voice, I kept my gun aimed. For all I knew, that was all a front to get my guard down. Criminals were getting craftier every time they attempted robbery in this building.

"Oh yeah? Where're your credentials?"

He sneered. "I don't have to show you nothing."

"Is that so? What kind of 'tax collecting' business are you up to that involves disturbing the peace?"

"What are you, a cop?"

"Not anymore, but I still have a gun. And you haven't answered my question. Your time is up. Beat it, or else."

His jaw tightened. "You ain't gonna shoot me, baby."

Baby... Gritting my teeth, I cocked the hammer. "Try me, turkey."

Beth's door flung open behind me. I looked over my shoulder in time to see her race out, holding a broom over her head, one of those old besom brooms I'd always associated with cartoon witches. I hadn't thought those brooms actually existed. Then again, in Beth's case, nothing surprised me.

"We're being robbed again!" Beth said, glancing at me. Then her hazel gaze swiveled toward the stranger, and she gasped. "You! You bastards just don't give up, do you?" She rushed at the man, screeching a hair-raising battle cry and swinging her broom wildly.

The man panicked, looking between me and Beth. Before he could react, Beth whacked him hard in the head, sending small pieces of besom straw flying. The man sank to his knees, covering his head.

"Stop! Stop it, you crazy bitch!" he cried.

"Bring our troops home! *Bring. Them. Home!*" Beth chanted, emphasizing each word with another whack.

For a moment, I wasn't sure what to do. Beth seemed to be handling the guy on her own. But I still wanted to know who he was and why he was here. Seeing that the situation was under control, I uncocked my gun and slipped it into my waistband. Then I grabbed Beth by the back of her shirt and pulled her away from the man.

"Hey, easy there. How about we give him one last chance to explain why he's here?" I said.

Beth panted heavily, looking back at me with fire in her eyes. "This suited heathen is a G-man! He's going to take us all in!" She tightened her grip on the broom and tried to pull away to dish out round two on him. "We must resist, Tootsie. We must not fight another rich man's war!"

I fisted the back of her shirt then returned my attention to the man. His sunglasses were crooked on his face as he regarded the both of us, half confused, half spooked.

"Better start talking," I warned him.

"I-I'm gonna sue you both for this! Sue you both for everything you got, just like I'm gonna sue that son of a bitch in there!" He thumbed toward Bob's door.

I arched an eyebrow. "What are you suing Bob for?"

"Defamation of character, that's what. I'm gonna rip him apart!" The man growled and looked toward Bob's door. "Come outta there, you fucking coward! Face me like a man!"

Beth let out another growl, and the man cowered again.

"Not good enough," I said. "Now, here's a tip: leave and don't come back, or else I'll have Beth here finish you off."

Beth raised the broom again, ready to strike. "That's right, get lost, you piece of shit!" she barked. "Go back to your dirtbag boss and tell him to end this fucking war!"

"Get away from me!" The man scrambled to his feet, grabbed his scattered papers, then bolted down the stairs. "This ain't over!" he yelled over his shoulder, barreling down another flight of stairs on the third floor. "I'm gonna sue all of you for attacking me!"

At last, I heard the main lobby's steel entrance door crash open, and the sounds of hurried footsteps disappeared. I finally let go of Beth's shirt. She white-knuckled the broom handle at her side as if daring the man to return.

Geez Louise! I'd never seen her that riled up before. I was beginning to wonder if she thought all men in suits were G-men. Or maybe she'd had herself a real good smoke earlier that morning.

"Hey, you all right?" I asked in a calm, soft voice.

Beth whirled and faced me, her eyes still burning with rage as though she was about to pummel me next.

"Whoa! It's me! Tootsie!" I assured her, raising my hands in surrender.

Beth's face softened. Her body relaxed, and she loosened her grip on the broom. "Oh, Tootsie, I'm sorry. I hope that son of a bitch didn't hurt you."

I gave her a reassuring smile. "No, I'm fine. I caught him loitering around Crazy Bob's apartment. He looked like he was up to something shady. You sure spooked him good."

She huffed. "Serves him right. How dare he come around here and try and recruit more innocent people to their deaths! I'm going to assemble a rally in front of city hall. We must speak out against this atrocity!"

"A... *rally?*" I slapped my forehead. "Ugh... for the last time, Beth, the war is over. When was the last time you read the newspaper?"

"It's all propaganda, Tootsie," Beth said. "The media is trying to distract us from what is important. They want us to believe the war is over."

"It is over, Beth. Saigon surrendered. Our troops are home. It was on the front page of practically every newspaper in the country last month. I have a clipping. I can show it to you."

She shook her head. "Don't get caught up in those lies. Stand with me during the rally, please."

I looked at her dubiously. "Do you even know what year this is?"

She regarded me with a slight raise of her eyebrow, as if she thought I was being facetious, but I really wasn't. I truly hoped to learn more about what went on in that wild mind of hers.

Finally, her expression hardened, and she marched back to her shop. "Don't mock me, Tootsie."

I followed her. "It's just a question. Do you know who our current president is?"

She opened her shop door. "Oh, for Pete's sake," she grumbled, shooting me an annoyed look. "Yes, Tootsie. It's Lyndon Johnson. Happy now? Goodbye." She stormed inside and slammed the door in my face. She flipped the sign suctioned to the glass from Open to Closed and rolled down the shade.

Dumbfounded, I stared at the door for a moment, then I rubbed my temples. My head hurt. I was thoroughly convinced that nothing could get Beth out of her weird, time-warped mind. Whether the cause was the drugs or that she really was a time-traveler or just plain crazy remained a mystery, one that not even *I* knew how to solve.

With Beth and the mysterious sue-happy stranger gone, I headed back toward my apartment. But I spotted the dropped ballpoint pen lying on the floor in front of Crazy Bob's door and carefully picked it up. I avoided handling it too much, to not disturb the fingerprints that were most likely present. I intended to do a little investigating later.

Crazy Bob's door had been replaced a couple months ago with a reinforced steel one after an attempted robbery that resulted in a stray bullet shattering the glass in his old door, which he'd kept covered with newspaper. This new door had no glass but a small peephole. It cost Sam the landlord a pretty penny to replace, but he hadn't had a problem since.

I listened at Bob's door for typewriter sounds but heard none. I chewed my bottom lip. *Is he even in there?* I wondered. I knocked on the door softly. "Bob? Are you okay? It's Tootsie Carter, your next-door neighbor."

I waited a beat. The silence continued.

I knocked again. "Bob? I just wanted to check on you. Someone was trying to break into your apartment, so I—"

The doorknob jiggled, and the door partially creaked open. The odor of cigarettes and whiskey flooded out from the dark apartment. I waited for someone to appear at the door, but nobody came into view. *Is he hiding?* I craned my neck, trying to get a peek behind the door, but it was open just far enough to cut off my line of sight. Bob sure was good at staying invisible.

"Uh... Bob?" I called meekly.

Another brief round of silence. Then a masculine arm snaked out from behind the door. The sleeve of a red-plaid flannel shirt was rolled up, revealing a thick, muscle-bound, olive-skinned forearm covered in dark hair. A big silver luxury watch decorated his wrist. His hairy sausage fingers held out a ten-dollar bill.

I looked at the money and furrowed my brow. "I'm not asking for money. I was just checking up on you and making sure you were okay in there."

No answer. Instead, the money was shoved closer.

"Hey, I told you I wasn't asking for money. I just wanted to make sure—"

Bob released the bill. It fluttered down and landed at my feet. Afterward, his arm snaked back inside the apartment, and the door closed.

I blinked several times. *Of all the...* I stared at the money at my feet. Unfortunately, I couldn't slip it back under his door. *What was all that about?* I thought, wondering if it was a tip or maybe a bribe. His gesture seemed kind enough, albeit strange. I seemed to be a magnet for all sorts of oddities. Never a dull moment in this building.

So much for today being a slow one.

CHAPTER 2

I left Crazy Bob's door and returned to my office. As I was about to close the door, a woman scurried up the stairs and headed my way. I hovered my fingers near my gun, in case the lady was up to no good. She slowed when she reached the hallway, scanning the doors with a timid gaze, her forehead knotted in concentration. She finally halted at my door, checked something on a small business card she was holding, and regarded me with curious green eyes.

"Yes?" I said, scanning the woman carefully from head to toe. She was young, more striking than beautiful, but the kind that would stand out in a crowded room. Her navy-blue pantsuit, her petite handbag, and the updo style of her curly dark-brown hair hinted that she'd recently clocked out at the office. She seemed harmless enough.

"Is Detective Carter in?" the woman asked.

"That depends," I said.

She lifted an eyebrow and curled her lip. "On what?" she spat.

"Depends on what services you need."

She pinned her gaze on me. "I *need* a private investigator to handle an urgent matter. Where is Detective Carter?"

Clearing my throat, I tugged the hem of my shirt down to conceal my gun. "You're looking at her," I said with a lopsided smile.

She did a double take, then her face lit up. "Oh, wow. My apologies. And here I thought female detectives were only Hollywood fantasies. Hot damn, women's lib at its finest."

"Heh. And I also have my own credit card too." I gestured her inside.

"Right on, honey." She entered and glanced around my small office.

I sat behind my desk and carefully laid the confiscated pen atop the newspaper. "Have a seat," I said, gesturing to the wooden chair in the front.

The woman approached and paused, eyeing the chair cautiously.

"It ain't gonna bite, y'know," I said. *Though it'll make your rear feel like a numb flapjack afterward.*

The woman finally sat in the chair. Her face contorted slightly as she shifted in the seat, trying to get comfortable.

I fought down my cynical smile. I always got a kick out of watching visitors squirm in that chair as if they were in a police interrogation room. "So, what can I do for you, Miss, uh…?" I discreetly removed the gun from my waistband, opened the bottom desk drawer, and returned the weapon to its holster.

She grunted. "*Miz* Allison Hays, and I'll give it to you straight." She gripped her purse in her lap. "I need you to take some pictures of a cheating husband."

I swore that old-fashioned wooden school chair was the best one-dollar investment I'd ever made. I was convinced it had some sort of magical powers because everyone who sat in it tended to make their requests short and sweet. I retrieved my pocket notebook from the center desk drawer and a pen from the coffee can on my desk and began writing.

"All right, Ms. Hays," I said. "That sounds simple enough. Do you know where your husband might be right now?"

Allison shook her head slowly. "You've misunderstood, Detective. This isn't my husband."

I arched an eyebrow. "Come again?"

"I'm here on behalf of my boss, Mrs. Paige Russell," Allison explained.

I furrowed my brow. "Paige Russell?" I repeated. *Why does that name sound familiar?*

"Yes. We'd like to be discreet."

Then it hit me. Paige Russell was CEO of Gatestar Media and Distribution, one of the largest media outlets in the city. If *that* wasn't women's lib at its finest, I didn't know what was. "Of course," I said, putting on my serious face. "I'm all about discretion."

"She's been stressed out these past couple months, trying to keep up with things at the company."

A woman in her position? I'd be stressed too. "You guys run the *Tri-City Beat*, right?"

She nodded. "That's right. We also distribute magazines and comics to small specialty stores."

I perked up. *Comics.* Now *that* was the part of Gatestar Media that interested me. "So you're the ones who used to deliver the *Dick Tracy Monthly* issues to Slap Jack's Comics over on Lenox Avenue years ago?"

"Most likely. They were popular. We delivered them just about everywhere."

I grinned and returned my attention to the notepad. "Good to know. All right, back to your boss."

Allison fidgeted with her purse straps. "I'm worried about her, Detective. She doesn't believe her husband, Joey, is cheating on her. But I know he is. She won't listen to me, though, so I want to give her some solid proof."

"That's swell of you to look out for her best interests like that, but what makes you think Paige wants or needs to know that her husband is cheating?"

"Because she's in such a high-profile position and she'd be easy pickings for a scandal story from a rival newspaper. I'm just trying to save her and the company's reputation before it's too late. If word got out about this, my job and livelihood is on the line, too, you know."

I wrote some more notes. "I see. Well, I understand how that can be quite a dilemma for you."

"Tell me about it."

"So does her husband work there too?" I asked.

"Yeah, he's one of the advertising executives. He's usually out and about, visiting our clients' facilities and doing market research for their advertising campaigns."

"So what's the problem? Where does the cheating come in?"

Allison growled. "Joey has been going off to non-work-related places while still on the clock, and Paige doesn't even bat an eye about it. She's stressed out over this company as it is. Why would he do that to her?"

Maybe Joey got bored watching his wife go crazy and decided to make himself useful elsewhere, I thought. With all the infidelity cases I'd dealt with in the past, one would think I'd have some sort of an understanding of unhappy couples. But the concept of love stumped me as much as my neighbor Beth's trippy time-warped mind.

I cocked my head, looking curiously at Allison. "Does Mr. Russell ever come back from his... excursions?" I asked.

"Yeah." Allison scowled. "After Paige is in bed. She says he comes in stinking like lipstick and perfume."

I raised my eyebrows. "So Paige knows he's cheating? And she's ignoring it?"

"She's in denial. I think she's too stressed and exhausted to accept it. I don't know. I thought if she saw the proof, she'd snap out of it and kick his sorry ass to the curb."

"Right. So where do you think Mr. Russell goes?"

She paused and looked left and right as though she sensed someone was eavesdropping. Then she leaned forward in her chair and lowered her voice. "Well, I've been told that son of a bitch goes to an hourly hotel called the Peacock House. Every day at lunchtime, he takes a bus over to Mott Haven, where he meets some young floozy at the hotel."

I flipped to a fresh page in my notebook and continued writing. *The Peacock House.* Just the name alone sounded shady. Fitting place for a cheating dirtbag of a husband to go for a little fun. "So he leaves the office at lunchtime and doesn't come back?"

"That's right."

"That sounds like some very detailed information. Who told you this?"

She looked thoughtful for a moment. "A man called me two nights ago. I think his name was Frank. He said he was a friend of my colleague Cindy, but I didn't recognize him or his voice. Anyway, he apparently knew Joey and shared his utter distaste for the man. He said that he could help me take care of Joey and the trouble at the paper and told me to get some pictures of Joey caught in in the act. I figured this job was best done by a private investigator."

"I see," I said, writing more notes. "This man, Frank... does he work at Gatestar Media too?"

Allison shook her head. "Not that I know of. I was surprised he said he was a friend of Cindy, though."

"Why's that?"

"Well, she and I are close friends, almost sisters. We know each other's friends and social circles. I don't understand why she wouldn't tell me about Frank."

"Maybe he's a secret lover or something?" I shrugged.

Allison smiled wistfully. "Maybe. But we usually confide in each other about stuff like that, y'know?"

"Well, you know, weird things can happen when people are in love." I flipped to a new page in my notebook. "How does this Frank guy know about Joey?"

"I don't know, Detective. The only thing I can think of is that maybe Cindy told him at some point. She and I talked about Joey and all this mess last week during lunch."

"And you still trust her?"

"'Still'? I've always trusted her, Detective. She's never lied to me, nor would she ever have a reason to."

"Has Cindy ever gone to Paige about this?"

Allison shook her head. "No. She may be all about the gossip, but she's not the confrontational type."

"Hmm..." I rolled the pencil between my fingers like a cigarette as I studied my notes. "Did Frank leave any contact information? A telephone number, maybe?"

"Nope."

Of course not. I rolled my eyes. "How can I contact Cindy?"

"You can't, unfortunately. She's vacationing in Mexico this week."

"Well ain't that great," I said flatly. "Okay, so let me get this straight. You know what Joey is up to, but Paige doesn't have a clue... or at least is trying to pretend she doesn't?"

Allison nodded. "That's the gist of it, Detective."

"Have you tried just taking Paige over to the Peacock House and letting her see for herself?"

"Plenty of times. She says she's too busy to go or she doesn't think he would be there and it would all be a waste of time."

"Maybe she knows he's there but doesn't know what to do about it."

Allison snorted. "If it were me, I would've divorced his sorry ass a long time ago. I don't know why she's so naïve about this. It's like she doesn't even care about the future of the company, you know?"

"Yeah, I get it. Divorce isn't always easy, though. Lots of legal headaches involved. How long have Paige and Joey been married?"

Allison shook her head solemnly. "About a year and a half."

"I see..." I tapped the eraser of my pencil against my lips. "And how long has Joey been cheating on Paige?"

Allison averted her gaze a moment and rubbed her chin. "I noticed it happening not long after Paige's father died nine months ago."

I stopped writing and gawked at her. "Seriously?"

"Yeah. Terrible, ain't it? Joey is scum, I tell you. No remorse or decency."

"No wonder she's stressed. The pressures of her father's death and having to shoulder a huge company on her own must be overwhelming."

"That's putting it mildly. Her stubbornness about avoiding the truth is damaging the company's reputation, financially and ethically. Ever since her father's death, the company's profits have slowly started tanking."

"Well, that's not good." If Gatestar Media went under, I'd probably never be able to get another *Dick Tracy* comic strip again. *This is beyond criminal.*

She looked at me intently. "Will you take this job?"

"You just need some photos? Sounds like something you can do, honestly. Why don't you just tail Joey on your own?"

"I've thought about it, but I can't risk Joey spotting me. There's no telling what he might do to me if he knew I was onto him like that. No, Detective, I need someone on the outside to do this. Besides, I would think a professional like you would be able to get some clear, undeniable evidence of Joey's infidelity."

"Okay." I shrugged. "My rate is one seventy-five a day, plus expenses."

"Sounds reasonable. I'd also like the negatives too."

I arched an eyebrow. I normally kept the negatives for my own legal liabilities. The only clients who'd ever requested both the photos and the negatives tended to be attorneys, paralegals, and others working in the law field. While I technically couldn't deny her the right to the negatives as a paying client, her request still gave me pause. "Um, sure. It's fifty bucks extra."

"I can dig it." Allison stood up from the chair, a wave of relief spreading across her face. I wasn't sure if the relief was due to the fact that I'd accepted the job or that she was just glad to be out of that chair. "I'll have the money wired to you. Please get me those photos as soon as you can."

"Absolutely. Can you give me a description of Joey Russell?"

"About six-one, medium build, brown hair, dark eyes. Wears really expensive-looking three-piece suits. He's pretty much the tall, dark, and handsome type. If you can make a pile of shit look irresistible, then that's Joey."

I made a sour face as I wrote down the vague description. "Anything else of note about him?"

She looked thoughtful for a moment. "Oh, he wears this godawful silver ring that looks like a panther's head eating a human skull. It's really creepy."

"Ew." I wrinkled my nose. "Well, that is definitely helpful to know."

"Trust me, you'll know him when you see him."

"Uh... okay, I guess I'll have to take your word for it."

Allison gave me her contact information, and I saw her to the door. This case was in the bag. I'd probably produced more photos in my entire detective career than the Kodak and Polaroid companies combined. I had the art of photography down to a science. I guessed if I ever got tired of the shamus life, I could join the paparazzi instead.

After seeing Allison off, I locked the door and went to my bedroom. Opening my armoire, I revealed a wide selection of cameras and lenses of various shapes, sizes, and types displayed on the top shelf. I chose the top-of-the-line Canon EF, which I'd bought the previous year at a camera expo for a whopping five hundred bucks. Yeah, I burned a serious hole in my wallet, but geez Louise, did this thing take the most gorgeous, detailed photos. Added to the fact that the camera itself wasn't too bulky to hide under my coat, it was the perfect tool for today's job.

After grabbing the telephoto lens and the rest of my essentials, I slipped on my trench coat and fedora and left my office, ready to be a *paparazza* for a day.

CHAPTER 3

Traffic crawled to a halt during the Tuesday afternoon lunch hour as I was taking the bus across town to Mott Haven. Around one thirty, I got off at my stop. The Peacock House was on East 134th Street, which was a block away from the bus stop.

Walking through the seedy neighborhood, I observed the condemned, graffiti-covered buildings dotting the garbage-littered streets, with drunks and drug addicts brawling in an alley and young thugs skulking around, giving me side-eyed glares. I brushed past an old woman pushing a metal shopping cart piled high with clothes and canned food. The somber look on her weathered face painted a bleak picture of the reality of this dying city. The plague of despair and urban decay squeezed its soul-sucking grip on the far reaches of these slums like the Grim Reaper. But that dark cloud hadn't yet extended beyond the Harlem River, where Manhattan's distant glittering executive high-rises and skyscrapers tore through the thick, smoggy skies like beacons of hopes and dreams. The contrasting view was a constant reminder of how much more work I had to do to take back my home. Fighting crime was tedious because it tended to spread faster than a virus. The madness didn't seem to have an end, but I would be out of a job otherwise.

Wearing a fedora and trench coat on this warm spring day was overkill, but I'd grown accustomed to it. It was practically my work uniform—a leftover habit from my childhood, back when I'd pretended to be a famous detective like my hero, Dick Tracy. Yeah, I got the quizzical stares and snickers, but my gun, wallet, telephoto lens, and other items were safely stashed in my coat's deep pockets, which meant I didn't have to carry a bulky handbag or purse. Hands-free was the way to be in my line of work.

I stood in front of a run-down four-story weathered brick building. A couple of its windows were boarded up with graffiti-covered plywood. The glass behind the bars of the front entrance bore an image of an elegant peacock. *This must be the place,* I thought.

I entered the establishment, which opened into a tiny, drab room. A metallic sign of a peacock's image hung on the nicotine-stained wall behind a frazzled-haired older woman sitting at the front desk. With a cigarette held between her skinny fingers, her red-painted nails longer than a werecat's, the woman was reading the newspaper. I approached the desk, and her gaze swiveled up.

"Yeah? Whatcha want, honey?" she said in her raspy Brooklyn accent. She tilted her thick red-framed glasses down her nose.

I furrowed my brow, giving the woman a once-over. "Hello. Um, you run this place?"

"Sure do. Name's Paula. Need a room?"

"Uh… well…" I scratched the back of my head. "Can I ask a question first?"

She stared at me blankly, not responding.

I cleared my throat. "Ah, um, what kind of place is this?"

Her thin penciled eyebrow rose. "It's an hourly hotel, sweetie."

"So, uh... what sort of... *amenities* do you offer?"

She smiled crookedly. "The only amenities we offer is a place to sleep and shit."

"Really? Not even a television? Or a telephone? Or a stove? Or—"

"Ya dreamin,' sweetie."

"Sounds a bit contradictory for a place called The Peacock House, don't you think?"

Her crooked smile became smug, and she took a long drag of her cigarette. "I have an interesting sense of humor."

That's putting it mildly. This place might be a great incognito spot for Crazy Bob to hide away without being bothered by random creeps trying to break into his apartment. "All right," I told Paula. "What are your rates?"

"Five bucks an hour for the normal rooms. Deluxe rooms are ten." She exhaled smoke from her nostrils.

"You have any private rooms upstairs?"

"Yup. Those are the deluxe rooms. Only got two vacant. Want one?"

I rubbed my chin. Joey Russell sounded like a deluxe-room kind of slimeball. It seemed like a logical place to start.

But I needed to be sure. "Actually, ah, I have another question first."

She rolled her eyes then regarded me with slight annoyance.

I recalled my earlier encounter with Beth and her utter dislike of men in suits, which gave me an idea to ramp up my charade a little more. "Did a man in a suit come in here?" I asked.

She snorted. "Honey, men in suits always come in here."

"Look, it's important. It's my husband, see? I think he's cheating on me, and somebody told me they saw him come in here."

The annoyance in her eyes turned to curiosity. "Yeah, there's a guy in a suit staying here. Brought a pretty young thing with him too." She paused and looked me over. "Guess he likes 'em young."

I swallowed, feigning shock. "R-Really? Was he tall? Medium build? Dark hair, dark eyes?"

She gave a half shrug. "Eh, maybe. Didn't notice."

"I bet he was still wearing our gold wedding ring, huh?"

She smirked and doused her finished cigarette in an ashtray on her desk. "Nice try, sweetie. He was wearing a silver ring, not gold. He ain't your man. Now, you want a room, or what?"

I quirked a smile as the woman had fallen right into my trap, giving me the information I needed. *Sounds like Joey's up there, all right.* I backtracked toward the front door. "Y'know, I think I'm gonna grab some lunch first."

Paula shook her head then readjusted her glasses and returned to her newspaper. "Whatever, honey. Thanks for wasting my time," she grumbled.

I rushed out the door and whipped around the corner of the building into an alleyway. I waded through the strewn garbage, the stench of rotting fish wafting through my nostrils and turning my stomach. Two of the second-floor windows were shut, their shades rolled down. The fire escape ran up along one of the windows that was opened slightly and a neighboring one that was closed. *Time to get to work.*

An overflowing dumpster was the perfect height to help me reach the fire escape's swinging ladder. But the dumpster wasn't directly underneath the ladder, and no way was I going to be able to push that stinking eight-hundred-pound behemoth closer.

One of the few highlights from my police academy days was that I excelled on the physical portion of basic training. My superiors had considered me "too advanced" to be graded under the women's general requirements but "not good enough" to be graded under the men's. I was a mutt, too in shape for my own good. I'd embarrassed a lot of men when I'd out-climbed, out-run, and even out-push-upped some of them in the timed endurance and agility tests. In the end, I'd graduated as top female of my class.

I was always putting those boot camp skills to use in this city. Whether as an officer of the law or a shamus, I tested my body's abilities in all sorts of ways.

I pulled out a pair of small leather gloves from the pockets of my jeans and slipped them on. Then I climbed atop the dumpster, balancing on the uneven mound of garbage. I'd noticed the sharp edges on the metal ladder. My gloves would keep me from slicing my hands open during my acrobatic attempts.

After another balancing act, I stood at the very edge of the dumpster and launched myself toward the ladder. I grasped the metal edge with my fingertips, holding on for dear life. I was careful not to jostle around too much, to protect my expensive camera, which was snuggled safely under my coat. Grunting, I used my legs to kick myself up an extra few inches. My midsection burned as it was awakened from this burst of new energy.

Finally, I secured myself on the step then shifted my weight, causing the other end of the ladder to teeter down with a loud creak. I grimaced and looked toward the open window above, but nobody peeked out. I slowly ascended the stairs until I was able to catch a view inside the room from the window with the partially rolled-up shade. Thankfully, the stench of the alley didn't reach this high. I didn't notice any movement and realized the room was empty when I got closer.

I moved on to the room to the right, which had the window partially cracked open. A shadow moved beyond, but I couldn't tell who it was. After creeping farther up the steps and pressing myself against the brick wall, I sank to my knees and looked inside the open window to my left. Two people were rolling around in a large bed that sat in the sparsely furnished room.

While watching the window, I unbuttoned the front of my trench coat, freeing the camera hanging securely around my neck. Fortunately for me, I wouldn't need to use my telephoto lens. I lowered my body to the fire escape's metal grating, discreetly pointing the camera toward the window's opening. I focused on the two people in bed, a man and woman. They were sprawled on a mass of white bedsheets, locked in a deep kiss. The woman moved on top of him, mounting him like he were a horse, exposing all her full-frontal-nude assets to him.

I finally got a good look at the man. He appeared to be in his thirties, with short wavy hair, calculating eyes, a five o'clock shadow, and a brooding, square-jawed face. A patch of dark hair covered his broad, toned chest. He was certainly the tall, dark, and handsome type. The woman, her face full of makeup, appeared half his age. With her petite body; small, round face; big, innocent, mascara-lined eyes; and her red hair done up in two pigtails, she looked like she could be his daughter.

A sinking feeling twisted in my gut. The young women these days tended to appear younger than they really were—myself included. I was often mistaken for a teenager, which was more annoying than anything. Go figure.

Still, I couldn't shake off the eeriness of what I was viewing through the camera lens. I studied the woman a bit more closely, noticing faint wrinkles around her neck where the makeup failed to conceal. A score of varicose veins streaked visibly along her bony arms and legs. Her nude body was more defined and rugged than a young girl's, which confirmed my suspicions about this woman being much older than she appeared. Apparently, the guy was just some creepy pervert who preferred his women to look like they were still in junior high school.

The man braced her shapeless hips, revealing a prominent silver ring on his left index finger. I zoomed in. The ring's inset appeared feline, but before I could focus on any more details, he moved his hand out of the camera's view. *It has to be him,* I thought. I moved the camera back to his face and snapped a photo. Then I quickly moved away from the window and waited. The camera was quiet enough, and I hoped that Joey was too wrapped up in his eye candy to hear or see anything out the window.

Joey's sex-laden voice filtered out. "I said, 'Call me Daddy.'"

I peered back into the room. The woman rode him like a cowgirl while Joey's hands explored her tiny breasts.

Click. Click. Click.

The two moaned then began twisting and moving around in the bed like professional wrestlers. They took turns pinning each other, and Joey took her from the front, back, side, and every other position that didn't seem humanly possible. Cringing, I shot a few more photos.

"Yes, Daddy! Yes! Yes! Yes!" the woman moaned.

I got several shots of her in the height of her sexual glory. At that point, all the bedding had made its way to the floor, and the two of them continued tumbling about. Finally, Joey stood, his back facing the window. He bent over, picking up the girl. A large black mole was present front and center on his right butt cheek, staring at me like an extra eye.

I grimaced. Evidence was evidence. *Click.*

The couple migrated to one of the far walls. I shuffled around, following them with my camera.

"Time for your spanking, baby," Joey rumbled. He had her pinned against the wall, taking her from behind like an alpha wolf claiming his mate.

Geez Louise. Aren't those two tired yet? My camera continued clicking away.

The woman's face contorted with pain and lust. Her eyes were closed, as if she was lost in her own fantasy.

I took a moment to check how many more shots I had left on the film roll. I'd taken a crazy amount already. If that wasn't enough evidence for Ms. Hays, I didn't know what would be. There was no denying these photos. Paige was in for a rude awakening once Allison showed her. Paige sounded like a good, loyal, optimistic wife. Unfortunately, those types tended to be mistreated the most. Such was the way of society, it seemed.

"Ahh! Who's that?" the woman suddenly yelled.

I started and looked back into the room. The woman's eyes were open, and she was staring straight at me, her face pale with horror.

Uh-oh.

Joey paused and turned his head toward me. His eyes widened, and he tore himself off the woman. "What the fuck!"

Time to go. Before he had a chance to identify me, I hightailed it back down the fire escape and raced out of the alley. I ran up Lincoln Avenue, not looking back. Passing under the Major Deegan Expressway, I spotted a bus picking up passengers ahead. Sucking in deep breaths, I sprinted faster as the last passenger began to board. I made it in the nick of time and found an empty seat on the bus. I plopped down in the seat and caught my breath as the bus sped farther up Lincoln Avenue and far away from The Peacock House.

Back at my apartment, I wasted no time getting the film developed and processed. I had a system for converting my tiny windowless bathroom into a darkroom, having all my photo-developing tools on hand. Several hours went by. Around six o'clock that evening, the prints and negatives hanging from clotheslines strung over my bathtub were dry. All the photos were as clear as day, detail upon cringy detail. I gave Allison a call.

"Oh my goodness, you're fast!" Allison squealed.

I winced. "All in a day's work, Ms. Hays."

"I hope you didn't have any trouble."

"Nothing I couldn't handle." That was easy money. *Maybe a little too easy.* My heart stuttered, a feeling of dread replacing those thoughts of victory.

Easy money never came without consequences.

CHAPTER 4

My alarm went off at 7:00 a.m. on the dot, jolting me out of a dream. I hadn't had a full night's sleep in months. After I washed up and dressed, I gathered my latest stack of hot tips on criminals on the loose for Chief Lewis. Most of the time, the chief sent them straight over to the district attorney, but some reports he kept if they had connections to open cases he was working on. I made sure my name was kept off unless the chief said otherwise. As long as the bad guys were brought to justice, I didn't mind that he and the rest of his boys took all the credit.

I tucked the papers into a leather folio and secured it with the attached string. I was supposed to meet Chief Lewis at nine o'clock at Maizy Jaye's Breakfast Café in Morris Heights, one of our many "secret" meeting spots around the city. The little hole-in-the-wall café was far enough away from the Fifty-Fourth Precinct that nobody we knew was likely to just happen by. My relationship with Chief Lewis was strictly off-the-record, a complicated business partnership that could get us both in deep trouble if either of us made a wrong move. Those who didn't understand our relationship could easily assume us to be a couple of crooked cops trying to skate the law.

I donned my trench coat, slipped on my dark-green fedora, and tucked the folio under one arm. I opened the front door and stepped into a pungent cloud of Beth's morning cannabis. She wasn't in the hallway, but she'd gone overboard with her "evil eye repellent." Dozens of hemlock sprigs hung all over her doorframe like Christmas garland. I rolled my eyes. *Guess I can add paranoia to her loony time-traveling antics.*

I paused at Crazy Bob's door. It was still intact, with no signs of a break-in. I approached the door and listened carefully. The *tappity-tap* sounds of typewriter keys continued, as much part of my apartment's background noise as the city's endless car horns and police sirens. *What is Bob typing all the time, anyway?* I wondered. *A book? News articles? A story for a pulp magazine?* Whatever it was, it sounded longer than a day without Tootsie Rolls.

Raw chill and drizzling clouds, as gloomy as the city's mood, hit me as I stepped out of the apartment building's front door. I headed down the street, making my way to the bus stop on the corner. I passed a newsstand, which displayed several editions of local papers. Slowing my steps, I glimpsed the headline in the *Metro Chronicle*: "Thousands of City Workers Lose Jobs!" I sighed. I usually skipped right to their extensive daily comics page, where the latest *Dick Tracy* strip appeared.

I picked up a copy and slipped the attendant two dimes. At least I'd have reading material for the bus ride. As I was about to leave, I spotted a racy photo in one of the gossip papers that sat among other tabloids on a separate rack at the end of the newsstand. Normally, I never paid those ridiculous papers a second thought. Plastered on the front page of the *National Esquire* was a familiar-looking photo of two silhouettes—a man and woman—locking lips. Two black Censored rectangles were placed strategically across the woman's upper and lower halves. The man's back was turned, hiding his identity, and a little black Censored heart was placed on his right butt cheek. A massive headline read, "Prominent CEO's Spouse Has Illicit Affair!"

I blinked. *What the...?* I snatched the paper and studied it. That was one of my photos, all right. But how did it get there? Did Ms. Hays send them to the *National Esquire*? It didn't make sense. Maybe the photos had been stolen. Still, I was annoyed that all my hard work had ended up in a paper that was best used for lining birdcages. I flipped open the paper and skimmed the cover story. I scowled at the author's name beneath the title: Chip Wilson.

Newsie... I growled, tightening my grip on the paper. That turkey was more irritating than a buzzing fly. He was the dark side of tabloid reporters, always looking for some cockamamie way to get his next big scoop. He was the kid in the neighborhood who was nothing but one big annoying megaphone, announcing the latest gossip or nosing around other people's business. Knowing he had something to do with this story gave me a bad feeling in my gut. *Does he even know I shot this photo?* I cringed. I would never hear the end of it. He would hound me day and night, trying to squeeze a story out of me.

"Hey, lady. Pay up. This ain't a public library," the newspaper clerk grumbled.

I gave him a sour look and shelled out thirty cents. Then I continued to the bus stop. As I waited, I read Newsie's article, which sounded as outrageous as his own personality. The article didn't mention names but talked about how a prominent CEO's husband was having an affair with an underage girl.

I knew what I'd seen at that hotel. That woman was *not* a child. It figured—the *National Esquire* was notorious for twisting the truth. What was Newsie's bag? I couldn't wrap my head around it. The more I read that jive article, the angrier I got. Something fishy was going on, and I was going to find out. That meant paying a visit to Newsie, which I was not looking forward to. *I should probably talk to Ms. Hays at some point too,* I figured.

But first, I needed to take care of things with Chief Lewis. The bus arrived, and I found my way to an empty seat. I scanned the long-faced riders, most of whom were dressed like they were on their way to the office. A few were reading newspapers. After the bus took off, I retrieved the *Metro Chronicle* from my trench coat pocket and pulled out the daily comics page. I settled more comfortably in my seat and relaxed as I indulged in Dick Tracy's latest exciting adventure and solved the fun little mystery puzzle at the end of the strip.

Before I knew it, I'd arrived at the Sedgwick Avenue stop in Morris Heights. I walked a short way to Maizy Jay's Breakfast Café, which sat on Cedar Avenue and overlooked the Major Deegan Expressway. The café, housed between a liquor store and a Laundromat, was easily missed since it had no conspicuous signage. Chief Lewis's little red Corona was parked among other cars along the curb. I smiled. *He's here.* I paused at the entrance and looked around, making sure no familiar faces, previous coworkers, or curious police rookies were near. When all was clear, I headed inside. A small bell jingled against the glass door as I entered. The smell of bacon, eggs, and doughnuts filled my nose. Back in the day, I remembered coming here occasionally on my way to the precinct. Their bagels were dynamite. Sometimes, the chief would bring a box of doughnuts from here to share with the department.

Carla, the clerk at the front counter, smiled warmly as I approached. The few tables inside were all occupied. This was definitely meant to be an "eat on the run" kind of place. In the back, however, was a small private room. I assumed that was where the chief was hiding.

I nodded in greeting to Carla then ordered a scrumptious bagel with cream cheese and a cup of hot chocolate.

While she prepared my order, she gave me another glance. Then, she did a double take. "Hmm. *Abrigo... sombrero verde,*" she mumbled in a rich Spanish accent.

"Excuse me?" I said.

She narrowed her eyes, scrutinizing me. "You... Tootsie?"

I straightened then glimpsed the suited patrons sitting at the tables. They didn't seem to pay me any mind.

I regarded Carla again and lowered my voice. "Yeah, why?" I asked warily.

"There is a man waiting in the back. He told me to tell you— the lady in the coat and green hat." Carla slid me the beverage and the hot bagel wrapped in red-and-white-checkered paper.

"Thanks," I said, assuming that was my official invitation to enter the restricted area. I headed toward the back of the café and opened the door to a room as tiny as my bedroom.

Chief Robert Lewis sat at a medium-sized six-seater table, reading the sports section of today's paper. He was a husky man, dressed in a professionally tailored brown suit, a white shirt, and a gold tie. His dark, square face bore rigid furrows around his forehead and brow, all the way down to his stern frown. He'd seen his share of battles, which had transformed him from the curious beat cop I'd first met as a kid into a full-blown leader.

The years had taken a toll on him, mentally and physically. Despite all that, he seemed to enjoy his work. With the amount of information I'd given him to help him make his job much easier, I might as well have still been on the force. He and my dad had been good friends since the time Dad let me ride in then-Officer Lewis's police cruiser for a day. It was my childhood dream come true. Rob was like the big brother I'd never had. He was also my guardian angel. I could always call on him for help and advice. Together, we made a pretty good team when it came to cleaning up these streets.

"Morning, Chief," I said. Sitting across from him, I set my breakfast and the folio on the table.

"You're late," he said, not looking up from his paper.

I checked my watch and sighed. "Sorry, I got sidetracked."

"Mm-hmm."

I unwrapped the hot bagel, tore off a bite-sized piece, and popped it into my mouth. It was nice and soft and melted on my tongue. "Ah, memories."

"Good ones, I hope," the chief said.

"Always."

He took a long sip of coffee, hiding his smile. "You got something for me?" he asked.

"Sure do." I slid the leather folio across the table. "The reports are ordered chronologically by the date each case was closed."

He unwound the security string and pulled out one of the manila folders. He took a few minutes to read one of the sheets inside while I finished the rest of my bagel. He stroked the sides of his thin mustache as his brown eyes moved left and right, scanning the paper. Finally, his thick eyebrows furrowed. "Dalton Cage," he muttered. "Man, I remember that son of a bitch. I thought we'd never catch him. Good to know where that dirty rat's hiding."

"He's all yours," I said, remembering that case vividly from the past month.

A client had needed me to find their missing watch, a family heirloom. The case led me straight to Dalton Cage's counterfeit operation, selling bogus watches, purses, and other "luxury" items. Mr. Cage already had a nice little rap sheet. He'd escaped the cops and had lain low for a while, but I eventually caught up with him.

"I hope he gets the book thrown at him, for a few years, at least," I said.

"We can only hope." Chief Lewis slid the paper back into the folio. "Impressive as always, Tootsie. I'd give you a raise for this, if I could."

Sipping my hot chocolate, I averted my gaze. "You had your chance."

He sighed. "Are you still going to hang that over my head?"

"Yeah, I am. Women's lib won, in case you forgot. You had the opportunity to make a difference and promote me as your first female detective at the Fifty-Fourth Precinct. Instead, you were too scared of what your male colleagues and superiors would think."

"Look, it was complicated at the time. I told you I was sorry. I learned my lesson, Tootsie. And yes, I was scared—not of what people would think of me but more for you. These idiots who have no respect for women in power would give you hell as a female police detective."

"Stop treating me like a delicate little flower. I thought you would've trusted by now that I could handle myself."

His shoulders slumped. "I do trust you. But during my time as chief, I've had to throw out a few knuckleheads who were exposed for being crooked cops. I would never forgive myself if one of those bastards hurt you. Things are bad right now. It's getting to the point you can't even trust your own brother. You're like a daughter to me, and I can't help but worry."

I smiled slightly. "You have more important things to worry about than my well-being. I'll be fine."

"Yeah, I get it. I get you. That's why you'll always be my number-one ace detective."

That drew a small chuckle out of me. It was a cute little pet name he'd given me when I was a kid. "Say, what do you think of today's news?" I asked, steering the conversation away from myself.

He arched an eyebrow. "Which news? A lot's happened."

"This one." I pulled out the *National Esquire* from my coat pocket and slid it across the table.

He glanced at the page dubiously. "An affair isn't news, Tootsie."

"No, it's not, but I don't like how this article was presented."

"Not many do when it comes to the *National Esquire*."

"However, I know the writer, and that photo was one of many that I shot for a recent client. It was for an infidelity case. What do you think?"

"I don't know what to think. Can't see any faces, but it's obvious what they're doing. Why are you asking me about this, anyway?"

"Because I'm trying to figure out how that photo made it on the front page so fast."

He took a sip of his coffee, looking thoughtful. "Someone must've submitted it to the paper."

"Why would they do that? I mean, if they're trying to prove a spouse is being unfaithful…" I frowned. *Could Allison have been using me for some other motive?* I couldn't understand it. Why would Allison go through all the trouble of getting a private eye involved? Maybe my gut instinct was right about that "easy money." Trying to make sense of everything wasn't easy at all.

Chief Lewis shrugged. "Who knows what happened? The person could've been robbed of the photos, for all we know."

Robbed… I chewed my bottom lip. That was possible, but I wasn't entirely sure.

"I'll check at the station to see if any ten-twenties came in recently," Chief Lewis finished.

"Thanks, Chief. One way or another, I intend to get to the bottom of this." *Even though I'm not getting paid.*

"I've no doubt you will." He winked.

I downed the rest of my hot chocolate and slid out of my chair. "Looks like I have some work to do. Will you be around later today?"

"I'm always a phone call away, Tootsie," he replied.

"Great. I might need your help in looking up some fingerprints."

"Oh?"

"Yeah, long story. I'll tell you about it later." I tossed my garbage then headed for the private room's exit but stopped at the doorway and turned around. "Oh… one more thing. This one's the most mind-boggling."

He grinned as though welcoming the challenge. "Let's hear it."

"Have you ever run across someone who thought they were living in a different day in time? A different year, perhaps?"

"All the time. They're usually strung out on something."

"Hmm…" No doubt, Beth was probably strung out on a lot of things.

"Or sometimes," he continued with a shrug, "they could genuinely not know what day it is. In which case, it sounds like they just need a calendar."

I rubbed my chin and perked up. "Say, you know what? That's a swell idea. Why didn't I think of that?" I made a mental note to stop at the stationery store on the way back to my apartment.

"Any other questions?" Chief Lewis asked, a hint of amusement on his face.

I shook my head, smiling graciously. "That's it for now, Chief. Thank you, as always."

"Mm-hmm." He picked up his newspaper.

As I left the private room, the chief called, "Hey."

I paused in the doorway again and looked over my shoulder.

"For the love of Saint Mary, be careful out there, okay?" he said.

I tipped my hat to him. "You don't have to tell me twice."

CHAPTER 5

After returning to my office apartment, I flipped through the *Yellow Pages* and located the number for the *National Esquire*. I called and asked for Chip, but the receptionist gave me the runaround. Eventually, I learned he was "on assignment" and wouldn't be back for several hours. *Swell.* I rolled my eyes. That bogus paper would print anything and everything, regardless of merit or quality. With a sigh, I hung up the phone.

I considered calling Ms. Hays. I'd never called a client back once I closed a case, as that was against my own personal code of ethics. But the mystery was getting stranger by the minute and was driving me crazy. Finally, gritting my teeth, I relented and dialed her number. The line rang and rang, but no one answered. I deflated and hung up. That must've been her home number. She was probably at work.

I tried Gatestar Media next. Just my luck, the receptionist said Allison had gone out to lunch. There went *that* idea.

I resorted to my last option: Roy. He and Newsie were childhood friends, and if anybody would know Newsie's whereabouts, it was Roy. I dialed Kronos Lounge, but nobody picked up. The place wouldn't open for several hours. Next, I called Roy's private number for his small apartment above the bar.

"Look, Tonya," Roy answered, skipping the greeting. "For the last time, the answer is no. You got your damned money, so stop calling!"

I blinked. "Excuse me?"

After a slight pause, he gasped. "Oh, shit. Tootsie? That you?"

"No, it's the Good Humor man," I said flatly. "Guess I was interrupting something?"

"No," Roy said quickly. "That crazy broad has been hounding me all morning."

"I'm sure she has."

"Hey, it's not what you think. There was a private birthday party last night downstairs, and my client had ordered a stripper. Well, now she's acting like she's entitled to perform in my bar whenever she damn well pleases."

I snorted. Roy was a terrible liar. He was too fine to be pushing strippers away. "Save it, Roy. I have something important I need to ask you."

"Sure, Tootsie. You know you can ask me anything," he said in a softer, more relaxed tone.

"Have you seen Newsie around?"

He paused again. "What do you want with him?"

"Answers. Didn't you see today's *National Esquire*?"

"You know I don't read that shit."

"Neither do I, but…" I explained the article to him. "Things aren't making sense, and I want to talk to Newsie about it."

"Did you call the head office?" Roy asked.

"Yeah. No dice. Look, I know you know where he is."

"I don't know where he is, Tootsie. I don't keep tabs on that cat twenty-four seven."

"But you know how to get in touch with him in a pinch, don't you?"

"And what if I do? Not like he'll come running."

I rolled my eyes. "Stop all that jive talking, Roy. You two are closer than a rat to a piece of cheddar. Tell him you got a hot lead on a new scoop, and he'll come to you faster than Superman."

"Oh, for crying out loud," he grumbled under his breath. "Fine. I'll see what I can do."

"Cool." I waited a beat, sensing he had more to say.

"What's in it for me?" Roy asked.

I smirked. *There it is.* "What do you want?"

"I want you to take a break and come to the bar this Friday night. I'm holding a watch party for the Ali-Lyle fight."

I groaned. "That's in three days. I don't know if I'll be done with this case by then."

"Well, you'd better, or else I'll find you and drag your ass here myself, dig?" Roy said.

I thought for a moment then let out a deep sigh. "Fine, Roy. You have a deal. Only because you agreed to help me with Newsie."

"I'm only agreeing to help you because I know that you know how I feel about you."

"Hmph. By the way you answered the phone a few minutes ago, I wonder how you feel about me."

"I told you, that shit with Tonya ain't what you think." He let out a flustered sigh. "Anyway, come to Kronos in about an hour."

I said a quick goodbye, hung up, and exhaled. Roy got on my nerves sometimes, but he was always there when I needed him. Still, taking him seriously was hard when he was always playing around with other women. I saw right through his sweet-talking, and I had no time for it.

I checked the clock above the front door. I could brave the lunchtime traffic and make it to Kronos Lounge in about forty-five minutes if I took a taxi. And I knew just the cabbie: my old friend and fellow Dick Tracy fan, Sid Bonato. I dialed the cab company and requested him. He was down in Brooklyn at the moment, which gave me time to take care of a few other matters. I called Chief Lewis's personal office number, gave him the skinny about yesterday's attempted break-in, and told him to stop by Kronos Lounge later that afternoon.

Afterward, I tucked away my .38, which fit snug in its holster within one of my trench coat pockets. I also gathered my mini notebook, the folded copy of the *National Esquire*, and for good measure, a couple of Tootsie Rolls from the candy jar. I retrieved a thin, floral-printed, wrapped square gift from atop my desk then headed for the door. On my way out, I picked up the paper lunch bag containing the pen the mysterious "tax collector" had dropped the day before.

After locking up my office, I went next door. The colorful hand-painted Open sign hung on the glass door of Beth's head shop. I held my breath and walked in. A little bell jingled above, announcing my presence. A variety of smoking paraphernalia and odd trinkets filled wooden bookshelves and glass display cases in the small room, which was the same size as my office. A clothes rack sported various styles of hippie clothing and patchwork sling bags. Colorful tie-dye banners and political, antiwar, and rock-band posters covered the walls. As I studied the place, I realized she had no calendars anywhere. *Maybe the chief was right,* I thought.

Beth walked out from an adjacent room, a bright smile on her fair-skinned face. She noticed me and stopped, giving me an odd look. "Oh, hello, Tootsie. Fancy seeing you here. Has the universe spoken to you at last? Are you ready to expand your mind and body?"

I finally exhaled and dared to take a tiny breath, ensuring that my nose wouldn't be overwhelmed by the tear-inducing cannabis stink. Thankfully, instead, I inhaled the pleasant scent of vanilla incense. "Ah, no, not today," I replied. "I just stopped by to—"

"Oh! Tootsie! Look!" She plucked a small bottle of yellowish liquid from a rack of others set on the front counter. "This is jojoba oil, straight from the Motherland. I got it yesterday. It's supposed to do wonders for extra-thick hair texture, like yours."

I cringed. "Eh, no thanks. I'll stick with my Blue Magic and pink oil. They haven't disappointed me yet. Anyway..." I held out the gift. "I wanted to give you this."

Her face lit up, and she approached. "You got me a present? How sweet of you, Tootsie. You shouldn't have."

I smiled. "Ah, well... just a little token of thanks for helping me stop that thug yesterday."

She took the gift, then her gaze hardened. "He hasn't been back again, has he?"

"Oh, no. I think you struck the fear of God in him." I laughed.

Her smile returned. "Serves him right. And I'll do the same for anyone else who thinks we're gullible enough to support this damned war."

I groaned. "Yeah…"

She tore open the gift, and her eyes widened. "Oh! I love Flavia Weedn's art. I will cherish this forever, Tootsie. Thank you."

"It's not just her artwork. It's also a wall calendar. Here." I flipped to the current month and pointed to the current date. "See?"

She nodded slowly, then her brow furrowed. "I see, but… that's strange…"

"What?" I asked.

"How did you manage to get a calendar from the future?"

I blinked. "It's not—"

She gasped. "Oh my gosh! Tootsie, have you been able to travel through time?"

I slapped my forehead. "Geez Louise. No, Beth. It's 1975. This calendar is correct. What year do you think this is?"

"'Think'? I know it's—"

Her telephone rang. She jolted to attention and went behind the small glass counter, where a cash register sat.

"I'm sorry, Tootsie, we'll have to talk later. Thank you again for the gift," Beth said and swiped up the receiver.

With a sigh, I shook my head and left the shop. *Well, there goes that idea.*

I didn't have to wait long for Sid after leaving my apartment building. The Italian bulldog was all smiles when he pulled up along the curb. I hopped into the backseat.

"How ya doin,' Ms. Carter?" Sid asked, his eyes trained on me from the rearview mirror.

"Great, thanks," I said. "Hope you're staying out of trouble."

He grinned. "'Ey, I'm an angel except when the knuckleheads wanna try me."

I laughed. "Right on."

"Where we goin' today, doll?"

"Punch it to Kronos Lounge."

"You got it."

As we zipped through the streets, Sid indulged me with another one of his old boxing stories. He sure had enough stories to write a novel. But I only half listened to him as my mind was more focused on the strange newspaper mystery. I took out my mini notebook to review the notes I'd taken during Ms. Hays's visit the day before.

We stopped at a red light. "Something wrong, Ms. Carter?" Sid asked, deep concern in his gruff voice.

I glanced up from my case notes, where I'd been idly staring at Ms. Hays's phone number. "Nothing... I'm fine."

He raised one of his thick eyebrows. "'Ey, now, you can't put nothin' past ol' Sid. But if ya don't wanna talk about it, then..."

I smiled slightly then glimpsed the floorboard of the front passenger seat, where several newspapers were strewn. Among them was a copy of that dreaded tabloid.

"You read the *National Esquire*?" I asked.

When the light turned green, Sid sped off. "Nah, not really. A rider left it in the backseat earlier this mornin', so I took it. I get lots of papers to read. Honestly, I don't remember the last time I paid for one. Hah!"

"Did you take a peek at the *National Esquire* at all?"

He chuckled. "Yeah, I caught a glimpse of the article. Some bum shacking up with a young dame. Disgusting piece of shit, if you ask me. If that were my little girl, I'd tear out that motherfucker's spine."

"Don't worry, it's not a kid. And that 'bum' is connected with one of the largest media distribution companies in the city," I said.

"Ya kiddin! Well what's he doin' actin' like a damn exhibitionist?"

"It's scandalous. Tabloids eat it up like candy. What's mortifying is that I, uh… happen to know the person who took that photo. She had no idea it was going to be used like this."

Both of his eyebrows shot up. "Is that right? Well, your friend's got some damn good camera skills. You ever thought about getting into photography, Ms. Carter?"

I tried to maintain a straight face. "I've considered it once or twice."

"I bet you'd make a swell photographer," Sid continued. "A little Brenda Starr and Friday Foster vibe going on."

"Ha. I'm not that glamorous."

"Jane Arden?"

I shook my head. "Too sophisticated." *And how the heck does she get around in those painful-looking heels?* I wondered.

"Hey, she also had spunk. Damn, I miss those comics," he said, bittersweet.

My smile returned. Talking comics with Sid was always refreshing. No one else I'd met seemed to appreciate them more than him. "In any event, I'm going to find out why my friend was duped."

"Your friend is lucky to have someone like you, Ms. Carter. Always out there helpin' the li'l guys. Much like a certain yellow-fedora-wearing detective I know." He winked.

"Speaking of which, you wouldn't happen to have issue three of *Dick Tracy Monthly*, would you?"

"Hmm…" He looked thoughtful a moment. "Not sure. Gotta check my stash. That one's an oldie, all right."

"Yeah, I've been trying to complete my collection. I started it around issue fifty or so, back when I was old enough to read and understand. It's been so hard to find some of those older issues."

"I hear ya. Well, don'tcha worry, doll. I'll keep an eye out."

"You're the best, Sid."

As we crossed over the Whitestone Bridge into Queens, my anxiety returned, quickly overshadowing my pleasant distraction like a dark cloud. I had one chance to get as much out of Newsie as I could. And knowing him, he wasn't going to talk willingly.

CHAPTER 6

By twelve fifteen, Sid had dropped me off behind Kronos Lounge, which was still closed until evening. I paid the fare—offering Sid a generous tip—hopped out of the cab, and headed for the alley. Roy's beat-up red '61 Corvair sat in the alley like a hunk of junk. I reached the building's side door and pounded on it with my fist.

"Open up! It's me," I announced.

Moments later, the door unlocked and swung open. Roy appeared, dressed in a gold abstract-print button-down shirt and dark-green slacks. Compared to how he dressed most nights, that was super casual for him. Yet, somehow, Roy managed to make even casual fashion look suave. His face softened as he held the door out for me. "Good to see you, Tootsie."

"Mm-hmm." I walked past him, hiding my smile.

He shut the door behind me and reset the locks. "Newsie's downstairs," he said.

"He came, huh? Good."

"He came faster than I could hang up the phone."

I smirked. "Told you."

"Yeah, yeah." Roy led me through his office.

As we passed his large desk, I set the paper bag on it. "Can you see that Chief Lewis gets that?"

Roy furrowed his brow. "What's in it?"

"A little present for the chief. I'll give him a call before I leave and remind him to stop by."

"Right."

We continued to a door at the back of the office leading down a set of stairs to the sublevel.

"So you got Newsie's personal telephone number, huh?" I asked.

"Yup."

I stopped at the top of the stairs. "Care to share it with me?"

"Nope." He crossed his arms and looked at me patiently.

I blinked. "Why not?"

"There are some things I can't share with you, Tootsie. This is one of them."

I raised my eyebrows. "Are you doing this as payback for me not telling you about my cases? You know they're confidential."

"I don't give a shit about your cases. I made a promise to a friend. Newsie is in a high-profile position, and as a friend, I give him the protection he needs."

"You don't trust me?"

"I trust you with all my heart, Tootsie. But a promise is a promise."

"I see." I frowned. "Listen, I get your being confidential with him like that and all, but Newsie may be a prime suspect in this case, and I might need him again."

"You just let me know when, and I'll handle the rest." Roy descended the stairs.

I followed, and when we reached the bottom, he unlocked and opened the door to the speakeasy. A lanky man was sprawled out on the couch with his polished, expensive-looking brown leather boots propped up on the octagonal wooden coffee table. He wore a black turtleneck sweater under a light-grey suit vest and grey plaid bell-bottoms. His signature burgundy newsboy hat topped his head. A cigarette dangled from his lips as he casually read a magazine. The half-naked pinup girl on the front cover indicated he was engaged in a little more than "light reading."

"There he is," Roy said, hiking a thumb at Newsie. Then he scowled. "Oh, for crying out loud!" Roy marched over and tossed Newsie's feet off the coffee table. "What are you, crazy, man? Keep your dirty-ass shoes off my table!"

Newsie lowered the magazine and gave him a dull gaze. "Hey, I just got these babies polished. C'mon, man. Where's the action? You know how much bread I'm losin' the longer I stay cooped up in this joint?" He plucked the cigarette from his lips and blew out a light stream of smoke.

"There's the action." Roy nodded toward me.

Newsie looked my way then popped up from the couch. He was tall—a little over six foot—but not quite as tall as Roy. Newsie's surprised face morphed to a mischievous grin that stretched from ear to ear. "Well, if it ain't good ol' Tootsie. Whatcha doin' here, foxy mama?"

"Cool it, Chip," I snapped, using his real name to emphasize my annoyance.

He drew back and took a long drag on his cigarette. "Same ol' Tootsie, huh?" he said to Roy.

"Eh…" Roy rolled his eyes.

Newsie smirked. "So to what do I owe this exclusive meeting with the world-famous Dick Tracy–wannabe sidekick, Tootsie Carter?"

Scowling, I stormed over to him. "Answers, that's what. I want to know about that photo. Where and how you got it."

Newsie gave me a curious look and took another drag of his bogey. "Photo? What photo? I don't know nothin' 'bout no photo."

I gritted my teeth.

"C'mon, man," Roy grumbled, elbowing Newsie in the ribs.

Newsie grunted, and his gaze bounced back to me. "Look, I deal with hundreds of pictures a day. If you're wantin' to know somethin' in particular, well... I can't give ya nothin' till I get the skinny. Can you dig it?"

I took out my folded copy of the *National Esquire* from my pocket. "Does this look familiar?" I showed him the front page.

Newsie's smile grew. "Sweet, ain't it? I'm next in line for a raise 'cause of that article. Finally, I got my big break. Front page, baby! It's been a long time coming, y'know that? All 'cause I was in the right place at the right time."

I snorted. "Oh, were you? Who gave you that photo, huh?"

He finished his cigarette and stabbed the butt in a glass ashtray set on the coffee table. "What makes you think somebody gave it to me?"

"Because you ain't no photographer," I said.

His mischievous smirk disappeared. "Oh yeah? Well, for your information, I happen to know how to take damn good pictures. It's part of my job."

I rolled my eyes. "It's a *photo*, not a picture, you jive turkey."

He bristled. "Whatever."

"And you didn't shoot this one. Trust me," I added.

"And how the hell would you know?"

"It lacks the amateurish, subpar quality that your photos tend to have."

Newsie grunted. "I resent that."

"Then admit you didn't shoot this photo. You have no eye for composition. You think just knowing how to press a button on a camera automatically makes you a photographer."

Newsie waved his hand dismissively. "Eh, you talk like you know your shit."

"I do. And before you ask, the answer is no, I didn't shoot this photo." I wasn't about to let him know it was me. I wouldn't get any sleep with him sniffing around like the desperate reporter he was, grilling me with a million-and-one questions about the photos.

"I wasn't intending on asking because I think it's plainly obvious you didn't."

I paused and looked at him with a straight face. Since he'd caught my bait, I wanted to learn more about this mystery. I took out my notebook and slid out the pen secured in its metal spirals. "Give it to me straight, Newsie."

"I think I'm gonna need a drink for this," Roy muttered, walking over to the minibar.

Newsie gave me a small shrug. "I'm tellin' ya, Tootsie. I don't know where the photo came from or who sent it. I returned to the office late yesterday afternoon, and Marcie, my secretary, said a man stopped by and dropped off a manila envelope. He didn't say nothin' while he was there. The envelope was full of scandalous photos of Joey Russell and his cute young thing."

"How did you know that was Joey in those photos?" I asked.

"There was a press release enclosed with tons of information about Joey, his wife, and Gatestar Media. Facts were cited and everything. I showed my boss, and he told me how to frame the story to make it pop—like not mentioning names—right down to what picture to use. He even tacked on a five-hundred-dollar bonus to it."

I blinked. "Your boss bribed you?"

Newsie flicked his hand dismissively. "Nah. He just values my hard work."

"Right…"

"Anyway, we held the presses for this article. We worked double time to get the story printed in today's issue."

I scribbled some notes. "Did your secretary remember what the man who dropped off the photos looked like?"

"Ehhh, she said it was a tall Black guy. He wore a short trench coat and a pair of dark sunglasses. That was about it. I think she was too distracted to notice anything else, to be honest."

"Why do you say that?" I asked.

"We had a new office assistant start today. A college intern named Rosa Timms." He let out a low whistle. "Fine-as-hell, slammin' young thing, she is. Marcie has this idea in her head that she's gonna get replaced, so she's been all anxious an' shit. I mean, Rosa's only temporary, but yeah… Maybe I can get Rosa to *tutor* me sometime, know what I mean?" He chuckled darkly.

"Back to the point," I said. "Marcie didn't remember anything else about the man?"

"Nope."

"Maybe the janitor saw something," I mused, rubbing my chin.

"Doubt it. We only have one janitor, and he works the graveyard shift. Believe me, I asked around. I wanted to know who sent the photos so that I could personally thank them. But nobody had any useful info."

I took down more notes. "So that man came exclusively to your building?"

"Yeah. It was weird. I guess word of my talents are starting to finally get around, eh?" He laughed.

I rolled my eyes. "The only thing you're talented at is being nosy and annoying."

Newsie smiled smugly. "Hey, y'know, Tootsie? I'm a reporter and you're a detective. We're not that different, you and I."

I snorted a laugh. "Trust me, you and I are worlds apart, and I intend to keep it that way."

"Agreed," Roy added from the minibar. "Tootsie gets in enough trouble as it is." He downed his mixed drink.

I gave Roy a sour look. "No one asked you." I turned back to Newsie. "Do you still have those photos?"

"Sure do, and I'm keepin' 'em forever."

"The negatives too?"

"There weren't any negatives."

I rubbed my temples. This mystery just took another confusing turn. If Allison still had the negatives, then she must've been the one behind everything. But why? Why jeopardize Gatestar Media's reputation over a personal vendetta against the CEO's husband? I had too much to think about.

"I want to take a look at the photos. There might be fingerprints or some other clue," I said.

"At least a dozen people touched them, Tootsie," Newsie said.

"I still want to check. I need to find a lead."

He cocked his head to the side. "Why are you so obsessed with these photos, anyway? What's your angle?"

"I, uh… want to find out who the photographer is so I can ask them to be my mentor. I wanna learn their secret." I smirked.

Newsie's smile grew. "Well, if you ever find out who took them, send 'em my way."

"I have a better idea: you give me that front-page photo, and I'll make sure you get a scoop bigger than this, that's sure to land you another promotion. I'll make sure it's kept exclusive to the *National Esquire* and nowhere else."

His eyes widened. "An exclusive? You ain't jivin' me, are you?"

"Nope. Let's meet back here after closing time." I cast Roy a glance.

Roy choked on his drink, returning the stare.

I smiled innocently. *You're the one who wanted to keep things secret.*

"All right. I'll be here," Newsie said. "You better have somethin' good for me, Tootsie. I mean it."

"Don't worry," I said.

"Now, wait a minute." Roy set down his empty glass and marched back over to us. "I oughtta get a say in this. It's my bar, after all."

"Make sure we're not disturbed," I said, playfully pinching Roy's cheek.

Roy grunted and pulled away. Scowling, he looked at Newsie. "You sure you're cool with this? I mean…"

Newsie gave him a dismissive wave. "It's cool. Ain't no one gonna be lookin' for me down here at three in the morning." He eyed me. "Tootsie just better come through."

I intended to because I had no choice. My time to gather the information just got cut in half. Still, I didn't fully trust that Newsie was being on the level about his end of the bargain. I figured it was probably best I did a little more digging on my own at the *National Esquire* headquarters. *Ugh. What did I just agree to?* I turned to Newsie and said, "Yeah. See you after closing time."

CHAPTER 7

I left Kronos Lounge and headed straight for the *National Esquire* headquarters in Manhattan. During the trip, I got my fabricated celebrity story straight. Tabloids loved celebrity gossip, and my plan for getting some real information was sound. Maybe I would be able to pick up some dirt for Newsie too.

Sid dropped me off in front of a luxurious brownstone on West Sixty-Eighth Street. A polished metal sign etched with the building's number over the mahogany front door told me I had the right address. Good thing, because I would've never thought this upscale-looking joint housed a sleazy newspaper. A few cars were parked along the curb, and another taxi was idling next to a fire hydrant ahead. The gruff-looking cabbie leaned against the hood of his yellow Torino, smoking a cigarillo.

I climbed the shallow steps flanked with flowerpots and a wrought-iron banister. When I reached for the door, it flung open with such force, inches away from my face, that I jumped back. A man of the tall-dark-and-handsome type stormed out of the building, his rigid face beet red. He wore a pair of dark sunglasses.

"You haven't seen the last of me, you motherfuckers!" the man shouted over his shoulder as the door began to close.

I froze, getting a good, hard look at the man up close. *That voice. Could it be?* My heart pounded. His voice was angry, but it still carried a smooth and alluring tone. I swore I'd heard that voice before.

The man brushed past me, giving my shoulder a light bump as he stormed down the stairs. Then he stopped and looked back at me. He lowered his sunglasses, and for a moment, we locked eyes.

I swallowed a lump in my throat. *Joey Russell.* I assumed he was here to confront the company about that front-page article. Did he know who took the photo too? I couldn't escape. All I could do was hope he didn't recognize me from the day before. I wanted to turn away, but something about him kept me compelled. He was a calculating man, someone hard to read. I hated people like that. Joey had a charismatic appearance. People like him also tended to have a way with words—a true diplomat and a perfect mask for someone who held secrets and motives. *No wonder Paige was so caught up in his charms,* I thought, trying to stay focused.

The anger on Joey's face ebbed, and he gave me a slow, attractive smile, dripping with friendly charm. His handsome facial features became more prominent, like the little dimple on his left cheek, which I'd just noticed. "Oh, sorry about that, miss," he said. But venom was dripping from those words.

I cleared my throat and, managing to resist his charms, spun my back to him. "No problem."

I reached for the door again while feeling his calculating eyes watching me. I turned my head slightly and saw Joey in my periphery. He hadn't budged from his spot on the stairs and was still looking at me.

"Wait... do I know you?" Joey asked.

"Nope," I muttered, opening the door and slipping inside before I could give him a chance to ask another question.

The door closed behind me, and I looked out the small glass window. Joey was gone. I exhaled a deep sigh. *That was close.*

The lobby was small, musty, and decked out in dark wooden trim and old, grimy mosaic porcelain tile flooring. The only sound came from a middle-aged woman with long, red, wavy hair, who was sitting at an L-shaped desk and clacking away at a typewriter. A telephone switchboard sat beside her on the desk, but no calls were coming through. I approached the desk, and the woman stopped typing and looked up at me.

"Yeah? Can I help ya?" she asked in a brassy North Jersey accent, adjusting her black-rimmed cat-eye glasses for a better look as she spoke.

"Hello," I said, tipping my fedora. "My name is Rita, and I have a hot scoop for News—er... Mr. Chip Wilson."

The woman pulled out a yellow legal pad from her desk drawer and picked up a pen. "Whatcha got, dearie?" she asked.

"I got a tip that the famous movie actress Stefanie Reed is flying in from Los Angeles to Westchester later today."

The woman stopped writing. "That all?" She arched an eyebrow.

"That's all I'm gonna tell you, lady. I need to talk to Mr. Wilson personally about this one. This tip's so hot it's smoking."

She gave me a long, thoughtful look, and I held my breath. "One moment," she said at last. She swiveled around to the switchboard, picked up the receiver, and pressed a few buttons. She waited a moment then said, "Hey, Marcie. Gotta hot one for ya..."

I exhaled and looked around the lobby. A few framed tabloid clippings decorated the walls, with bizarre headlines like a woman in Iowa giving birth to identical "twelve-uplets" at once, a Pennsylvania coal miner who fought Bigfoot with his bare hands, and one about a man claiming to be Elvis's evil twin. *I can't believe people actually believe this stuff,* I thought, resisting the urge to roll my eyes. Just like Newsie to work at a crooked place like this, full of lies, stretched-out truths, and way-out-there gossip.

The woman hung up the receiver and swiveled back to me. "Mr. Wilson ain't back yet," she said. "Talk to Marcie, his secretary, and she'll get your story to him." She pointed toward a set of narrow wooden stairs that rose beside a short hallway. "Upstairs, third door on your right."

I gave the woman another hat tip in thanks. "Appreciate it. By the way, did anyone happen to stop by here sometime yesterday afternoon to deliver some photos?"

"What's it to ya?" The woman eyed me up and down with a pebble-hard stare behind those gaudy frames. "Look, sweetie, this is a newspaper office. Photos get delivered here all the time. I don't keep track of who brings what. I'm just Sharon, the nice desk lady who smiles and tells people where to go." She emphasized the point, smiling awkwardly, revealing lipstick stains like smears of blood on her crooked teeth.

I grimaced. "Yeah. Um, right... look, Sharon. I need to know the person who did the blind drop of the photos."

"You with that rude son of a bitch that came by a couple minutes ago asking about some photos? Look, I'm gonna tell you what I told him. Ain't no one important enough coming through here that would make me blink."

"Noted. And no, I'm here of my own accord. I don't know that person you're talking about."

"Good." She turned back to her baby-blue Smith-Corona. "Then get goin', sweetie. I got work to do." She resumed typing.

Attempting to get any more information out of her would be useless. I left the lobby and climbed the stairs, which creaked slightly under my weight. Reaching the top, I entered a narrow hallway full of closed office doors with names painted on frosted glass panels. I reached the third door on my right, where Newsie's name was displayed prominently. As I reached for the gold door handle, I heard several voices in the room beyond. I quietly opened the door a crack and peeked in. The smell of freshly brewed coffee hit my nose.

Three people were grouped around a large wooden secretary desk, chatting loudly enough to make me cringe. Beyond the desk was a closed door to a private office, which I assumed belonged to Newsie. He must've been doing really well for himself to have his own office and personal secretary. Still, I assumed that was more due to his charisma and persuasion skills and less about his actual work. Like Roy, he could talk his way out of anything. Those two were cut from the same cloth.

"You're dreaming, Marcie," a young, college-aged girl with wavy blond hair said, sitting on the corner-edge of the desk, holding an unopened can of soda. "Ain't no way you're gonna get a promotion without something spectacular to bring to the table."

The older, auburn-haired woman sitting at the desk huffed. "Let's get it straight, Trish. I would've had a promotion today if that bastard Aaron wasn't around when I mentioned that UFO story to you guys this morning."

"You mean that story about the guy in Long Island with the tape recording?" a short young man with a dark, shaggy haircut asked, leaning against the side of the desk. "Oh yeah, that one was smokin.' I keep telling you that you need to keep that shit to yourself. Everyone's competition around here."

'Everyone is competition.' Interesting way of looking at it, I thought. I was starting to understand why Roy was acting all weird with me about Newsie. Their relationship wasn't so different from me and Chief Lewis. *Gee, Roy is a great friend to Newsie, looking out for him like that.* I looked left and right, making sure I was still alone in the hallway, and continued to eavesdrop on the three.

Marcie scowled. "Don't remind me, Patrick. I just better not get passed up by that new kid, Timms. That little runt just started college." She took a sip from a white mug with the *National Esquire* logo on the side.

"Don't worry," Patrick assured her, cracking a thin smile. "You'll land yourself a big scoop. Just make sure it doesn't involve Elvis." He groaned. "You've no idea how many news inquiries come through the mail room every day about that fat old has-been. The boss just tosses them straight in the garbage."

Marcie sighed. "Who knows when I'll get another hot story?"

"Hang around the coffee shops sometime," Patrick suggested. "You'd be surprised at what people talk about over a cup of joe. Better yet, hit the bars. Nothing makes people talk like a few too many." He smirked.

Marcie shook her head. "I doubt you'd get anything newsworthy from a drunk. Eye-catching is what it's all about for this newspaper."

"I've discovered some possible eye-catching stories from some pieces of mail that came in last week. I can let you in on them, if you want," Patrick said.

"No, I'd rather do this on my own," Marcie insisted. She paused and checked her watch. "Hmm. I thought Sharon said there was another visitor coming."

"Hope it's not that weird guy again," Trish grumbled.

Uh-oh. I quietly let myself in and approached the three. "Hello," I said, giving them a brief tip of my fedora.

The group swiveled their gazes to me, giving me the once-over.

Then Marcie smiled and said, "Hey, you must be Rita, right? The one who has a tip about Stefanie Reed?"

"That's right."

"What! No way!" Trish exclaimed. "You have dirt on *the* Stefanie Reed?"

"Didn't she recently get divorced?" Patrick added, rubbing his chin in thought.

"Yeah, for like, the eleventh time." Trish snickered. "I swear, she goes through men like I do my laundry."

"Yeah. Well, I got something for Mr. Wilson. A big scoop," I said.

Marcie whipped out a yellow notepad and began scribbling notes. "Where and how did you get this information?"

"I have, uh… friends. They prefer to remain anonymous."

Marcie stopped writing and frowned. "Hmm… you're not one of Mr. Wilson's regulars. How do I know you're on the level?"

"Mr. Wilson and I go way back. When I got this tip, I figured I'd do him a solid. Plus, I wanted to know about the photos he got yesterday."

Marcie's eyebrows shot up. "Those photos were yours?"

"Uh, no, but a little birdie told me that someone gave Mr. Wilson some racy photos."

"Not long ago, some guy came storming up in here demanding the photos and negatives. You ain't with him, are you?"

I shook my head. "Nope. I work independently. I have no idea who you're talking about."

Marcie tilted her head up and looked down her nose at me dubiously. "Okay…"

"But now that you mention it, who was the guy, and why did he want the photos?" I asked.

"He didn't give a name. He was wearing dark shades, so I couldn't recognize his face. He was a smooth talker, though—until he got angry, that is. Anyway, he was demanding we give him the photos and negatives from today's front-page story."

"And?" I raised my eyebrows, eyeing Marcie expectantly.

Marcie mirrored my gaze. "And what? We didn't give him shit. Besides, we don't even have the negatives."

I rubbed my chin. *No negatives…* That confirmed my suspicion that Allison must've still had them. Or her robber did if the photos were, indeed, stolen.

"Interesting," I said. "So where did that photo come from in the first place?"

"Some cat in dark shades dropped off the photos last night." Marcie studied me a moment. "Actually, he wore a trench coat that looked a little like yours."

"What did this guy look like?" I slid my mini notebook out of my trench coat pocket.

"Black guy. Average height. Kinda cute." She paused then quirked a smile. "But not as cute as Mr. Wilson."

"Wait in line, Marcie. He's mine first." Trish giggled.

"Hey, what about us, Trish?" Patrick said, frowning.

Trish rolled her eyes. "There was never 'us.' Mr. Wilson's got it all in the bag. No one can top that silky-smooth Casanova."

I cringed. "Er…"

Trish looked at me as if I were from another planet. "What's with that face? Mr. Wilson is so dreamy. I'd drop off my photo in his office any day."

I tightened my jaw, using every ounce of my willpower to maintain a straight face. "You can't possibly mean that," I said flatly.

Trish blinked at me. "Have you seen him? He's a fine, sweet-talking piece of work."

Ugh… I think I'm going to be sick.

"Give it a rest, Trish," Marcie said. "It's obvious that he's into the new reporter, Rosa. Lucky bitch…"

Rosa… Rosa Timms? I grimaced slightly. *Poor girl.* "Right. So, uh… did this mysterious man in the trench coat say anything to you guys when he stopped by Mr. Wilson's office?" I asked, attempting to steer the conversation in a different direction.

Trish and Patrick shook their heads.

Then Marcie said, "A few of us were working overtime yesterday when he stopped by. Sharon was already gone for the day. I went downstairs to put something on her desk, when I saw a man—a man I didn't know—outside the building, taping a manila envelope to the glass of the front door.

"I opened the door to confront him. It was so strange. He didn't say anything. Simply pointed at the taped envelope then turned and walked away."

"Which way did he go?" I asked, taking more notes.

Marcie shrugged. "Somewhere down Sixty-eighth, I guess. I didn't stick around to find out."

"Interesting. So you're certain this guy wasn't some mail courier or delivery person?"

"Nah, I'm pretty sure this was just a random stranger off the streets," Marcie assured me. "You sure you don't know him?"

"Positive. Sounds like he was doing a blind drop." The three of them furrowed their brows in confusion, and I gave them all a dismissive wave. "It means," I continued, hoping to clear up the police lingo, "whoever the photographer was didn't want those photos traced back to them, so they sent an anonymous person to deliver them."

"I see," Marcie said, nodding slowly. "Well, sorry I couldn't be much help in identifying him."

"Yeah." I sighed. Dark glasses and a trench coat told me nothing. Looked like I might've reached a dead-end already. "What's with that article, anyway? You didn't even mention names or show faces. I mean, surely there were some clear, identifiable photos in that envelope, right?"

Marcie shrugged. "That's what the boss told us to print. I gave the envelope to Mr. Wilson, and he showed the boss."

I scrunched my nose. "That sounds like a very odd decision on your boss's part. Or was it meant to look mysterious to drum up reader intrigue?"

"Maybe there were no names disclosed in that envelope," Patrick suggested. "I don't think anyone knows who the hell those people are in the photo, if you ask me. But it looked scandalous enough for an eye-catching story, so why not dress it up a bit with a controversial article?"

"It's smart marketing, if you ask me," Trish said.

Marketing... I rubbed my chin. *Of course. Follow the money.* "So, hypothetically speaking, if I gave you a story about me marrying Bigfoot, you'd run it on the front page?"

The three of them exchanged dubious looks, then Marcie said to me, "Sure, if the price is right."

"Five hundred bucks?" I asked.

Trish snorted a laugh.

I arched an eyebrow. "A thousand?"

Patrick gave me an amused smile. "Maybe for three-quarters of the front page, and that's only if it's on a slow news day."

"You're looking at a minimum of three thousand dollars for a featured full front-page article," Marcie said.

"And that's *if* it's a slow news day," Patrick restated, waving an index finger.

My jaw dropped. "Three *thousand* dollars?" *Follow the money, indeed.* "So let me get this straight. Someone paid you to run that article with that photo?" I asked.

"Hey, it made a great story, didn't it?" Marcie shrugged.

"I suppose..."

The fact that she didn't answer my question made this mystery even more convoluted. The minutes were ticking by, and before I knew it, I would have to face Newsie and give him the story of a lifetime like I'd agreed—whatever story that might be. In the meantime, I needed to pay a visit to Gatestar Media headquarters and talk to Allison Hays and Paige Russell. I just hoped I wouldn't run into Joey again. But if Joey was smart, he'd probably stay away from there for a while.

Trish slid off the desk and headed for the exit. "Welp. Better get back to work before Mr. Fisher gives me the third degree."

"Hey, wait, let me walk you out," Patrick said, following.

She groaned. "I know how to get to my office, Patrick."

Marcie perked up. "Oh, before I forget. Trish, here." She opened a drawer in her desk, pulled out a small baggie filled with tiny red granules, and handed it to Trish. "My brother snuck more of that stuff in my lunch bag again."

Trish spun, and her eyes went wide with delight. She rushed back to the desk and snatched up the bag. "Yes! I love these so much!" She scooped out a handful of the granules and poured them into her mouth.

Patrick scrunched his nose in disgust. "Ugh! How can you eat those things? They make my mouth feel weird."

I blinked several times. "Um... what is that stuff?" I asked, my former-cop senses assuming the worst.

"My brother calls it Pebble Poppers. It's candy," Marcie explained. "He works at a candy company, and he thinks he's some mad scientist or something, always experimenting and making odd sweets. Lately, he's been obsessed with these Pebble Poppers. They're a prototype. Not even on the market yet."

"What's so special about them?" I asked.

Marcie shrugged. "Who knows? He's weird like that. The candy is carbonated or something. It does funny things to your mouth."

Faint crackling sounds filled the room. Trish stuck out her tongue, which was covered with red Pebble Poppers. "Hey hop hwen yu hut hem hon yur hongue," she said.

I furrowed my brow. "Popping, carbonated candy? Now, there's a new one."

Trish swallowed the Poppers and held the bag out to me. "Try it! They taste like cherry."

I stared suspiciously at the red granules. *Huh. Why not?* I reached into the bag and took out a small pinch. I sniffed the granules then sprinkled them on my tongue and waited for something to happen. They did have a sweet, pleasant cherry taste. Suddenly, I felt tiny pops and crackles on my tongue and the roof of my mouth. I grimaced. "Ah! That smarts!"

"That's the point," Marcie said. "Like I said, my brother is weird."

The popping slowly subsided as the candy melted away on my tongue. "Is he going to actually try and market this to the public?"

"I sure as hell hope not!" Marcie said.

"Are you kidding?" Trish said. "This stuff is gold. My four-year-old cousin would go crazy over it. They kinda make you thirsty afterward, though." She popped open her soda and brought the can to her lips.

Marcie gasped. "No, Trish!" She hopped out of her chair, deftly vaulted over the desk with a gymnast's speed and agility, and slapped the drink out of her friend's hand. The can went flying onto the wooden floor and spilled a frothing puddle of dark-brown liquid.

Trish and Patrick started. I tensed.

"What'd you go and do that for?" Trish asked, glaring at Marcie.

"Never, ever, *ever* drink soda right after eating Pebble Poppers," Marcie said. "That was the number-one rule my brother warned me about."

"What happens if you do?" I asked, my curiosity piqued.

Marcie looked at each of us solemnly. "Your stomach explodes."

I blinked. "What?"

"No way," Patrick said.

Trish rolled her eyes. "That's the most ridiculous thing I ever heard."

"It's true," Marcie persisted. "My brother told me the horror story. He fed some Pebble Poppers to a lab rat. He accidentally spilled his soda, and some of it went into the rat's cage. The rat drank some, and... boom! Guts everywhere."

Patrick grimaced. "Damn... that's nasty."

Trish stared warily at the soda puddle and chewed her bottom lip.

"That's... unbelievable," I said, trying to wrap my head around the unlikely phenomenon. I had a special place in my heart for science, thanks to my childhood hero, Dick Tracy. No way could such a thing happen, based on the basic rules of science. But I had a feeling I'd be wasting my breath trying to explain that to these three.

"It's true, I tell you," Marcie said. "My brother gets into some weird shit sometimes."

"It's so unbelievable, it..." I paused and smirked at an idea. "It sounds like a perfect news story you should write," I finished. If they weren't going to believe me, I'd simply use their ignorance to my advantage.

Marcie perked up at that. "You think so?"

"Yeah. Think of the front-page headline: 'Candy Company Exposed! Makes Dangerous Exploding Candy for Children!'"

Marcie smiled briefly. "Yeah... I like that. It'll teach my brother a lesson and maybe get him off his crazy obsession."

"And you'll be saving millions of children," I added. "Your exposé will be talked about around here for months, maybe years."

"Maybe I'll finally get that promotion." Marcie's smile grew.

Trish grunted. "Hmph. I should be the one to write that story. If it wasn't for me about to drink the soda, you wouldn't have had the idea."

"Why don't the both of you collaborate on it?" I suggested. "Oh, and I bet Mr. Wilson would *love* to have a story like that. Think of how much it would flatter him if you two wrote an exclusive article just for him."

Trish's and Marcie's eyes lit up.

Patrick groaned. "I could give you a way better story than that, Trish," he muttered.

"You can't top this, especially when kids are involved," Trish argued. "This story might as well be a public service announcement. Definitely front page worthy, if you ask me."

"If you say so." Patrick hung his head and quietly left.

"You guys really have something here—I know it," I told Marcie and Trish then headed for the exit.

"Hey, wait, Rita. You never told me that Stefanie Reed story," Marcie called.

Cringing, I stopped and spun around. "Uh, yeah, about that. Wouldn't you know it? I forgot. Guess I'll have to come back later."

Marcie's expression fell. "Oh…"

"But hey, you have a new story to focus on. I'd say get to it!" I continued then quickly left. I shut the door behind me and exhaled a deep sigh. I could hear the excited muffled voices of the two women talking at once.

Looks like I just gained an ace up my sleeve.

CHAPTER 8

My next stop was the Gatestar Media headquarters, located on the corner of East Forty-Sixth Street and Lexington Avenue in Midtown East Manhattan. The trip was a short subway ride across town. I tended to avoid the subways, especially at night, because I was always having to put some knucklehead in their place. The last incident had involved me walking right into the middle of a gang war. Thankfully, I cut that trip short and managed to get out of there in one piece. Today, the crowds were extra thick with tourists and cops and office workers heading home. The lowlife punks wouldn't crawl out of their dirty rat holes for a few hours yet.

I paused at the entrance and looked back at the busy street. Crowds of people walked to and fro, some hopping into waiting taxicabs and others boarding a bus on the corner. I couldn't shake off the feeling of running into Joey earlier. It seemed unlikely I would find him showing his face around here with his giant scandal hanging over his head. Then again, I wasn't sure how dumb or smart he really was. *Well, he didn't recognize me before. So he probably doesn't know I took those photos.*

I stepped through the revolving glass door of Gatestar Media's exquisite eleven-story high rise and entered another world. Unlike the rustic, cramped *National Esquire*, there were no creaky stairs or cranky-looking receptionists. Instead, the cavernous lobby was all mahogany wood, brass, and echoing black marble that turned the hectic rush of high heels and men's hard soles into an overpowering din. Three perfectly coiffed women in sleek business suits manned a semicircular reception desk, and young college-aged kids wearing white badges with Intern under their names wove through the chaos, folders and envelopes jammed under their arms. Some of the interns were dressed in business attire, while others dressed casually. One intern wearing a dark-brown trench coat zipped out of the crowd and brushed past me, a bulky camera hanging around his neck. He rushed through the entrance doors and out of sight.

I walked in with my head held high, like I belonged there, and slid around to a bank of wall telephones with reporters gabbling their hot scoops into the receivers. The nearest one had a tip about a stabbing that had happened on the 6 Train en route to Parkchester late last night. Another reported an arson incident in Jackson Heights earlier that morning.

Lowering the brim of my fedora, I spun away from the reporters then strode toward a mahogany half-round desk, where a uniformed security guard sat.

"Hey, there, missy. You lost?" the pudgy older man asked, scrutinizing me with his narrow gaze.

I gave him a small hat tip and eyed the silver name badge affixed to his breast pocket, which read Miller. "The name's

Carter. Tootsie Carter," I said. "I'm here to see Ms. Allison Hays." I paused and raised my eyebrows. "She *is* here, isn't she?"

Mr. Miller relaxed and sat back in his swivel chair, which gave a light creak. "Yeah, she's here. You another one of those college interns? I swear, there are so many of you people running around this place like ants."

I opened my mouth to recite my canned story, but his question had caught me off-guard. *Ugh. This again.* A day didn't go by that I wasn't mistaken for some kid barely out of high school. Usually, I didn't care, but at times, those mistakes interfered with my job. People either tended not to talk to a runt like me, or I'd get shooed off like some nosy little kid so the "adults" could have some privacy. In this case, however, perhaps a youthful disguise would come in handy in helping me find some clues. I was desperate for anything. I quickly backtracked my prepared statement, cleared my throat, and then said, "Well, I, uh... I just need Ms. Hays to finalize my application. I also have some important information for her. She and I talked the other day, so she knows who I am."

His brow furrowed, then he nodded slowly. "All right." He pointed toward the semicircular desk. "One of the receptionists over there will get you squared away."

"Swell. Thanks," I said then quickly strode to the reception desk, where the three women had their telephone receivers to their ears.

One of them, a brunette with a short bob, finally ended her call and turned to me. "Hello, miss. Do you have an appointment?"

"Sure do." I repeated my rehearsed spiel about Allison Hays and myself.

"All right. Wait a moment." The receptionist picked up a cream-colored receiver attached to a large switchboard and pressed a button then dialed on a rotary. "Ms. Hays, there's a Ms. Tootsie Carter to see you…"

While the woman talked, I scanned an open logbook sitting atop the desk. A list of names was scrawled there, along with the times the people entered and left the building. I didn't see any names I recognized—not even Allison's. Then again, the logbook was probably for visitors only, not employees, but I wasn't certain. The earliest time written on the pages currently open was 1:20 p.m., but I could see the ghosting of more logs on the previous page. As tempted as I was to flip the page over, I kept my hand still. I didn't need to draw any suspicion to my idle investigating.

The receptionist hung up the receiver and looked back at me. "All right, Ms. Carter. Ms. Hays is waiting. Sixth floor, Office 605-A." She tapped the open logbook. "Don't forget to sign in."

"Thanks," I said. I scribbled my John Hancock and the current time, 3:24 p.m., on the last empty space and headed toward the back of the lobby, where three brass-colored elevators sat. People entered and exited, causing the elevator doors to open and close with an awkward synchronization. Three of the interns I'd spotted earlier moved my way, chatting as they gripped their Gatestar Media–branded coffee mugs.

"So is Mr. Santano letting you go out in the field yet?" a girl with long dark hair asked one of her companions, a curly redhead.

Ms. Red let out a snort. "Yeah, right, Nikki. He's making me read papers published in the last three weeks. Then I have to discuss with him five articles I liked. It's such a drag."

"Well, at least you get to do some actual work," Nikki said. "I spent over four hours this morning listening to my mentor drone on about improving my photojournalism skills."

One of the elevators opened and disgorged a group of suited men carrying briefcases. I hurried inside the car before it had a chance to fill up again. The interns followed, seemingly not paying me any mind as they continued their conversation. I pushed the button for the sixth floor. One of the interns, a young Black girl with a short afro, pressed the fifth-floor button. She cast me a curious glance. She had a cute round face and smooth, dark, flawless skin. She looked like she was barely pushing eighteen. *Do people really think I look that young?*

The doors closed, and the elevator began its slow ascent. The strong smell of coffee filled the small space.

"You new around here?" Afro Girl asked me.

I rubbed the back of my head. "Uh, yeah. I'm hoping I get my internship application finalized today. I have a meeting with Ms. Hays."

"Ms. Allison Hays?" She grimaced. "Ooh... good luck, girl. I heard she don't play."

I furrowed my brow. *What does she mean by that?* I wondered.

"I'm Sandra, by the way."

"Nice to meet you. I'm Tootsie," I replied.

Sandra turned back to her chatty friends. "I don't know why they're not letting us write something more exciting and relevant—like about that one girl from Brooklyn who OD'd last night."

Ms. Red frowned. "Another one? Ugh. I hate writing stories like that."

"How else are we gonna get tough around here?" Sandra glanced up at the lighted numbers, which had just passed floor three. "I think it's worthy news, especially with the heroin epidemic going on."

"Was it actually heroin that killed her?" Nikki asked.

"I don't know. I just remembered hearing on the morning news broadcast that the police found little packets with purple circles stamped on them... or were they stars? Either way, they were drugs."

"They're not gonna let any of us write an article like that, Sandra," Ms. Red said. "Those are left up to the big dogs."

The elevator dinged at the fifth floor. The girls left, still chatting away. Their conversation sparked some curiosity, but I knew I couldn't do anything about it. So many types of narcotics were being circulated on the streets that I'd lost track of what was what. The war on drugs was rampant, one of the things keeping the city's law enforcement constantly on their toes. We'd gone from one war overseas to another war right in our own backyard.

Finally, at the sixth floor, I stepped off the elevator and into a long hallway lined with office doors. Unlike the chaos in the lobby, this floor was quieter, with occasional suited passersby walking to and from offices. At the end of the hall, a blue-clad janitor wheeled a supply cart in front of a door and wiped the glass with a white cloth.

A nearby office door was propped wide open, where I caught a glimpse of a large, busy room full of people—mostly women— sitting at several rows of desks, typing away like a paper assembly line. The scene sparked grueling memories of Ms. Ball's high school typing class, where she'd made us all type synchronously while blindfolded. After taking her class, I swore I would never take up any profession that required typing. Of course, I decided to be a cop and a private eye instead, two professions that dealt with more typing than any journalism job.

I found my way to Allison's office. The frosted glass displayed her name and the office's room number. I gave a small knock on the glass then opened the door a crack. "Ms. Hays?" I called. "It's me, Tootsie Carter."

"Come in, Ms. Carter," Allison replied.

I let myself into the medium-sized windowless office littered with loose and crumpled paper, half-opened filing cabinets, and a wooden bookshelf used for storing more stacked manila folders and coffee mugs than books.

Ms. Hays sat behind a typewriter on an L-shaped wooden desk. A pair of large, black-rimmed reading glasses sat atop her head, nestled in her curly, bun-tied brown hair. Her fair-skinned face was caked with makeup, and her lips bled with a rose-colored lipstick two shades too bright. She frowned at me. "What do you want, Detective?"

Her cold tone struck me unawares. Compared to the day before, Allison was like an entirely different woman. I cautiously approached the desk and briefly scanned the mess of papers scattered around her typewriter. A few framed photos of her and an attractive Black man in a suit decorated the desk. A small photobooth strip of her and another woman with a mushroom-style hairdo was pinned to a small thumbtack board with other notecards hanging on the wall by the desk.

"Uh, I wanted to talk to you about those photos from the other day," I said.

Her frown deepened to a scowl. "You mean the one that appeared on the front page of today's *National Esquire?*"

"Yeah. How did—"

"I am furious. And confused. It wasn't supposed to go down like this. I may lose my job. We all might if someone connects the dots and outs Joey. I never asked to be a part of a scandal."

I blinked then whipped out my notebook. "Wait a minute. You have no idea how those photos ended up in the hands of that tabloid?"

"No! Why would I do such a silly thing? I was just trying to get Joey and show Paige that he was no good. I never asked for all this..."

I scribbled down some notes. "Who put you up to this? Frank?"

"Yeah..."

"Okay. Start from the beginning."

She deflated and hung her head. "When I first noticed Joey playing around, I sensed he was bad news. I could tell it was bothering Paige, because she would be a little distant whenever he wasn't around. But she still kept clinging to him like glue. I wanted to help her see that Joey was no good. Cindy and I talked for a long time about it.

"Shortly after that was when I got the telephone call from Frank. He said he could take care of Joey and instructed me to get some photos of him, put the photos and negatives in an envelope, and leave the package under the Alice in Wonderland statue in Central Park."

I stopped writing and arched an eyebrow. "Those are some pretty elaborate instructions just to expose a cheating husband."

"Tell me about it," Allison said. "But I was desperate to help Paige."

"Around what time did Frank call you?"

Allison thought for a moment. "Around six in the evening last Friday, I think. I spent the next few days looking for an available private investigator. That was when I found you."

"So after you left my office yesterday, where did you go? What did you do?"

"I did as Frank instructed. I put them in an envelope, went to Central Park, and left them under the statue."

"What time was that?"

Allison tapped her chin. "I don't know. Maybe around eight o'clock? It was dark."

"You're lucky you didn't get mugged out there. Or worse."

She grimaced. "I was scared, but I knew it had to be done for Paige's sake. I didn't stick around. Anyway, my fiancé Mike was with me."

"So you didn't see anyone come by and pick up the package?"

"Nope. Mike and I left the park and went home."

"Did Mike see anyone?"

Allison shook her head. "No, unfortunately."

"And you didn't have Frank's number, so you couldn't call him to let him know the package was there, right?"

"That's right." She perked up. "Say, I wonder how Frank knew I had delivered the package?"

I twirled the pen between my fingers. "Maybe he didn't. Maybe someone else did."

Allison chewed her bottom lip. "You're saying someone else might've taken it?"

"Could be. But if that's the case, then it sounds like sloppy work on Frank's part. Especially for someone who gives such elaborate drop-off instructions. No, something ain't right."

"Yeah. That damned tabloid knows what's going on with Joey and this company. They'll hang this scandal over our heads for who knows how long. I don't know what kind of message was supposed to be conveyed with this article."

I rubbed my chin. "Maybe it's a subtle message. A warning, perhaps. Does Joey have any enemies?"

"Hmph. Cindy's not too keen on him. I don't know about everyone else in the company, but I personally think he's a first-class asshole. I want Paige to get rid of him. He's a plague on this company and on my life."

"What did he do to you?"

"What didn't he do? He's a total racist and pig."

I arched an eyebrow. "Racist against you?" I looked at her quizzically. Allison was a White chick. Joey was a White dude. That didn't make a whole lot of sense to me.

She shook her head. "Not against me. Against Mike, my fiancé. Joey doesn't think a White woman should date a Black man."

I wrinkled my nose as if I could smell the racism. "Your fiancé's Black?" Allison Hays was just full of impressive surprises.

"Yeah. But Joey ain't having none of it. He's always saying that I need to find myself a 'good, full-blooded American man who will treat me right.'"

"You're right. Joey sounds like a first-class pig."

"Yeah. Fuck him. Joey still thinks *Loving v. Virginia* was a conspiracy theorist's fairy tale. But we're getting married in two months. I love Mike with all my heart."

"Right on, and congratulations," I said.

"Thanks. Ever since Joey has been at this company and said those terrible things to me, I've hated coming to work."

"So why don't you quit?"

Allison shook her head. "Quitting is a coward's way out. I'm not letting some racist, male chauvinist dirtbag dictate my life. And Paige is a good person. I'm going to free her from this nightmare if it's the last thing I do."

"Whoa. Hey now. I get that you have an axe to grind with him, but let's be rational about this. Someone on the outside has their hands in this pot. They have the photos and negatives. They can do a lot of damage."

Her eyes widened slightly. "What if... what if Joey's behind all this? What if he's the one who stole the photos?"

"What?"

"Joey's a slick mother. I wouldn't put it past him to sabotage this company, even at the cost of his own reputation."

"Why would he do that? Would he really go that far to take down his wife's company?"

She snorted. "The way he's been acting? I doubt he gives two shits about his wife."

That seemed like a far-fetched conclusion but perhaps not impossible. I still needed to find more pieces of this puzzle in order to clear things up a little.

Allison's expression dulled. "I'm at a loss, Detective. Maybe you can talk some sense into Paige."

"Me? If she won't even listen to her own employees, why would she listen to an outsider like me?"

"Maybe if you let her know you're a detective, she might listen to you. Look, I'm pulling at straws here. I don't know how else to get her to wake up. I don't think we'll ever know what became of those photos or how they ended up at the *National Esquire*."

"Well, incidentally, I visited the *National Esquire* headquarters earlier, and the staff said that a Black man in a trench coat and dark glasses left the photos."

Allison bristled. "Well that wasn't Mike, if that's what you're driving at."

"Of course not. The photos had to have been taken sometime during the night, but you were with your fiancé all night, right?"

"Yes, we took the cab back to our apartment after we left the park. Neither of us went anywhere else."

"Okay." I flipped to a fresh page and scribbled more notes—Allison seemed to have a sound alibi. "Do you know where else Joey likes to hang out?"

"Other than the Peacock House? I have no idea. But I'm sure that bastard gets around."

"What about Paige? Where does she like to go?"

"Paige is a workaholic. She's usually here working until late at night. I've tried to get her out to a bar or discotheque, but she always makes excuses."

I tapped the clicker end of my pen against my lips. A wife in charge who never left her office sounded like a perfect recipe for any adulterous husband. "Does Paige get a lot of visitors in her office?"

Allison snorted. "Are you kidding? Her office penthouse might as well have a revolving door. All business, mind you. She's been pretty busy today, with all the investor meetings."

I raised my eyebrow skeptically. "Are you sure that's all that's been going down in her office?"

"I'd bet my life on it, Detective. She loves Joey unconditionally."

"I see." I stared at my notes and frowned.

"I just want all this to go away. I should've not let Joey get to me so much."

"What's done is done," I said. "I'm going to find a way to get those photos back."

"I appreciate you giving a damn to want to help me."

I wrinkled my nose. "Yeah..." My reasons were twofold. One, I had a business reputation to maintain. I didn't need anyone—especially Newsie—to find out those tabloid photos were mine. And two, I didn't want to see this company go under on account of some scandal. Where else was I going to get my daily dose of *Dick Tracy* strips?

Allison chewed her bottom lip. "I guess I should compensate you for your time."

I opened my mouth to decline the offer but rethought things. I felt like I was on the butt-end of someone's sick joke. But whose? What started as 'easy money' was growing into a big, giant pain. And now that Newsie was somehow involved, I wasn't about to be destroyed by some wannabe journalist who built his career on lies. This was war.

"Yeah," I finally said. "Given the extent of this problem, I think compensation is gonna be necessary for this one."

"Of course. I wouldn't expect anything less from a professional. One seventy-five a day, right?"

"Plus expenses."

"Okay. I'll have the money ready."

"Good. Now, in the meantime, you lay low and stay out of trouble. I'll be in touch. If that Frank guy calls you again, let me know."

She nodded. "Right on." Her desk phone rang. Her gaze turned to the phone, and she told me in an apologetic voice, "I think we're done here, Detective." She picked up the black receiver.

"Yeah, I guess we are," I said. "Have a good day, Ms. Hays." I spun on my heel and left her office. As I slowly closed the door, I tried to take a small listen of Allison's conversation. Frank's name wasn't mentioned, and from the newspaper lingo she used—like "gutters," "real estate," and "mastheads"—it sounded like she was talking to another employee. I trusted that she'd let me know if she heard from Frank. After all, she wanted to see the matter go away as soon as possible. And so did I.

Making my way back to the elevators, I whipped out my mini notebook and wrote down a few more interesting notes from my conversation with Allison. It might be worthwhile to pay Paige a visit. But how was I going to get in there without making a scene?

"*Hola, jovencita,*" someone muttered nearby.

I shoved aside my thoughts and looked up at the janitor, whom I'd spotted farther down the hall earlier. Now, the older Puerto Rican man was busily wiping the brass trim on one of the elevators to a shine.

"You talking to me, sir?" I asked the man, who didn't look up from his work.

"*Sí.*" He glided the rag along the sides of the brass trim, removing grime and stray handprints. The man had a receding hairline, and his weathered profile sported a full salt-and-pepper beard. "You mind taking the stairs?" he continued in heavily accented English.

I exhaled a small breath of relief, realizing I wouldn't have to rack my brain trying to use my weak high-school-level Spanish. "Uh, sure. Is there something wrong with the elevator?" I looked toward the flashing floor numbers.

"No," the janitor replied. He took a step closer and casually wiped down the brass button panel in circular motions. "Can we... talk?" he asked in a lower volume, keeping his eyes averted.

I chewed my bottom lip. The sharp sound in his voice indicated he had information to share. I gave him a quick once-over. He was dressed in a blue-grey worker's uniform with an oval name patch that read Luis in dark-blue script.

"Okay," I said with a nod. I stepped away from the elevators and walked down to the opposite end of the hallway. I brushed past a frazzled-looking woman carrying an armful of papers, who scrambled off as though she was late for a meeting. I reached the stairwell entrance and stood next to the closed door.

Luis the Janitor joined me. He glanced behind himself, his dark-brown eyes filled with a spark of concern, then returned his attention to me. "I overheard you talking with Allison. You're a detective?" he whispered.

My ears perked. Interesting—he didn't refer to Ms. Hays formally. I leaned in closer and whispered back, "That's right."

"*Muy bien.* I need to talk to someone that's not the police."

I furrowed my brow. "What do you need to talk about?"

"About Allison. About a lot of things." He nervously looked around again.

He sounded like he knew something—something good. I was at odds with this convoluted mystery, so I would take anything I could get. "Okay. I'm listening."

"Not here. Let's meet at Twin Kettles Coffee Shop on East Thirty-Sixth Street and Third Avenue. It's easier this way. Nine o'clock okay?"

I gave him another careful once-over. He sounded sincere, that what he had to say was strictly business. Still, I had to be on my guard. I didn't know anything about him or his motives. "Why so late?"

"I get off at eight o'clock. I have some family business to take care of, and then I will go to Twin Kettles."

"Okay. Nine o'clock's fine. I got a favor to ask of you in return, though."

He nervously looked over his shoulder again then back at me. "What is it? I must get back to work."

"I need to talk to Paige Russell. Can you find a way to get me to her office without any trouble?"

His eyes widened. "*¡Mierda!* You crazy? I'll get fired."

"Hey, this is important. This entire company may be in danger if I don't talk to her soon. I'll agree to your terms if you agree to mine."

He pursed his lips, his gaze faltering from mine again. "Okay. Okay. I'll… I'll see what I can do."

"Is she working tonight?"

"*Sí*, she works late most nights."

I nodded. "All right. I'll meet you at Twin Kettles at nine tonight, then." I checked my watch. "What time you got?"

He held out his left wrist, revealing a small watch with a worn leather strap. I synchronized my time with his.

"*Ven solo.* Come alone. Just you. Okay?" he stressed.

"Yeah, sure. I got it. I'll be there at nine o'clock sharp. Just me."

One corner of his lips tugged upward to a small smile, revealing more wrinkles around his eyes and cheeks. "*Gracias*, Detective." He spun and returned to his janitor's cart sitting by the elevators. He retrieved the rag sticking out from his back pocket and resumed polishing the brass trim.

I pushed open the door to the stairwell. Stagnant, musty air seeped out. I peered down toward the ten flights of stairs. The sounds of doors opening and closing several floors above and below me echoed off the concrete walls.

As I made my way down the stairs, I let my mind wander. Tonight's meeting with Luis the Janitor might prove lucrative. He could be the key—literally—to getting inside Ms. Russell's office. If she was as busy as Allison said, then I'd most likely find a clue about those missing photographs. About Joey. *About a lot of things*, as Luis had put it so eloquently.

Finally reaching the first-floor lobby, I stopped at the receptionist desk and signed out. Then I quickly escaped the building before I was spotted by some suspicious reporter that might stop me and give me the third degree. I had a few hours before evening to prepare for my meeting with Luis, so I headed back home. Sid wasn't around to take me this time, but another Checker cabbie who picked me up drove just as quickly. Thank goodness, because I needed all the time I could spare to make sure tonight's plan was flawless.

CHAPTER 9

Returning to my Leland Avenue apartment, I checked my mailbox in the vestibule—empty. *Now, there's a nice surprise, for a change.* I climbed the stairs to the fourth floor. As I walked toward my apartment, I spotted a note taped to Crazy Bob's door. Curious, I approached it. I knew that note was none of my business, but Bob, for someone who, as far as I knew, barely—if ever—left his apartment, sure seemed to be getting a lot of visitors lately. *Who's coming to his door now?* I was beginning to wonder if Bob was some famous celebrity.

The note was a neatly folded piece of white paper with an embossed seal affixed. It looked important. It looked... official. I blinked. *Did that guy from earlier really sue him?* Well, the least I could do was give Bob the note. I edged closer to the door and listened. The clackity typing noise made me relax a little, confirming that Bob was home. I knocked on the door.

"Hey, Bob. It's Tootsie," I called. "I just wanted to let you know that you have a note on your door."

The typing stopped. Moments later, muffled footsteps shuffled toward the door. After a series of clicks and slides from the locks, the door opened a crack. A whiff of cigarettes and liquor seeped out, but Bob didn't appear. Instead, his hairy arm appeared, snaking around the edge of the door, and his grubby fingers ripped off the taped note. He gripped the crisp paper, crinkling it, and then pulled his arm back.

"Uh..." I said to the invisible man as I rubbed the back of my head sheepishly, "sorry, I wasn't trying to be nosy or anything. I just happened to see it on my way back to my apartment. It looked important, so I wanted to let you know. Don't worry, I didn't open it."

Seconds later, Bob's hand returned, holding out a five-dollar bill.

I blinked. "Hey, I'm not asking for tips or anything. I'm just trying to be a good neighbor."

Again, he shoved the bill toward me insistently, saying nothing.

I rolled my eyes then finally swiped the money. "Geez Louise. Fine. If that's how you feel about me letting you know about one little note."

Still silent, he retracted his arm again. The door slowly closed with an eerie creak.

I remained in front of his door, staring at the money in my hand, trying to make sense of the strange encounter. But my brain was currently preoccupied with more important matters, like tonight. I returned to my apartment.

After locking the door, I plopped down at my desk and sighed. *What a day.* And it wasn't even done yet. I had a little over five hours until my meeting with Luis the Janitor at the coffee shop. I figured I'd better take advantage of the downtime

and get some lunch. As I was deciding between a grilled cheese
or a ham sandwich, a man's silhouette appeared beyond the
closed blinds of my front door. The silhouette stood there for a
few moments, then his head moved slightly. Moments later, the
doorknob jiggled, and I heard a firm yet nervous knock on the
glass.

I straightened in my chair. *Another potential client?* I thought.
I rarely took on multiple cases at once, depending on the
situation. I would hate to turn away a person in desperate need
for help, but I would listen to their story, at least. I got up from
the desk and walked to the door. I swiveled the blinds open and
froze. My jaw dropped as I stared wide-eyed at the last man I
hoped to see.

Joey Russell.

His charming olive face was beet red again. He looked as
furious as he had when I bumped into him earlier at the *National
Esquire.* My heart pounded so quickly that I felt it was going to
tear out of my chest.

Joey stared at me long and hard then mirrored my shocked
expression. "You! It *was* you!"

I swallowed. I tried swiveling the blinds closed again, but my
hand was shaking too much. *He knows. Darn it, he knows.* "I-I
don't know wh-what you're talking about," I said, fumbling with
the swivel wand.

"You know exactly what I'm talking about, you nosy bitch."
He gritted his teeth. "Open this fucking door."

"I will not. Now go away."

"I know who you are, and I know what you did. I ain't
leaving."

"Then I'm going to call the police."

He growled. "My life's already a living hell right now. I don't need cops involved." The anger in his tone ebbed.

"That's your problem, not mine," I said. "Now, this is your last chance. Leave, or else."

He pressed his hands and forehead against the glass. "Look. I'm unarmed. Give me five minutes, and I'll explain. I swear, no bullshit. Let me in, damn it."

He was pleading at that point, but I remained vigilant. I abandoned the door a moment, grabbed my gun from my desk drawer, and tucked it into my waistband. Then I returned to the door. I couldn't trust that he was really unarmed, so I had to protect myself, just in case. "Five minutes," I said. "And don't even think about trying to get slick with me. I have a gun, and I know how to use it."

He looked at me with trepidation and nodded.

I took a deep breath and undid the locks. Then I slowly opened the door. Joey stood there a moment, looking at me with a half-confused, half-intrigued expression.

"You own this joint?" he asked, waving his finger, indicating my office apartment.

"No, I'm just the maid," I said dryly, rolling my eyes. "Your stupid question cost you four minutes. Now you only got one minute to explain yourself. You better start talking some sense, turkey."

He nodded and walked inside. "Okay. Here it is. I'm being blackmailed, all right? I'm in hot water, and those photos you took made this problem even worse."

I crossed my arms and arched an eyebrow. "What did you do?"

He frowned. "Nothing. Look, I'm not gonna talk about that. All I want are the negatives. The people at the *National Esquire* had a couple of the photos but none of the negatives. So I assumed they were still at the source of the problem."

"What makes you think I took them? And how did you know where to find me?"

"I saw you peeking through the window at the Peacock House before you made a run for it. I recognized you again at the *National Esquire*, so I took a taxi and followed you."

The Torino cab at the National Esquire office. I wonder…

"I waited while you went for a visit at Gatestar Media headquarters and then followed you back here," he finished. "And I'm not leaving until I get those negatives."

"Sorry to disappoint you, but I don't have them. I'm trying to find them also."

"Who hired you to take those pictures?"

"I don't discuss my clients. But I can assure you they don't have the negatives either."

Joey combed his fingers through his dark hair. Light reflected off that gaudy panther ring on his right finger, the ugly face looking like the boogeyman rearing its gruesome mug in the dark. "Are you really on the level, Ms. Carter? Are you actually trying to get those negatives back?"

"I am, but not for the same reasons you have. I can't believe your poor wife has to be subject to men like you."

"Hey, I love her, all right?"

"You know and I know that's a load of bull." I paused and wrinkled my nose, thinking about his eyesore fashion sense. "Especially from someone who wears an ugly ring like that."

He arched an eyebrow. "What's wrong with my ring?"

"It's creepier than Frankenstein."

He snorted out a laugh. "For your information, this is a Dionysus ring, named after the Greek god of wine and debauchery. It symbolizes living life to the fullest and not giving a shit."

"How ironic and fitting for a dirtbag like you."

"Whatever. I don't give a fuck what you think. Paige is my wife."

"Some husband you are, playing around like a spoiled kid with too many toys."

He sighed and clenched his fists. "Paige fucked up. She made a bad decision by sticking her nose where it don't belong. Now we're all in deep shit."

"The only bad decision I see she's made was marrying you."

He glared at me. "Look, I ain't risking my neck no more."

"What are you talking about?"

"This shit runs deep. Far deeper than you think. If you really want to know what's going on, then go to this place after eleven tonight. Tell them you want the Bubblegum Special." He rapped out an address to somewhere in Queens.

I went to my desk and transcribed the address onto a piece of paper. "What is that, some kind of secret drink?"

He followed me and stood before the desk. "Just... go there, and you'll know."

"Okay, Joey. I'll bite. You better not be jiving me."

"I'm not. Hell, what is it gonna take for you to find those negatives? Money? How much?"

Now he was desperate. But no price could undo the pain he'd given his wife. "Three hundred bucks a day, plus expenses," I spat.

His eyes widened. "That's insane."

"No, that's business. I thought you'd know all about that."

He grumbled under his breath.

"How badly do you want those negatives?" I urged.

After another round of grumbling, he jammed a hand into one of his pants pockets, yanked out a wad of twenties secured with a rubber band, and tossed it to me. "Here. Take it."

I caught the wad and thumbed through the bills—far more than three hundred dollars. I thought about saying something about it but decided not to. Joey's infidelity had gone from a small, easy-money problem to a full-blown crisis in very little time. "All right. Give me your telephone number. I'll be keeping in touch, so you better not try and run out on me, thinking you're gonna leave me in the middle of your mess."

"I'm not going anywhere. Not until I get those damned negatives back." He gave me his number, which I wrote down.

"Okay, we're done here. Now, leave and let me work." I pointed at the door. "And don't you ever come around here harassing me like that again, or I *will* call the police next time, you dig?"

He lifted his chin, looking down his nose at me. One corner of his mouth tugged upward into a small, crooked smirk. "Yeah. I dig it. You got your shit together. Reminds me of Paige. Let's just hope you don't make bad decisions too."

I narrowed my eyes. "Get out."

He looked at me for a few moments then turned and left. He walked with a bit of swagger in his step as if he owned the world. After all the chaos he'd caused his wife, perhaps he did. But even beneath all that charm and charisma, he was still a wolf.

I followed him and stopped at my doorway, watching him go down the hallway stairs until he was out of sight. I waited a beat in case the slickster tried sneaking back upstairs. When I was fully convinced he was gone for good, I closed and locked my office apartment door, reset all the locks, and swiveled the blinds closed. My brain was mush. I shut out my encounter with Joey for a little while and spent the next few hours on myself before I went out to meet Luis the Janitor tonight.

I fixed a grilled cheese sandwich on my hot plate for lunch and scarfed it down as if I hadn't eaten in days—but I barely tasted it. I took a power nap, hoping to reset my brain—but I tossed and turned every minute. Lastly, I reviewed my case notes—but I couldn't focus. My mind was swimming from all the information I'd gleaned. Joey seemed to have a possible lead, but as with everyone else I'd run into today, I wasn't fully convinced he was on the level.

Around eight o'clock, my telephone rang. I looked up from my notebook and grabbed the receiver from the desk telephone.

"Good evening. Detective Carter speaking," I said.

"Hey, Tootsie. I got those fingerprint results for you," Chief Lewis said.

I relaxed a little. "Wow, that was fast."

"He already had a yellow sheet, so it sped up the process. One of my rookies found the match."

"Terrific. What'd you find?"

"They belong to a guy named Harry Lawton. He's some kind of small-time political pundit. He had a counterfeiting charge from late last year. Other than that, he's been clean as a whistle."

I snorted. "There's no such thing as a 'clean' political pundit, Chief."

"Touché."

"And that guy definitely ain't clean after what I caught him doing outside my neighbor's apartment."

"Well, you know I can't do anything without some solid proof. Get me something good, and I'll get him off the street."

I deflated. *Great. Who knows when that guy will be back again?* I wondered about that note on Crazy Bob's door. *Could Harry have put that there?* "Yeah, sure... I'll get you something," I said. "Thanks for looking into it, Chief." I paused, hesitating to ask him for another favor. "Um... I was wondering if you can help me with one last thing."

Chief Lewis sighed. "Spit it out, Tootsie."

"Can you get a list of all incoming calls made to this number around 6:00 p.m. last Friday?" I gave him Allison's telephone number.

"I'll see what I can do. What's this about?"

"It's for a case." I left it at that and hoped the chief wouldn't ask any more about it.

"All right. Be careful out there. Don't go and get in over your head again with your cases."

I smiled. "I'm not. It's just some simple detective work, that's all. Thanks again."

"Sure. Oh, by the way. It's called 'anachronistic displacement.'"

I scrunched my brow. "Huh?"

"That friend of yours who doesn't know what day it is. Carmen, the precinct's behavioral psychologist, told me all about it. Anachronistic displacement is a mental condition where a person actually believes they are existing in a certain time period and they're pretty much unaware of what's going on in the here and now."

Sounds like Beth, all right. "Is there any cure?" I asked.

"Carmen didn't mention a cure," the chief said. "She said it's a state of mind. So I guess it could be one of those things where something just suddenly clicks in your friend's head one day, and *poof!* They're back to living in the right time. Apparently, this condition occurs more in the elderly. The modern world moves too fast for them to keep up, I guess."

"My friend is only a couple years older than me, so I doubt that's the case."

"Did you try the calendar?"

"Yeah. Didn't work. She actually thought I was a time-traveler from the future." I sighed. "I guess there really is no hope for her, huh?"

"For now, no. But don't sweat it," he said. "I'm sure she'll come around one of these days. Maybe."

"That's reassuring," I said flatly.

We talked a little while longer. No reports of photo robberies had come in to the precinct the day before. Allison seemed to be telling the truth about not being robbed of the photos. Then again, she could've neglected to go to the police. Either way, it led me nowhere.

I didn't mention anything to the chief about Joey. I didn't want to discuss all that mess yet—not until I had some good, solid leads.

The more I thought about this convoluted mystery, the more I believed that someone—or multiple someones—wasn't telling the truth, and I was caught in the middle of this web of lies, being knocked around like a pinball. One thing I hated more than someone bad-mouthing the name of Dick Tracy—being played.

CHAPTER 10

By 8:30 p.m., I'd left my apartment. My favorite cabbie was all smiles as he pulled up to the curb in front of my building. But his smile didn't do much to ease my nerves as I hopped into the backseat. I wasn't sure what to expect, if I was walking into a trap or worse. I brought along my .38 just in case, but I hoped and prayed I didn't have to use it. Soon, we were off, headed downtown.

"Hey, Ms. Carter," Sid said, breaking me out of my thoughts. "I was thinking earlier today about how you can complete your *Dick Tracy Monthly* collection."

"Oh?" I said, half of my mind piqued with interest while the other half focused on the task at hand.

"The Comic Art Convention is coming up in July at the Commodore Hotel. I bet you'll be able to snag some old issues there. But if you're feeling really ambitious, there's always San Diego Comic Con."

I grimaced. "Ah, yeah, I think I'll stay local for now." I'd missed the last year's Comic Art Convention because of a case. I felt torn, part of me regretting that I'd missed one of my most anticipated events of the year. But duty had called, especially when it had involved a case of a missing child. That case wrapped up nicely, and I was stuck with reading the recap of the convention in the paper the next day. Oh well.

"I hear ya," Sid said. "Last time I've been outta this city was back in '43. It's a long way to Salerno from here, I'll tell ya what."

We pulled up in front of Twin Kettles Coffee Shop. The place was housed in a two-story brick building and sandwiched between a boutique clothing store and a law firm. Both businesses were shuttered for the day, the metal doors rolled down in front of their entrances. An Open sign flashed from the glass door of the coffee shop. From my distance, the place looked empty. I sure hoped Luis wasn't leading me on.

"On another case again, I take it, Ms. Carter?" Sid asked, looking at me from the rearview mirror.

"Something like that."

I checked my watch—ten minutes until nine. Sid had blazed through the streets like a racecar driver.

"You gonna be around this area for a while?" I asked.

He quirked a smile. "I can be. Or, y'know, I could just wait on ya, doll." He flipped off the meter, which halted at two dollars.

I smiled as well then slipped him a five-dollar bill through the bulletproof partition. "You don't have to wait. You have a job to do, after all. I wouldn't want you to get in trouble with your boss."

"Psh. It's all right, Ms. Carter. My boss knows I'm one of the best drivers he's got. Nobody knows this city better than me. He ain't never gonna give me a hard time. Besides, with all these crazy gas prices, my boss better be glad I'm saving the company a li'l dough."

Touché. "All right," I conceded, realizing there was no point in arguing with him. "I swear, one of these days, I'll have to pay you back somehow for all the times you've helped me."

"Don't worry about it, doll. You just keep on getting these knuckleheads off the streets, 'cause the cops can't do it all alone."

I chuckled. "I try. But sometimes things get so tough I just wanna give up. But then I think about all the people out there who don't have help. All those families... it reminds me why I do this."

Sid's smile faltered. "Huh. Well, you fight the good fight. Like I once did. Ain't got no more family to fight for, though, so I just fight for me."

I cocked my head. "No family? Not even siblings? No kids of your own?"

He laughed. "Nah. My family disowned me when I was sixteen, when my pops found out I was dating an Irish girl. But then I later found out that she was cheating on me, which really messed me up. I joined the Army after that."

I opened my mouth then closed it. I couldn't even begin to understand how it felt to not be loved by one's own family—betrayed by the people they loved. Poor Sid. He seemed like a great guy who deserved a better life, a happier life.

"I'm sorry," was all I could say.

"Me too," he said. "I'm sorry I put all my trust in that lying broad. And I haven't talked to my family since the day I left home. They probably think I'm dead by now, anyway. The last thing Pops told me when I walked out the door was to go to hell.

Whatever. That's what the past is meant for—to stay outta my way."

My throat tightened. His rigid tone indicated he'd made up his mind about his life a long time before. I thought for a moment. "Hey, are you working this Friday night?" I asked, trying to lighten the mood.

The dark cloud over his face lifted a little as his smile slowly returned. "I work every Friday night, doll."

"Well, clock out early and come down to Kronos Lounge. My friend is hosting a watch party for the Ali-Lyle fight. It'd be great if you could come."

His face got a little brighter. "Yeah? Damn, I heard that's supposed to be a good fight. All right, li'l lady. I'll see what I can do."

"Swell." I checked my watch. *Five minutes left.* I opened the door. "Gotta go now. Thanks for the chat."

"Anytime, Ms. Carter. I'll be waitin' here."

"I might be in there a while. You really don't have to—"

"I'll be waitin' *here*," he insisted in his no-nonsense bulldog tone, giving me a stern gaze.

I hesitated then got out of the cab. "A-All right."

The mildly cool night air graced my cheeks as I walked into the coffee shop. The aroma of fresh coffee beans hit my nose and perked me up a little. The place was dead. A lone waitress poured coffee for a man sitting at the counter. He was young—too young to be Luis—and dressed in a snazzy yellow button-down shirt and matching plaid pants. Leaning on his elbows at the counter, he stared at his cup of joe like he was deep in thought.

Toward the back of the shop at a tiny two-seater table was Luis, smoking a cigarette while reading the Sports section of the paper. He was out of his blue janitor's uniform and wore a casual tan shirt, black slacks, and a faded grey baseball cap. I approached the table and stood behind the empty chair across from him.

"I'm here," I said, wrapping my fingers around the top of the chair.

Luis looked up and smiled. "*Hola*," he said, folding the paper and setting it aside. He tapped some ash from his cigarette into the ashtray on the table and gestured for me to sit. "Please."

I waited a beat, took one last look around the place, then pointed at his chair. "I want to sit there."

He furrowed his brow. "Uh... okay..." He got up and sat in the other chair.

I plopped down in my preferred seat, where I had my back to the wall and a good look at the place. These old police habits were going to follow me until the day I died. "All right, Luis. Let's talk," I said.

"I'm glad you came, Ms. Detective," Luis began, smiling slightly.

"Just call me Tootsie," I said. "What kind of information do you have for me?"

His smile fell, and he lowered his voice. "It's about... what you and Allison talked about earlier. Joey Russell. I don't like him. Things ain't never been the same since he started working at Gatestar."

I whipped out my notebook to a fresh page and began writing. "What's changed around there?" I asked.

"Everyone's in a bad mood. I think they're scared. Those investors... they started coming around a lot more, meeting with Ms. Russell. She's been nervous. I think the newspaper's gonna shut down. I think Joey did this."

"I haven't formally met the man, and I already hate his guts. You ever talk to him?"

Luis shook his head. "No... and I'm glad I don't. I'd punch him in the nose, otherwise, for talking to Allison the way he does. Allison is a good woman. She's trying to help Ms. Russell get over Joey. I just wish Ms. Russell will listen..."

"What's your beef with Joey?"

"*Ay*... I don't like the way he talks to me. Just 'cause I'm the janitor. And I don't like the way he treats Allison. Sometimes I wonder if he treats Ms. Russell like that too."

I blinked. "You think so?"

Maybe that was why Paige was so reluctant to learn the truth. Maybe she already knew and Joey had threatened her to stay silent. Could she have known about the photos? Maybe she knew about the negatives. It could've been the only thing she had over Joey without his knowing. Talking to her about it—or at least trying—might be worthwhile.

"Ms. Russell is a good lady. A good boss," Luis said. "I've been working here for over seven years, since back when her *padre* was running things. He was a good boss too."

The yellow-clad stranger at the counter finally slid off his stool, left some change on the counter, and walked out. The waitress swiped up the money and cleared away the dishes. She cast Luis and me a brief glance then stood behind the register going through guest checks. At last, Luis and I were alone, and I let my body relax a little.

"Ms. Tootsie," Luis said, "since you're a detective, can you find out what's going on? But please do it quietly. I don't want the police around."

"I'll do my best. I'll need your help, though." I raised my eyebrows at him, hoping he'd remembered to hold up his end of the bargain.

Luis took a long, nervous drag of his cigarette and exhaled. "*Sí*, I know. My coworker Edwin works the janitorial night shift. He don't like what's going on around there, either. I told him I was meeting a detective tonight to hopefully investigate and that they would need to get into the building unnoticed."

I took some notes. "Is this Edwin guy on the level?"

"*Sí*. I swear to you, Ms. Tootsie, Edwin hates Joey as much as I do. He also thinks Joey is trying to take down the company. We don't want to lose our jobs."

"I get it. So is Edwin willing to let me in?"

Luis nodded. "*Sí*. He said for you to come to headquarters at ten thirty tonight. Come around through the alley. He'll have the side door propped open for a few minutes for when he takes out the garbage."

I nodded once but had a strange feeling in my gut. I wasn't foolish enough to walk around in a dark alley unprepared, especially in this city. I couldn't take any chances, no matter how straight Luis or his friend seemed. I checked my watch. I had a little over an hour. "Okay. Got it."

"I told him what you looked like, so he'll keep an eye out for you," Luis said.

"And what does Edwin look like?"

"He's short. Black guy. Wears glasses. Got a small beard. He's a little older than me."

I wrote down more notes. "Okay."

Luis finished his cigarette and doused the butt in the ashtray. "I'm taking a big risk with my job, *jovencita*, I got bills to pay. I also need this money to help out my brother Ricky and his family. They're trying to adopt a kid. I can't believe how damn expensive it is…"

"Yeah, one of those unfortunate things. What does your brother do, anyway?"

"He and his family own a small restaurant up in Mott Haven. They sent in their adoption application six months ago, but they need more money to cover the extra expenses. Business has been slow, and they haven't been able to get enough money saved before the deadline."

"I see. Well, you're a good brother to want to help him out like that." I finished writing then looked up at him carefully. "I don't want to see this company fold. And I don't want to see you lose your job."

"Just be careful, okay?"

"Would Edwin be able to sneak me up to her office?"

"No, but you should be fine if you take the stairs. The security guard mostly hangs out in the lobby during the night and don't do the rounds while the janitorial staff are cleaning."

"The building doesn't have CCTV, does it?"

"No."

That was a relief. I reviewed my notes. Looked like I would be off to Gatestar Media Headquarters next. But then I spotted the address that Joey had given me earlier. My next idea was a long shot, but Luis seemed the observant type. Maybe he'd overheard Joey talk about this address before. "One last question," I said, showing Luis the address. "Do you know this place?"

Luis stared at it a moment then wrinkled his nose. "That's my uncle Diego's thrift store in Jackson Heights. It's called Thrifty World… well, his store's address ends in nine, not eleven. Maybe it's next door or across the street."

"Hmm…" I rubbed my chin.

"Why do you ask?"

"Joey gave it to me."

Luis frowned. "*Bastardo…*" He perked up a little. "I wonder if…"

"What?"

"*Tío* Diego once told me about his rude next-door neighbors. A beauty parlor, I think. They kept making noise, and sometimes, he hears strange sounds under the floor."

I arched an eyebrow. "Sounds under the floor?"

Luis shrugged. "My uncle couldn't explain it. He just said it bothered him."

"Did he complain to the landlord? Or the police?"

"No, *Tío* Diego didn't want to cause problems. He's a simple man, Detective. He likes to mind his own business."

"I understand."

"If Joey gave you that address, then maybe he has something to do with whatever's going on next door."

That was a possibility, but I wondered what sort of business a slimeball like Joey would have with a beauty parlor. "I'll check it out."

"I hope Joey stays far away from my family. If you ever stop by *Tío* Diego's shop, please check on him and tell him hi for me. He closes the shop at eight, though."

I checked my watch—already ten o'clock. "Okay. Maybe I'll visit him tomorrow. For now, I'm going to see what I can get out of Ms. Russell." I slid out of my chair. "Thanks for all the information."

Luis nodded. "Will you let me know what happens?"

I wrinkled my nose slightly. "It depends on the information. Can't make any promises. Give me your telephone number."

He spat it out, and I wrote it down in my notebook. Then his smile returned a little brighter this time. "*Gracias*, Tootsie. I appreciate your help."

I said my goodbyes and left. Sid was still waiting outside. I hopped in the cab, and we were off again.

Around ten twenty, we pulled up along the curb across the street from the Gatestar Media building. A few windows inside the eleven-story building burned with a soft, fluorescent glow. The lobby was dimly lit, and I spotted occasional movement inside. I looked toward the dark alley beside the building. A streetlamp flickering its dim amber glow nearby wasn't enough to penetrate the gloomy opening. Occasionally, people walked by, some dressed lavishly as though they were coming or going to the nearest discotheque, while other dark figures slinked along the sidewalks, scanning over their shoulders like they were up to no good.

I slipped my payment and tip to Sid through the bulletproof partition. "Thanks." I said and opened the door. "You don't need to stick around this time. I might be in there for a while. Go earn your bread."

He rolled his eyes. "All right, Ms. Carter. But I'm gonna try and stay in the area. Let me know when you need to go someplace else."

"Will do." I got out of the cab and waved him off. Once he disappeared around the corner, I hustled across the street and headed to the alley. I slipped my hand into my trench coat and rested it over the butt of my holstered gun. The dim halo of light from the nearby streetlamp stopped just shy of the alley's entrance. I casually leaned against the wall and watched a handsome couple walk past, and then I slipped into the alley's pitch-blackness. My heart pounded. I hated feeling anxious uncertainty. My fingers curled around my gun. The seconds ticked by like an eternity as I waited and listened.

A door swung open, and light from inside the building poured out, spearing through the darkness. A man appeared and kicked a wooden wedge under the door to prop it open. He disappeared inside the building then reappeared moments later lugging a large garbage bag over his shoulder. The light touched the man's dark face, revealing a short white beard. As he walked toward a nearby dumpster, the light swept over his janitor's uniform and the white name patch, which said Edwin in simple cursive.

Letting go of the gun, I pulled my hand out from my trench coat. I emerged from the shadows and approached Edwin the janitor as he heaved the garbage bag into the dumpster. "Hello, Edwin," I said. "I'm Detective Carter."

He flipped the dumpster's lid closed and turned to me. "I've seen it, and I still don't believe it. I thought Luis was just making up some jive story about a detective who was also a sister."

I rolled my eyes. I'd half a mind to show him my police badge, but then I remembered that I purposely hadn't brought it. While it'd had its uses during some of my past investigations, I was trying to wean myself away from that crutch as a means of gathering information. Besides, the more I used it, the riskier the chance of me getting in trouble. Chief Lewis had let me keep it on the off chance I needed to get out of a pinch, but I was taking things too far, bringing it along with me on almost every case like a security blanket. That badge was becoming more and more of a liability for me and for Chief Lewis.

Besides all that, even if I did have my badge, flashing it right then would have been a bad idea, especially when I was trying to be discreet and Luis was worried about involving cops. Instead, I whipped out my wallet, retrieved my private investigator ID badge, and stuck it in Edwin's face. "Well, believe it. This sister's trying to save your job," I spat. "I need to get inside so I can talk to Paige."

He glanced at the badge, then his attention flicked back to me. "Shiiit. That thing real?"

"I worked my butt off to earn it, so yeah, I'd say it is." I put the badge away.

"Okay. Okay. I'm just trying to be careful. Can't trust nobody around here."

"Frankly, I don't trust anyone around here, either. But at some point, we're going to have to come to some sort of agreement. You don't like Joey, and neither do I. We have a common enemy. Help me so I can help you."

He looked at me long and hard then nodded once. "I can dig it. Follow me." He brushed past me and went back inside.

I waited a few moments before following. So far, so good. Once I was inside, he closed and locked the side door. My heart thumped. The offices along the short hallway were dark, but I wondered if someone was still in there, burning the midnight oil.

We walked a short way down the hallway and stopped in front of the door leading to the brightly lit stairwell.

"Is the security guard doing his rounds yet?" I whispered.

"Nah, Brandon's still hanging out in the lobby until I finish up here," Edwin whispered back. "I'll keep him busy for a while. Take the stairs up to the eleventh floor."

"Okay," I said, preparing my legs to hate me.

"And don't go snooping around other offices. If someone don't recognize you, they're gonna call security. Just go straight to Ms. Russell's office like you planned."

"Yeah, no detours. Promise."

Edwin frowned. "And don't tell her or nobody else that we talked."

"Don't worry. My lips are sealed." I made a zipper gesture across my lips.

I opened the stairwell door while Edwin continued down the long hallway toward the main lobby area. As I climbed the stairs, my heart pounded. I'd assumed that Ms. Russell would be understanding of all this, but it seemed I was being met by all sorts of surprises. At that point, I couldn't tell who or what would be waiting for me in her office.

CHAPTER 11

My trek up the twenty-two flights of stairs was uneventful, thankfully, but my nerves remained on edge. At last, I reached the eleventh floor landing, my legs throbbing and burning as if I'd run a marathon. The fiery sensation in my lungs reminded me of those grueling months spent training for the physical abilities test in the police academy. I paused to catch my breath. I eased the eleventh floor's steel door open, and the crisp scent of fresh paper and ink cut through the musty, stale air of the stairwell. I stepped into a dark and quiet hallway, my feet sinking into the plush carpeting. The doors to the few offices were shut. Near the end of the hallway was a soft white glow coming from one of the offices. I quietly padded down the hallway, my ears ringing from the unnerving silence. The walls seemed to hide the sounds of the city outside as well. I sure could use some walls like those back at my apartment.

I passed the other offices, which were large conference rooms. I peeked inside one and spotted grand floor-to-ceiling windows that displayed the colorful, twinkling city lights reflecting off the Hudson far in the distance. I stopped in front of the office that had a glow of light coming from inside. It illuminated the frosted glass window, highlighting Paige Russell's name in elegant gold script. Affixed to the wall next to the door was a wooden drop box. A couple of stapled papers and a white envelope stuck out from the box. I paused at the door to listen but couldn't hear whether anyone was inside. I took several deep breaths, going over everything I'd planned to say, then I knocked softly. I waited a few moments, but no one answered. My stomach did flip-flops. *Is she even in there?* I knocked a little more loudly.

"Not now, Edwin, I'm busy," a woman called in a sharp voice.

I exhaled and knocked again. I decided to keep quiet and make her open the door on her own. If she heard my voice, nothing would stop her from calling security.

"Damn it, Edwin, I said I'm busy!" the woman barked.

I gave another obnoxious rap on the door.

She growled. Finally, the sounds of muffled footsteps approached, followed by the click of a lock. The door flung open. The light from the office highlighted tiny pearls of sweat beaded along the woman's forehead and soft, fair-skinned cheeks. A red hairband accentuated her dark, shoulder-length flipped hair. She was dressed in a fashionable, multicolored one-piece knit dress and open-toed platform shoes with lipstick to match. Her big brown eyes scrutinized me from head to toe, and she started.

"Mrs. Russell, I presume?" I greeted with a polite hat tip.

She blinked. "Who the hell are you? How did you get past security?"

"My name is Detective Tootsie Carter. And I, uh... found my own way up here. Anyway, I need to talk with you. It's urgent."

Paige frowned. "Detective? Who hired you?"

Technically, Joey. And Allison, but I probably shouldn't tell her that. "Nobody hired me," I assured her, raising my hands in surrender. "I'm here of my own accord. I wanted to talk to you about your husband, Joey."

Her expression grew dark. "Who put you up to this? Who do you work for? I'm not telling you shit. Now get out of here before I call the cops on you for trespassing!"

Uh-oh... So she wasn't as understanding as I'd hoped. "Wait, Mrs. Russell. I swear to you, I'm alone. I'm a private investigator, and I work for myself." I showed her my P.I. card.

Paige skimmed the card, and her nostrils flared. "What do you want with Joey?" she asked.

"He paid me a visit recently."

Her jaw muscles tightened. "You're lying. I'm calling security." She attempted to slam the door in my face, but I quickly wedged my foot between the door and the frame. The door smacked against my steel-toed boot and rebounded, swiping inches past Paige's face. She jumped backward.

I marched into the office and closed and locked the door behind me. Her office was immaculate, with a spectacular view of the sparkling lights of Midtown East Manhattan—a fitting view for the queen that she was, sitting on top of the corporate world, looking down at her minions. The office smelled like new leather and wood and a hint of rose. Her mahogany executive desk and the rest of her furniture were designed with a contemporary modern flair. Several bouquets of fresh, red roses set in decorative vases were strategically placed throughout the office. An open box of chocolates and a dozen red and white long-stem roses sat atop the desk.

Paige glared at me for a moment then rushed to her desk and snatched at the phone. "I'm calling security!"

Oh, geez Louise... I rushed after her, grabbed the back of her dress and yanked her away before she could dial. "No!" I said. "Will you please listen?"

"Let go of me!" She tugged and pulled, trying to break free, but I fisted the knitted material of the back of her dress. "Let *go*! This dress is a Missoni Exclusive! If you rip it, I'll fucking kill you!"

I continued to hold on. "Give me five minutes. That's all. Then I promise I'll leave, and you'll never see me again."

Finally, she calmed down. "All right, Detective," she said in a huff. "Five minutes, and not a minute more."

"Great." I let go of her precious Missoni and guided her toward the leather sectional couch in the middle of the room—far away from the telephone. "Let's sit over here and talk."

Frowning, she reluctantly walked over to the couch and sat. "Anything said in this office stays in this office. If word of our meeting leaks out to anyone else, I will sue you for everything you got, so don't fuck with me."

"My lips are sealed, Mrs. Russell." I planted myself right next to her in case she decided to make a quick getaway. She gave me the stink eye but stayed put.

"So here's the skinny," I began. "Joey came to me recently, asking for some photos and negatives because he claimed he was being blackmailed or something. Of course, I had no idea what he was talking about, but I didn't like the way he was making those demands. So what's up with him? I figured you might know, being his wife, and all."

Paige rubbed her chin, her expression thoughtful. "I don't know anything about a blackmail, and I don't know why he would have any business going to you... unless..." Her brow furrowed.

"Unless?" I repeated, taking out my notebook.

She pursed her lips. Her gaze darted around the office a moment, and she let out a deep sigh. Her body relaxed. "I'm working on a story, a big story about a large drug operation that I believe has ties to the OD deaths over the past several months. I feel like I'm getting close, but Joey keeps telling me to leave this story alone. I can't leave it alone when the deaths keep piling up. The *Tri-City Beat* hasn't had a big, sensational story like this in a long time, and it's the kind of story we need to bring this company back in the black."

I wrote down some notes. "What info have you found out about this drug operation?"

She sneered. "That's confidential until the story is released. I don't even talk to Joey about it anymore. If he's not going to help me with this story, then I'll do it myself."

"You think he has some ties with the operation?"

"I'm only speculating that someone on the inside who might happen to know Joey might suspect something. I've been trying to gather evidence as discreetly as possible. As far as I know, no one knows what I'm doing. Except Joey."

"You think he would go so far as to compromise your story?"

"I don't know what he's doing, if he's doing anything at all. You could say this a passion project. I would've liked Joey to help me with it, being my husband and all, but he's obviously not interested. My father—rest his soul—not only owned this paper, he was a world-class journalist. A lot of his exposés made a huge splash in the media industry and were what set this paper apart from all the others in this city. We haven't had that since his death in August last year. I'm trying to revitalize my father's legacy. And this is the story that will do it."

I frowned. "I'm sorry about your father."

"It was his time. He ran this paper for over forty years, and I learned everything I know from him."

I thought back to Joey's visit and how it related to Paige and her woes. I was trying to connect the pieces, but nothing was fitting quite right. Joey was after the photos and negatives of his infidelity. It had nothing to do with Paige's goals. Maybe he did have some secret ties to a drug organization. But what was the purpose of his feature in the *National Esquire*? Someone else was obviously involved. Frank, perhaps? Maybe it had something to do with Paige being the president of the company. Women in power were such a rare sight that one tended to make more enemies than friends.

"Is Joey cool with you being the president?" I asked.

She glared. "What are you insinuating?"

"Hey, it's a fact that some men can't stand women being above them, especially in the workplace."

"Joey respects me. And so do my employees. I'm just as capable of running this company as my father was."

"Hey, you don't have to convince me of anything. I admire anyone in your position, man or woman. I can't imagine how stressful it must be, having so many responsibilities on your shoulders like that."

Her expression softened a little. "I watched my father do it for all twenty-six years of my life."

"So I guess, technically, since you and Joey are married, that means he owns part of this company, too, right?"

"Usually, that would be the case. But my lawyer said that, based on my father's will, the company is fully entrusted to me."

"I see." I filled another blank page with more notes. "No stipulations?"

She looked thoughtful. "The only stipulation would be if I died or was rendered completely incapable of running the company."

"Hmm…" I stopped writing. "You haven't gotten any death threats, have you?"

"No. And I am also perfectly capable of running this company."

I tapped the pen against my notebook and thought. "I still don't understand why Joey would want to discourage you from writing this story. Especially if it will bring a positive outcome for the paper's finances."

She shrugged. "I don't know, Detective. I love him with all my heart. I'm a good wife to him, but I have to do what I have to do, with or without him."

I glanced around the room at all the numerous rose-filled vases. "Are all those roses from him?"

Her gaze flicked to a bundle of white roses sitting on the end table next to the couch, and she quirked a smile. "Yeah. He's a real smooth Casanova."

I wrinkled my nose slightly. No wonder she was so wrapped up in his charms. The slimy snake lived a double life. And since Paige was so wrapped up in her big story, she was none the wiser to his secret affair. "And he's always been faithful to you?" I asked, though I had a feeling that was a wasted effort.

Paige frowned. "You sound as annoying as Allison. She's nice and damned good at her job, but I wish she'd stop with all these conspiracy theories about Joey. I don't know what she's upset with him about, but I don't have time to deal with that bullshit."

I assumed it was because of Joey's disapproval of Allison's fiancée, but I didn't want to tip Paige off too much about my conversation with Allison earlier. "Well, y'know, I wouldn't dismiss this completely, Mrs. Russell. As you said, you're a busy woman. A man in his position might find some fun elsewhere if he can't get any attention from his wife."

"I know Joey wouldn't do that. He loves me and treats me well." She gestured to the roses. "He has no reason to go elsewhere."

"When was the last time you two talked?"

She scowled and averted her gaze. "Not since yesterday. And honestly, I don't have time to talk to him."

"You say you're a good wife to him," I countered with an arched eyebrow, "but you're here working late tonight. Where is he?"

"He goes out to the bar with his friends on the nights I work late."

I rolled my eyes. "Wow, you really put a lot of trust in this guy. He can do no wrong, huh?"

She went silent a moment then cocked her head. "Are you married, Detective?"

"Nah. Men can't keep up with me."

She furrowed her brow and gave me a puzzled look. "Right. Well, listen, honey. When you love somebody—I mean, really love somebody with all your heart, you just know that person isn't the ugly picture that the world paints."

Geez Louise. This woman's more stubborn than a chocolate stain. I decided to let that matter rest. Allison was right: Paige was truly blinded by love, and nobody could convince her otherwise.

"Listen, Mrs. Russell," I said, changing the subject. "I'm all about stopping bad guys. This story you're writing sounds like a lot of criminals are involved, so why not let me help you? Let's help each other."

Paige shook her head. "No. This is my project. I'll handle things my own way."

I sighed. "All right. If that's the way you want it."

"That's the way it's going to be."

"I know you still don't fully trust me. I get it. But I'll just say that I'm in the business of helping people in this city, and I haven't let anybody down yet."

"Good for you, Detective. I'm in the business of making money. I have a story to write, so see your way out." She stood from the couch and pointed toward the door.

A piece of the puzzle was still missing, and I was wracking my brain over it. My next stop would be Joey's mysterious address. At this point, it was all I had left to go on since Paige seemed convinced Joey was being a good husband and having a couple drinks with the boys. *If only she knew.*

"Yeah, sure," I said, standing. "I appreciate your letting me stay and talk to you for longer than five minutes. I know I promised before that you wouldn't see me again after this, but would it be okay to at least give you a call, in case I have any more questions?"

She flicked her gaze to me, scanning me up and down a second time, and she huffed. "If it'll help you sleep at night, Detective, then fine. I don't know what you're up to, but whatever it is, you better not drag this paper into it, or I'll sue you out of business."

"I swear, I'm on the level. And your paper has nothing to do with my agenda, so you can rest assured."

"All right, Detective. I trust you. Don't make me regret it." She rapped out her direct office telephone number.

I took down the number then put my notebook away. "And I'm going to have to trust that you won't call the cops on me." I looked at her expectantly.

"Like I said earlier, what is said in this office stays in this office."

"Right on." I nodded and headed for the door. "Have a good evening, Mrs. Russell." As I left the office, my heart began to pound furiously. Someone in her position could easily shut me down for good in a snap. I only had one chance to make things right, and I couldn't turn back.

CHAPTER 12

Sid drove me to the address Joey had given me. It was in Jackson Heights. Sid knew these streets like I knew Dick Tracy's life story. It was almost midnight. I had a little over three hours before my meeting with Newsie. We were stopped at a red light on the corner of Thirty-First Avenue and Eighty-Ninth Street, and my ears perked at the muffled sounds of a scuffle. I glanced around, trying to locate the commotion, but saw only small groups of people shuffling along the crosswalk and sidewalks. Then my eyes cut to movement in an alley. A man in a denim vest and black bandanna scrambled out and zipped down the sidewalk, dodging passersby like he was on the run from the law. In seconds, he disappeared farther down the street.

Sid huffed. "Damn punks," he muttered. "Say, Ms. Carter. Did I ever tell you the story of how I first got into boxin'?"

I met his gaze in the rearview mirror. "Don't think so."

"During the second war, I was captured and shipped off to a German POW camp in Barth." When the light turned green,

Sid sped off again. "There was an underground boxing ring set up, where those fucking Nazi officers would gamble on fights between the prisoners that they'd throw in there like dogs. Just my luck, I was one of the dopes who had to keep those sons of bitches entertained. The more I won, the better chance I had to survive."

I blinked. "That sounds like a terrible nightmare. I'm sorry you had to go through that."

Reaching our destination, Sid slowed the cab and parallel parked along a curb, behind another car. "Eh, it was a shitty time in my life back then," he continued. "I was undefeated in the ring, and the officers got bored, so they started making me fight some of their own people. I'll tell you something, doll. There ain't no greater feeling than knocking the shit out of Nazis. Left and right, those fucking bastards hit the mat and didn't get up. I caught the boxing bug after that. When I finally came back home, I became a fighting machine."

"Well, I'm just glad you made it back in one piece," I said.

He cracked a smile. "Me too, doll. Talkin' to you reminds me that there're still some good people left in this fucked-up world." He paused and glanced out the passenger's window. Then his gaze swiveled back to me. "Got a case around here?"

"Ah, you could say that," I said, staring at a weathered old two-story brick building sitting on the corner of Thirty-First Avenue and Ninety-First Street.

"It's pretty rough out in these parts, y'know. Had to bust up a bum trying to jack me a couple days ago."

I slipped him a five-dollar bill. "Thanks, but I can handle myself just fine." I opened the door and climbed out of the cab.

"Yeah, yeah, I know. You're good people, Ms. Carter. One of the few good people left in this town. Watch your back out here, eh?"

"I always do. See you around." I shut the door.

After Sid sped off, I stood in front of the building, which housed four units, but only two of them were occupied. One of the occupied units was Thrifty World. A large red-and-yellow plastic sign sat above the store, which was currently closed. A steel roll-down security door and shutters covered the entrance and windows. An iron folding gate stood in front of the security door, and a giant padlock hung from a chain attached to it.

Geez Louise, is Diego selling diamonds in there or something? I wondered. I would make a point to pay him a visit the next day. Next to Diego's shop was the other occupied unit, a massage parlor. A long red awning dividing the first and second floors stretched from one end of the parlor to the other. Faint, soft light glowed from the second-story windows. It was after midnight, and the place was still open, not to my surprise. During my time on the force, I was privy to plenty of stories from female coworkers on the vice squad about some of their disturbing undercover work at massage parlors, gentlemen's clubs, and other places. No amount of money in the world could have ever gotten me to work in that department. And Chief Lewis made certain of that too.

After what I'd caught Joey doing the other day, this seemed like the kind of place he would hang out. But why would he willingly give the address of his favorite shady place to a private eye? I smelled a trap. Joey had picked the wrong woman to cross.

I marched through the door. A set of iron bars shielded the door, which had Hands of Paradise Luxury Spa written in elegant script on the tinted glass. Inside, I breathed in the pleasant aroma of incense and sweet-smelling perfume. Warm, atmospheric light from a hanging chandelier filled the tiny lobby area. Against the wall, two plush red chairs flanked a wooden end table, where a large red candle burned steadily.

Luxury, indeed. I took off my fedora then shrugged off my trench coat and draped it across my arm.

Behind the counter, a woman dressed in a black catsuit had her back to me while she arranged some fancy bottles of oil on a glass wall shelf. Affixed to the wall next to the shelf was a wooden pegboard full of hooks. A few of the hooks had decorative keys hanging from them. A set of stairs leading up sat beside the counter, its entrance decorated with a large tasseled red-and-gold curtain. On the other side of the room was a closed door covered with a hanging beaded curtain.

I could feel the money dripping from this place. It definitely seemed like Joey's bag. But again, I wondered why he would spend time at a cheap hole-in-the-wall place like the Peacock House. Maybe to throw any of his potential stalkers off his trail. Or maybe it was nothing at all, and he simply came here after work to get a quick, stress-relieving massage. That made sense even though massage parlors tended to have more than one function. A thought struck me. *Could it be that Joey is having an affair with one of the hostesses?* At that point, anything was possible.

I approached the front counter. The woman was still busy with her bottle arranging, so I gently cleared my throat.

"Hello," I said.

The woman paused and looked over her shoulder, her long, feathered blond hair giving a little bounce. Her thin eyebrows shot up. "Well, hello to you," she said in a smooth, brooding alto. She faced me fully, revealing the plunging neckline and sultry curves of her skin-tight catsuit. "I'm Kimberly. How may I serve you?"

I grimaced. *Yeah, that definitely ain't no typical masseuse's uniform.* I cleared my throat. "I'm looking to relax. It's been a while since I've been out this way. I know this place is the bee's knees when it comes to relaxing."

Kimberly's gaze traveled up and down as she gave me a once-over. Then her full rose-red lips turned upward into a small smirk. "Oh, you better believe it." She reached behind the counter, retrieved a thick leather binder branded with the Hands of Paradise lotus logo, and set it on top. "Here are our services. Take your time browsing."

I stared at the binder's thickness with trepidation. That sure was a lot of "services."

I thumbed through the pages, which were contained in plastic sheet protectors. The services included various types of massages, from the most basic to the most exotic. Then I checked the prices... *Sweet Saint Mary...* Inflation had hit this place harder than the H-bomb. I kept a straight face as I flipped to the spa section. Spending an hour doing the "hydro massage" would cost me almost a month's worth of rent. The prices got higher the farther I went through the book. I gave up after seeing the four-figure price tag of a red wine bath. "Actually," I said, closing the binder. "All I want is the Bubblegum Special."

Kimberly paused. A small crease appeared at her brow. "Excuse me?"

"The Bubblegum Special," I repeated, already devising a new script in case Joey really was lying to me. "What? Don't tell me you don't offer that anymore."

She moistened her lips. Her gaze briefly flicked to the staircase then returned to me. "Ah... I believe you're mistaken."

Noting her hesitation, I sensed I was on to something. Maybe Joey was being honest after all. "I ain't been gone that long. The Bubblegum Special was the one thing I loved about this place."

Light footsteps thumped on the floor above.

"Well…" Kimberly paused and looked toward the stairs.

Moments later, a man descended. He was average height and build, sported a brown moustache, and was dressed casually in slacks and a polo shirt. He was joined by a shorter, lanky, balding man with a pug nose. He was dressed sharply in a dark-grey three-piece suit.

"What a doll she is, Frank. An absolute doll," Pug Nose said.

I blinked. *Frank? I wonder…*

"I know," Frank chuckled darkly. He went behind the counter and slipped something into a drawer.

Kimberly's face brightened. "One moment, Mr. Bailey, while I get your hat." She disappeared through the beaded curtain and returned moments later with a black fedora with a little brown feather tucked into the band.

"Next week, then," Mr. Pug Nose Bailey said, taking his hat. He turned, scanned me up and down, then grinned a piano-key smile.

I forced a small smile then diverted my attention back to Kimberly.

After Mr. Bailey left, Kimberly looked back at me, and her hesitation resurfaced. "Frankie, this… *woman* is asking about B. G."

Frank opened another drawer, paused, and looked up.

I met his cold gaze, and a chill ran up my spine. The way he looked at me with those calculating dark-brown eyes, I sensed something strange about him—sinister. He reminded me of Joey except he was more creepy than suave. I swallowed once, took a deep breath, and regained my composure. "Y-Yeah, what gives? I loved that service. Don't tell me you stopped offering it."

Frank shut the drawer. He assessed me from head to toe. "Never had a broad ask about that."

"Well, your memory must be shot," I said. "You telling me women aren't allowed to get that service now? What a drag."

"My memory's fine. Who are you?"

"The name's Rosa. Rosa Timms," I replied, not batting an eye. "I know what I got last time, and I wanna get it again. So hook me up already."

Frank went silent for a beat. "I don't know no Rosa."

"Think harder." I scowled. "Oh, I get it. You raised your prices. Don't think I can afford it, that it?"

He rubbed his chin and eyed me carefully. "Yeah, it's gone up a little."

"Okay." I reached into my trench coat pocket, pulled out my wallet, and retrieved three hundred dollars from the stack of bills Joey had given me earlier. "Is this enough?" I laid the money on the counter.

Kimberly swiped up the money and counted it. "It'll get you fifteen minutes' worth," she told me.

I blinked. *Fifteen minutes? What kind of cockamamie massage is this?* Maybe some famous *Playboy* model was going to give me a massage. It must've meant something if Joey was so insistent about it. "That's more than enough time for me to relax."

Frank regarded me dubiously. "I guess times are changin', huh?"

I raised my eyebrows. "What do you mean by that?"

"Nothin.' Get her what she wants, Kim." He left through the beaded curtain and disappeared down a dark hallway beyond.

Kimberly opened the drawer that Frank had gone into earlier and pulled out a gold key with a pink-and-white polka-dotted bow tied to it. She discreetly slipped the key down her abundant cleavage like a slotted piggy bank, and the key disappeared like magic.

Then she went to the pegboard and unhooked a silver key with an Eiffel Tower charm. Finally, she turned to me. "Shall I take your coat and hat, Ms. Timms?"

"Just the hat, please," I said, surrendering my fedora. I didn't trust these people enough to leave my coat unattended when I had my gun, wallet, and other items stashed inside. "I want to keep my coat with me, in case I get cold."

Kimberly gave me a funny look then shrugged. "Right." She left through the beaded curtain for a moment with my hat then returned. She beckoned me toward the stairs. "Follow me, please."

I hesitated before trailing behind her. "I swear, with this new price hike, the service had better be more than five stars' worth. I'm talking absolute diamond quality, can you dig it?"

"Of course, Ms. Timms. We offer nothing less."

I remained on edge as I ascended the staircase, which creaked under my weight. I held onto the banister, keeping Kimberly a few paces ahead.

"Have there really been no other women asking for the Bubblegum Special?" I asked.

"It is not really a service our female patrons tend to ask for."

I blew a raspberry. "Geez Louise. Well, they don't know what they're missing, then."

She glanced over her shoulder, giving me a confused look. "Right."

Reaching the second floor, we were met with a long hallway of closed doors. Each had two keyholes, one on top of the other. The faint, muffled sounds of voices filtered out from beyond each door. Kimberly led me to the very end of the hall, to the last door.

"You're in luck. This is our last available room," Kimberly said, gesturing to the ornate wooden door affixed with a brass nameplate that read Paris.

"Hmm, is this the quickest way to France?" I quipped, nodding toward the sign.

"No. All of the massage rooms are themed," Kimberly said in an unamused tone. "You happened to luck out and get our most romantic room."

"Great. Then I'd say it's money well spent."

She magically produced the key with the pink bow from her cleavage and stuck it in the top lock. Then she inserted the Eiffel Tower key into the bottom lock, turned it once, and opened the door. "Your fifteen-minute special will begin as soon as your masseuse arrives."

"Okay."

I stepped inside the quaint, dimly lit room. A curlicue-iron-framed king-sized bed topped with a floral-patterned duvet sat in one corner. Sheer white curtains decorated the room's window, which overlooked Thirty-First Avenue. Beneath the window was a plush white Victorian-style chaise lounge. A gaudy chandelier hung from the popcorn ceiling by a silver chain, swaying ever so slightly at our presence. Strategically placed sconces decorated the floral-patterned walls. The room carried a fresh lemon aroma of cleaning chemicals.

Kimberly took her leave, closing the door behind her. There I stood, alone in the room, unsure of what would happen next.

While I waited for my masseuse, I explored every inch of the room, including the furniture, and the Eiffel Tower–shaped decorative centerpieces and picture frames. With all the searching, I wasn't sure what I was looking for. I peered out the window at the people passing by under the amber halo of the streetlamp along the sidewalk. I laid my coat over the back of a chair then approached the bed with caution. I ran my hand along the soft duvet and heard the faint sound of a door close from the room next to mine. I retracted my hand and spun around.

"Mmm, you got magic hands, Cin," a man muttered in the hallway. "Sunday still good?"

A woman chuckled. "Yeah, but let's make it before five. My plane comes in from Mexico at six."

"Oh yeah, baby. My feet will be ready for you before then."

Mexico... I approached the door and slowly opened it a crack. The couple walked toward the stairs leading down, their arms interlocked. The woman was lean, average height, and sported a blond mushroom-cut hairstyle. I widened my eyes, recalling the photobooth picture I'd seen on the wall in Allison's office. *Cindy?* She was the same woman, all right. But what was she doing here? I shut my door and paced around the room, trying to figure things out.

The doorknob jiggled, snapping me out of my thoughts. The door opened, and a short, petite, fair-skinned girl wearing a red bikini and a black waist-apron stood in the doorway. Her mousy brown hair covered her ears and cascaded just below her jawline. She had a cute, round face, a button nose, and big, bright eyes that sparkled like two sapphires. Her glossy, full lips puckered and inched upward to an adorable little smile. She looked young, all right.

"Hi, I'm Sherry. I will be taking care of you," she said in an off-putting high-pitched voice.

I cringed. "Nice to meet you, Sherry. I'm Rosa."

"Hi, Rosa." Her creamy skin flushed a light shade of pink. "Um, where would you like me to perform your Bubblegum Special?"

If that wasn't a loaded question, I didn't know what was. I gestured to the chaise bench. "Let's do it there."

She nodded once then kept her head lowered as she walked to the window. Her shyness made her look cute and innocent. That must've been her quirk. Sad that a pretty girl like her was stuck in a seedy place like this instead of putting those looks to better use in a fashion magazine.

I followed her to the bench and sat, and she stood before me in silence, keeping her head inclined like a small child who was about to get scolded.

"Hey, you okay?" I asked.

She swallowed once then gave a timid nod. "Yeah, um. I just never done this with a lady before. I hope I will be able to meet your needs."

Frowning, I studied her. Her thin body was stiff, and she didn't so much as fidget. Something was bothering her. She seemed to be masking something else. I was beginning to sense what this service would entail. Not surprising that a pervert like Joey would have a girl like her take care of his "needs."

"How about I make it easier for your first time, eh?" I held out a hand. "Ever done a hand massage?"

She smiled slightly. "Those are easy. That's all you wanna do?"

"Sure."

"Okay." She retrieved a sample-sized vial of clear liquid from her apron's pocket. She twisted the vial open, releasing a pleasant lavender scent. She dabbed a small amount of the liquid in her palms then gently took my hand in hers. Her skin was soft, smooth, and cool to the touch. Despite the awkward stiffness in the rest of her body, she expertly rubbed along the tight muscles in my hand.

"So, uh, how long have you been working here, Sherry?" I asked, not taking my eyes off her work.

She fell silent for a moment then said, "About six months."

"You like it here?"

She chewed her bottom lip, inclining her head lower, and gave a soft nod. "Uh-huh…"

"Hey, you don't have to be nervous. I don't bite," I assured.

She turned my hand over and began rubbing around my palm with her thumbs. It felt surprisingly good. I hadn't realized how many tense muscles I had.

"Sorry. Am I doing okay?" she asked.

"You're doing fine."

Her small smile returned, and she released my left hand. "Your other hand, please."

I gave Sherry another once-over and frowned. My heart gave a wary thump. Something was very strange. Finally, I reached out and touched her chin, forcing her to look at me.

"Hey," I said.

She looked back at me with pretty eyes wider than a frightened deer's, and I sensed that didn't have anything to do with her having to massage a woman. She tried to pull her face away, inadvertently rubbing some sandstone-colored makeup onto my hand. Then I realized, under the dim glow of the room's ambience, just how many layers of makeup were caked onto her pretty face. But the makeup was trying to hide something faint on her cheek—a line. No, something else. I released her and examined the makeup smear. Then I frowned. The spot of makeup wiped away from her jawline revealed the bottom of that line—a deep Frankenstein-looking scar. That explained why she wasn't auditioning at a modeling agency.

"What? What did I do?" she whined, her eyes glassy. "Did I make you mad?"

"No. Calm down." I pointed to the scar. "How did you get that?"

She sank her teeth into her bottom lip again. "P-Please, can I just finish the massage?"

I cocked my head. *So many masks,* I thought. Her questions, her mannerisms carried childlike tendencies. She was either really good at acting, or... I gasped. *No. Could she be...?* Only one way to find out.

"You're not tending to all my needs," I said.

She looked at me pleadingly. "Wh-What do you need, Ms. Rosa?"

"Just Rosa's fine. I need you to talk to me. Can you do that?"

"Um, sure."

"You go to school?"

"Yes, I go to college," she replied without hesitation.

"Oh? Which college do you go to?"

"The one in Queens."

I looked at her skeptically. "You mean Queens College?"

"Yeah."

"How do you not know the name of the college you go to?"

"It's my first year."

"Yeah? How old are you?"

"Twenty-two," she said almost immediately.

I raised my eyebrows. "Starting college a little late, huh?"

"Yeah."

"What year were you born?"

"Nineteen forty—" She paused then rubbed the back of her head. "I mean... nineteen fifty-five."

I exhaled a deep sigh. A sinking feeling lurched in my gut. "I really hate liars."

She took a step backward and rubbed her forearm, her small frame trembling. "P-Please. Let me finish your massage. I will get in trouble if Ms. Kim finds out the session ended early."

"Don't worry, the session won't end early. I still have eight minutes left for this session. We're going to spend every minute of it chatting. You're going to tell me everything I want to know."

She winced. "Wh-What do you want to know?"

"I want to know how old you are—how old you *really* are."

She lowered her head and slumped her shoulders in defeat. "Twelve," she muttered, her voice barely audible.

My mouth slowly hung open. "Did I hear that correctly? *Twelve*? As in one two?"

Sherry nodded.

"And you work at a place like this?"

Her bottom lip quivered. "Are you upset? I don't want Ms. Kim to get mad at me for not meeting your needs."

"Did Ms. Kim give you that scar?" I asked.

Sherry averted her gaze again, her expression going blank. She didn't reply. There was my answer.

"You don't belong in a place like this," I continued. "Where are your parents?"

"I don't got nobody," she muttered. "Can I finish your massage now?"

"No," I said.

She swallowed. "P-Please don't tell Ms. Kim we ended the session early. Please…"

I cringed, hearing that distinct cry for help in the young girl's pleading voice. This situation felt like one big nightmare. How did I end up in the middle of it? What other despicable things was this place hiding in plain sight? Chief Lewis needed to know about everything, but first, I had to find out more. I took a breath to calm my nerves then gently took her hands in mine and walked her back to the bench. "We're not done talking." I sat her down on the bench then knelt before her so we met at eye level. "Tell me what's going on around here, Sherry. Who else works here? Are there other little girls like you servicing adults?"

She paled. "I-I, um…"

"Did Ms. Kim warn you not to tell?"

Sherry chewed her bottom lip and fell silent again.

"Do you know a man named Joey Russell?" I asked.

She cocked her head curiously. "No. Who's that?"

"He's a bad man. A very bad man. Are you sure you don't know him? Never heard his name mentioned before?"

She tapped her temple, looking deep in thought. Then she shook her head. "No, I don't know him. Maybe Ms. Kim knows. Or Mr. Audrey."

"Who's Mr. Audrey?"

"The boss."

Great. Just when I thought Joey was the only dirtbag I had to worry about. I took some mental notes. I wanted to get them down in my notepad but resisted the urge to budge from my spot while I had Sherry talking. "What does Mr. Audrey do?"

She chewed her bottom lip. "He tells people to make things."

"What kind of things?" I asked.

"I don't know what they are."

"What do they look like?"

She scratched the side of her head. "Um… they're little white things with pretty purple flowers on them. He calls them Sherries. He named them after me." She smiled proudly.

A bitter taste formed in my mouth. "Are there a lot of people who work for Mr. Audrey?" I asked.

She shrugged. "I dunno."

"Do you ever talk to Mr. Audrey?"

"Um…" Her gaze swiveled fearfully toward the closed door, as if she'd heard someone listening on the other side. Then she turned back to me. "Not really. He usually just wants me to make him feel good."

I shuddered. There was a special place in the fiery pits for disgusting scum like Mr. Audrey. Joey too. Sherry denied knowing Joey, but she had to have some connection with him since Joey seemed to know the secret code word for her services. Maybe he'd threatened her life if she told. I would find out from that dirtbag soon enough. I took another slow breath to keep my nerves calm.

"Where do you live?" I asked.

"In the basement." She pointed down.

I blinked several times. *Are my ears deceiving me?* "You live in a cold, dark basement?"

She smiled reassuringly. "It's warm. Ms. Kim gives me lots of blankets. Mr. Audrey likes it when I stay down there. He calls me his favorite princess."

I'd heard enough. I was getting sick to my stomach. I wasn't sure how I was going to begin to explain everything to Chief Lewis. "Look. I'm gonna get you out of here, all right? Mr.

Audrey and everyone who works for him are bad people, and you shouldn't be around them."

Sherry raised her eyebrows. "They're not bad people. They love me. Mr. Audrey tells me that every day. And guess what? He's taking me on a vacation next week."

I blinked. "What kind of vacation?"

"We're going to California. He said I'm going to be a star. I can't wait."

"Just you and him are going on this... vacation?"

"Well..." She rubbed the side of her neck. "I'm going with one of his friends, and then Mr. Audrey will meet us there later."

The sickness in my stomach was rising in my throat. "Don't do this, Sherry. There's nothing good waiting for you in California, where Mr. Audrey and his friends are concerned. What these people are doing to you is not love. You deserve much better."

"No. They'll get mad if I say or do anything. Please..."

"If they loved you, they shouldn't be getting mad at you. I want to show you a better life, where people won't be mad at you and you can do whatever you want and be whoever you want to be."

She looked thoughtful for a moment then tilted her head. "H-How can you do that?"

"What do you want to be when you're older?" I asked.

A small smile returned to her lips. "I wanna be a baker or pastry chef and make the prettiest, most delicious cakes for people."

"That sounds wonderful. Well, guess what? I'll find a way to make your dream come true. I'll find you the biggest bakery shop, and you can make all the cakes you want."

Her face brightened. "R-Really?"

I nodded then opened my mouth to respond, but a firm knock came at the door.

"Three minutes," Kimberly called from the other side of the door.

Sherry's face turned snow white, and she gasped and took my hand in hers.

"Massage my hands and answer your boss," I whispered to the girl.

Sherry hesitated then fumbled with my right palm as she struggled to stay focused. "O-Okay, Ms. Kim. I'm just finishing up now."

I waited a few moments, listening to Kimberly's footsteps fade away then snatched my hand away from Sherry. I stood and marched over to the bed to retrieve my coat. "Can you keep a secret?" I asked Sherry in a hushed tone.

She watched me for a moment. "Yes…"

"Good. Tell no one about what you told me. If you want that bakery, you have to promise me. People like Mr. Audrey would be very angry if he found out I was getting you your own bakery."

"Yeah, he would be. He never lets me have anything."

"Leave it to me," I said, checking myself in a nearby mirror. I watched her reflection looking back at me. "Can I be your friend?" I asked her.

She gave a firm nod and a broad smile. "Yeah. Thank you, Rosa. You're very nice."

I half smiled. "I have another secret for you too. But I can't tell you until after I get you out of here."

Her eyes glittered with curiosity. "So when can we go?"

"Very soon. I need you to stay strong for me in the meantime. I will be back again."

Her happy expression faltered slightly. "Okay." She headed for the door. "I need to go fix my makeup before Ms. Kim sees me. Bye, Rosa."

After she left, I exhaled a long, deep sigh. *What did I just walk into?* My mind was swimming. I whipped out my notebook and hastily took down all the information I remembered. It was going to be another long talk with the chief, and not one I was particularly looking forward to. I also planned to give Joey a call. I'd dealt with similar cases in the past, and each time, it always made me furiously sick. How could such despicable evil run rampant in my city for so long? Seeing things like this reminded me of why I'd decided to become a shamus long ago. Too many Sherries were in trouble out there, and people like me needed to free them.

I just hoped I wasn't too late...

CHAPTER 13

Kronos Lounge was practically dead by the time the cab driver dropped me off around a quarter to three in the morning. Sid had clocked out of work after midnight, so I took my chances with another driver who was just as efficient. Thinking about that dreaded so-called massage parlor left me mentally exhausted. *That poor girl.* I was going to get little twelve-year-old Sherry out of there somehow and bring Mr. Audrey and the rest of his perverted dirtbags to justice.

The lounge's front door was unmanned and unlocked, and I slipped inside. The ambient-lit bar was trashed, confetti and balloons everywhere. A hired three-man cleaning crew were scrubbing away with their push brooms and mops and filling garbage bags while a Gladys Knight song crooned from the colorful flashing jukebox in the corner.

Roy's star barmaid, Stella Holson, was behind the bar, counting her tips, her lush curves bulging out of a sheer lace blouse. A plastic tiara sparkled in her tight afro. Collins, one of the bouncers, was cleaning off the wooden stools then flipping them over and setting them upside down on the bar. He, too, wore a festive multicolored party hat.

"We're closed," Collins said firmly without looking up.

I kicked a balloon out of the way, and it popped like a firecracker.

He glanced my way and did a double take. "Oh, hey, Tootsie."

I gave him and Stella a small salute. "Hey. What happened here? Looks like a tornado ripped through this joint."

"It was my birthday," Stella said with a crooked smile. "Roy threw me a surprise party. He's such a sweetheart."

Anything for his gorgeous bombshells, I thought, resisting the urge to roll my eyes. "Yeah, he sure is. Happy birthday, Stella."

She winked and continued counting her tips.

"Roy's in his office," Collins told me, stabbing his thumb over his shoulder.

"Thanks," I said, carefully maneuvering around a pile of confetti. I walked to the back of the lounge and knocked on the door to Roy's private office. "Roy, open up. It's me."

No answer. I waited a few moments then knocked again, to no avail. Out of the corner of my eye, I spotted Roy descending the stairs from his apartment. The shirt of his gaudy light-green leisure suit was half unbuttoned, revealing a peek of his thick chest hair and a heavy gold chain. He held the hand of a young, pale-faced woman dressed in an orange Halston dress and matching high-heeled shoes. She was holding the back of her other hand to her forehead like a weepy damsel in a cheesy Gothic romance. I couldn't believe Roy would fall for such a cheap act.

Why do I care what Roy does in his spare time? I frowned. Part of me wished he would see me as something more than just another entry in his Rolodex of women. Then again, who was I to compete with drop-dead-gorgeous, curvaceous rock stars like Stella?

"Did I come at a bad time?" I asked, trying to keep the disgust out of my voice.

Roy looked up at me with a start, like a child who'd been caught with his hand in the cookie jar. "Ah! T-Tootsie, you're here!" he stammered.

"Yeah, I'm here."

"Oh." Roy grinned and tried to pull his gaping shirt closed. "Great to see you. I was just helping Chanelle here. She wasn't feeling well." He gave the woman a concerned look.

Chanelle groaned and stumbled down another step. I could've sworn she smiled.

"Easy, baby," Roy cooed. "I'll have Collins call you a cab, all right?" He helped her down the last step then guided her toward the main lounge.

"Uh-huh," Chanelle muttered. She staggered toward the bar and into Collins's arms.

I turned back to Roy. "You didn't have to do that on account of me," I said.

Roy's eyebrows lifted. "Do what? Chanelle had a headache. I took her upstairs so she could get an aspirin."

"You don't have to explain yourself to me, Roy."

He paused a moment. "Hey, it's not what it looks like. She really was feeling bad. I guess she partied a little too hard." He fell silent a moment, then his eyes went wide. "Wait... you don't honestly think she and I were... oh, for crying out loud, Tootsie. You know me better than that."

I shrugged. "Honestly, these days, I don't know about you anymore."

His expression hardened. "Look, whatever you think I am, you can just forget it. Other than my own mother, there's only one woman in the world that matters to me, and I'm looking at her right now."

I rolled my eyes. "Don't start, Roy. I had a long day today. I'm not in the mood for your jive-talking. I need to see Newsie. Is he here yet?"

Roy sighed and unlocked the door to his private office. "Yeah, he's down in the speakeasy." He opened the door and went inside. At the back of the office, another door opened to stairs leading down to the sublevel. I followed him.

I discovered Newsie lounging in his usual spot on the couch, his feet propped up on the coffee table while he indulged in another dirty magazine. Scowling, Roy shut the door firmly behind us. Newsie jumped and looked up from the magazine. Roy marched over to the coffee table and tossed Newsie's feet off. "If I gotta tell you about that one more time..." Roy warned.

"Oh, for fuck's sake, man. You sound like a damned square. Give it a rest," Newsie said, waving his hand dismissively. He looked at me and grinned. "Hey, Tootsie. So here I am. What's the skinny, baby?" he asked, rolling up the magazine and tucking it away in the inner pocket of his blazer.

I approached the couch and stared down at him. "Call me baby again, and I ain't tellin' you nothing."

"Hey, now. I can dig it." He held up his hands and cracked a crooked smile. "By the way, I got your picture." He nodded toward the coffee table where a manila envelope sat.

I glanced at the envelope then back at him. "At least you're good for something." I reached for the envelope, but before I could touch it, he swiped it up.

"Uh-uh-uh," he said, waggling his finger like a scolding parent. "We had a deal."

"Yeah…" I conjured up the bogus story I'd heard earlier, one I knew would sate a vulture like him. "So word on the street is that there's a company making exploding candy for children. It's called Pebble Poppers."

Roy looked at me with an arched eyebrow. "What?"

"What?" Newsie repeated, mirroring Roy's expression.

I nodded. "Yup. It's already happened to one kid, apparently. They ate Pebble Poppers and drank some soda, and they exploded. I'm surprised the *National Esquire* hasn't covered this already."

Newsie scrunched his nose. "No way. I ain't covering a story about some stupid kid's candy."

"Not used to publishing actual *truthful* news, are you?" I countered.

"That can't be true, Tootsie. Where did you hear that?" Roy asked.

"I'm not disclosing my sources. But I'm sure if you ask around, you'll find out quick enough." I nodded to Newsie. "I bet—no, I *know* someone in your office is probably on top of it. If they publish that story first, who do you think will get the bigger recognition for saving thousands of children in this city?"

Newsie rubbed his clean-shaven chin thoughtfully. His gaze swiveled to me then back to the manila envelope. "All right. This shit better be legit, or I'm gonna come find you. And you won't like it when I do."

Roy fumed. I could tell he was about to explode on Newsie, so I intervened and firmly pressed my hand against Roy's chest.

"No, Roy," I said. When he calmed down, I withdrew my hand and confronted Newsie straight on. "Listen, Chip. Don't write checks your butt can't cash. I ain't afraid of you or your lying, scamming, fake newspaper. I've had a long day today, and I'm not in the mood, so don't try me."

Newsie fell silent and scowled. Then he tightened his jaw.

I snatched the envelope from Newsie's hands and took a peek inside. "These are all the photos used in the article?" I asked.

"Yeah," he spat.

"Good. Then we're done here. I got my photos—you got your scoop. Now, scram."

Newsie made a sour face. He adjusted his newsboy hat then shoved his hands in his pants pockets. "I feel like I wasted a trip down here."

"Hey, I held up my end of the bargain. Take that story or leave it," I said.

"Sounds like a buncha jive to me," he muttered, glaring. He looked at Roy. "I still don't know what you see in this broad, man. All those fine honeybees you got hangin' out in this joint? You're a damned fool, Roy. A damned fool."

Roy shook his head and stabbed his thumb toward the door. "Get outta here, man."

Newsie spun on his heel and marched out the door. Roy waited a beat then went to the door and opened it, making sure Newsie wasn't eavesdropping. To my relief, the annoying reporter was actually gone.

Roy closed and locked the door then approached me. "Exploding candy? Really?"

"Heard it with my own ears, Roy." I shrugged. "Anyway, enough of that. I got what I came here for. You mind driving me home?" Wow, I really must've been tired, to ask Roy to drive me around in his beat-up ticking time bomb of a car.

Roy perked up. "I'll drive you to the moon and back if you want, Tootsie."

"Just to my apartment for now. I'm beat. I don't feel like waiting around for the bus or another taxi, and I definitely ain't taking the subway at this time of morning."

Roy fished his car keys from his pocket. "You've just put the cherry on top of my wonderful evening."

I frowned. If only he knew the nightmare I'd had to endure earlier. But I would make sure he never found out. It was about time he enjoyed his own life for a change and stopped getting caught up in mine.

"That's great," I said half-heartedly.

His expression faltered. "You okay?"

"Like I said, I'm tired. Can we go now?"

"Sure." He ushered me out of the speakeasy and toward the stairs.

Exhaustion was quickly overtaking me as we left the sublevel, said our goodbyes to the remaining staff and cleaning crew, and exited through the back door of the lounge. We emerged into the alley, where Roy's '61 Corvair sat like a rusted heap of scrap metal. The red paint was almost completely chipped away, and the front bumper hung on for dear life by a few bolts. I found it embarrassing to be seen riding around in this jalopy, but Roy apparently didn't have a care in the world. I would've expected a classy cat like him to have a bit more pride in his ride, but for as long as I'd known him, I still never understood him most of the time.

The trip back to my Bronx apartment was quiet. I could barely stay awake, with the hypnotizing flashes of streetlights whisking over my face. Before I knew it, we were parked outside of my building. Roy left the engine running, and the car's rough idle made my rear tingle.

"Here we are," Roy announced.

I yawned and reached for the door handle. "Thanks."

"Need me to walk you up?"

"No, I'll be okay," I assured him, opening the door.

As I scooted out, Roy touched my hand. "Hey. Get some rest. You're still coming to the fight on Friday, right?"

I grimaced. *I did sort of say I was coming, didn't I?* That was before I met Sherry. "Yeah, I'll be there," I mumbled, moving my hand away from his. "Bye, Roy. And... thanks for being there for me." I got out of the car and trudged up the stoop of my apartment building. I had two days to keep my disturbing discovery under wraps from the likes of Roy.

Two days to make things right before the police moved in.

But if saving Sherry ended up taking two days, then I was already too late.

CHAPTER 14

A good night's sleep was impossible with that nightmare haunting my mind. The hours ticked by, and around seven, the morning light peeked through the slats of the closed blinds. Groaning, I stared up at the plaster ceiling of my apartment. *How much sleep did I get?* I wondered, still feeling groggy. No way was I was getting another wink—I couldn't stop thinking about little Sherry and the others, trapped like her, who needed my help.

After getting washed up and dressed and forcing down a meager bowl of Corn Flakes, I called Chief Lewis. It was almost eight o'clock, and I knew the chief was getting another early start at the office. I sucked in a breath. My heart pounded as I listened to the insistent ringing of the line and waited patiently for him to pick up. Three rings. Four rings. Five. I'd half lowered the receiver, about to hang up, when a man said, "Hello, Robert Lewis speaking."

Heaving a deep sigh, I pressed the receiver back to my ear. "Chief! I'm glad you're there."

"I just walked in the office, Tootsie. What's up?"

"We need to talk." My voice went solemn. "Can you stop by my place as soon as you can?"

There was a brief pause.

"What did you do now?" he asked.

"It's a long story, Chief. I need to talk to you face-to-face."

He let out a deep sigh. "All right. I'll head over as soon as I put out a couple fires here in the office."

"Thanks. See you soon."

I hung up and leaned back in my chair, my chest tightening with growing anxiety. I needed to make that *other* call, the one to Joey. Just thinking about it left a bad taste in my mouth. I found his telephone number in my notebook and dialed it. The line rang six times, then I heard a click. Silence.

Did he pick up? I wondered. "Joey?"

"Detective?" Joey asked, his voice sounding uncertain.

I frowned. "Joey Russell, give me one good reason why I shouldn't report you to the police, the FBI, and every news outlet in the country."

Joey went silent a moment. "What the hell are you talking about?"

"You know exactly what I'm talking about, you sick, perverted piece of scum. She was a child. A *child*! The authorities are gonna have a field day with you. You'll never see the light of day."

"Oh. So you went to the place? You saw?"

"Yeah, I saw. I knew you liked them young, but you are an absolutely despicable human being. There's a special place in the fiery pits for evil people like you."

"Evil? Now wait a minute, baby—"

"Don't call me baby again. That's your one and only warning. I hope the judge throws the book at you for all the despicable things you've done. The way you've treated people. The way you've treated your own wife. And what you did to that child."

"Hold the fuck up. I never laid a finger on that kid. I swear on my life."

"Yeah, I hope you get a life sentence at Sing Sing."

"I'm serious. I ain't into that kid shit. I've got morals, too, you know."

I snorted. "Morals? Ha! You of all people have no right to talk about morals. Especially what I witnessed at The Peacock House with you and your little floozy who was dressed like a high school student."

"Mary's thirty-nine—older than me. We were role-playing, for fuck's sake."

I grimaced. The conversation just took an awkward turn.

"Look," Joey continued. "Believe me when I tell you that I ain't got nothing to do with what's going down at that massage parlor."

"Okay, then. Why did you give me that address? And how did you know about Sherry?"

He let out a deep sigh. "All right. I'll tell you."

Cradling the receiver between my ear and shoulder, I flipped to a fresh page in my notebook and prepared to write.

"My wife, Paige, has been working on an exposé about the Hands of Paradise parlor for several months. She dug around and found some old overseas financial documents linked to a man named Felix Audrey. She eventually traced him back here in New York, at that parlor, specifically."

I furiously took down some notes. *Felix Audrey... the same Audrey as Sherry's boss?*

Joey continued. "At that time, I didn't know what she was getting herself into, so I helped her with her investigation. I have a couple of... friends in high places who know someone on the inside. That's how I learned about the Bubblegum Special."

"Who are these 'friends' of yours? More perverts who like little girls?" I asked.

"No! They don't fuck with kids. These are my trusted friends whom I can call on in a pinch. They follow the law as they see it."

"What's that supposed to mean?"

"It means they know how to legally do things without getting caught."

My frown deepened. *Ugh... those kinds of people.* Nailing down an arrest for people like them was always hard because they knew how to play legal loopholes against the system. Back when I was on the force, Chief Lewis told me they were the least of our problems even though they were the biggest pain. In most cases, our hands were tied, and those guys knew it.

"All right," I told Joey. "You and your... *friends* learned about the kid. What happened next?"

"I was gonna tell Paige about it, when I got this mysterious phone call, a man's voice I couldn't recognize because it was disguised like a robot. The guy didn't give a name but an ultimatum. He ordered me to cease and desist Paige's investigation, or else he would destroy her, the paper, and everything—and everyone—she loves."

I stopped writing. "He threatened you?"

"It sounded more like a promise."

"Okay, so Paige was poking her nose where it didn't belong, and this robot-voice guy caught wind of it and is now threatening to take her out?"

"That's the gist of it, Detective," Joey said.

"You think the man that called you might be Felix Audrey?"

"I suspect it is, but I'm not sure. I don't think I want to know. I've been trying to dissuade Paige from working on the story anymore so all this shit could go away quietly, but she's as stubborn as her father. Once she puts her mind to something, she doesn't back down.

"Well, her stubbornness is what got my damned photo on the front page of the *National Esquire*. Thank God my face and body were censored. The same day the article came out, the robot-man called again. He said that scandalous article was a warning—that if I didn't stop Paige from her investigations, things would get far worse for me."

"So it's gone from threats to blackmail," I concluded. *And that must've been what Joey meant yesterday.*

"Yeah," he said. "That's why I was trying to find those damned negatives. But after that threatening telephone call, I realized who probably had them."

I skimmed my notes. Things were starting to piece together. *So Allison doesn't have the negatives—this Audrey guy does.* "Sounds like Audrey's scared that Paige might be onto him about the kid."

"Paige don't know anything about the kid. She only suspects Audrey of being connected to a secret drug operation, but she's still trying to find some more proof."

"And you're trying to stop her from doing that."

He sighed. "Yeah. She thinks I don't care. But I do. I really do."

"You can tell her until you're blue in the face how much you love her, and you can shower her with all the flowers and chocolates in the world, but you're still a cheater."

"Look, what I do in my own private time is my own business, and I would appreciate it if you don't tell Paige or anyone else."

"Oh, don't worry. I'm not in the business of ruining marriages. That usually falls on the adulterer anyway. I'm just doing a job. You'll have to face Paige at some point and air out this dirty laundry. Anyway, if what all you said about Audrey and the parlor is true, then it's time to get the police involved."

"No. Fuck no. Paige might as well wear a neon sign for Audrey. No cops, Detective. I don't know what kind of man Audrey is, but he sounds like someone who doesn't break promises."

"Then what do you propose? This problem ain't gonna go away on its own."

"He's blackmailing me with those negatives, so if there was a way to somehow get them back, then he'd lose some of that bargaining power."

"Okay, I'll figure out a way. And what about Paige's article?"

"I can't stop her. She's bent on it being connected with a drug operation. I don't think Audrey knows the extent of her knowledge. She's been focused on the drugs side of things, which I could see Audrey hiding in plain sight if he did have some involvement."

"It's all speculation," I said. "I need to know exactly what's going on behind the scenes before I make a potentially dangerous move."

"If you find something—anything in that parlor related to a drug operation—then we can be the ones with leverage over Audrey."

I huffed. *Like it's going to be that easy.* "Stay by the phone, Joey. I'll be calling you back later."

"I'm not goin' nowhere, Detective."

"Where are you, anyway?"

"I'm at an apartment somewhere in this city, and that's all you're gonna know."

I rolled my eyes. "Fine. Stay there. I mean it." I hung up the phone and exhaled a deep sigh.

I spent the rest of the morning trying to go over my notes from the night before, as well as my five-page transcription of Joey's story.

A loud series of thumps coming from next door made me jump. I looked up at the clock over my front door and sighed. It read just after noon, and the thumping sounded like Crazy Bob had another disgruntled visitor. Or maybe a robber—no telling who the person was. I had to remain alert. The building was never safe from robberies, and I couldn't take a chance that this was yet another attempt at lawbreaking.

I grabbed my gun from my desk drawer, crept to the front door, and peered out the blinds. Two men were in the hallway. One of them was Harry Lawton, who was pounding furiously on Crazy Bob's door. I didn't recognize the other man. He was shorter than Harry, was dressed similarly in his Wall Street–style suit, and sported a comb-over that looked too neat to be real. Looked like Sue-Happy Harry had decided to bring along one of his crooked friends.

"I know you're in there, motherfucker," Harry said. "Come outta there!"

Unfortunately, Beth was out at another one of her imaginary protests at City Hall, or she would've had a field day with these two stooges. I gripped my gun, concealed it behind my back, and flung open my door. "I thought I told you to leave and don't come back," I demanded.

The pounding stopped, and the two men spun to face me.

Harry scowled. "This ain't none of your business, girl. And you better not try nothing this time, either. This guy right here's my lawyer!"

I blinked. *Geez Louise. What in the world did Crazy Bob do to get all this harassment?* "Look, I know who you are, Mr. Harry Lawton. And I know about your previous run-in with the law. So I suggest you move along before I get the police involved."

Harry sneered. "You don't know shit about me. And go ahead and call the cops. I'll sue you for everything you got if you get me arrested for just standing outside a place of business."

"You're loitering. That's a violation," I corrected. "And you're disturbing the peace."

Harry leaned over to his "lawyer" and whispered something in his ear.

I lifted my chin and kept my gun concealed behind me. "This is your last warning, Harry. Leave, or else."

"Or else what?" Harry jeered. "You gonna sic your crazy girlfriend on me again? Just try it, bitch. I'm warning you I got my lawyer here, so you better stay cool if you know what's good for you. I have every right to be here, and I'm not leaving till I get what's owed to me!" He turned and pounded his fist on Crazy Bob's door. "Come outta there! I got my lawyer this time. I'm taking you to court, and I'm gonna burn every last one of those fucking books!"

I perked up. *Book? Did Crazy Bob write a book?* I wondered. That would certainly make sense, hearing the typewriter sounds all day and night. But why the big secret?

"Okay, I get it," I said. "You're suing him for defamation of character because he put something about you in a book?"

"That's right, sweetheart, and it's a legal offense," the "lawyer" said. "My client here is within his rights to sue for damages."

"How do you know Bob wrote about you?" I asked Harry.

"How? Have you even read his last fucking book? Urgh. Why am I even talking to you about this?" He spun back to the door and pounded harder with his fist.

"The proof is on those printed pages," the "lawyer" said.

Scowling, I confronted Harry's friend. "So tell me. Where'd you get your law degree from?" I asked.

The man looked at me quizzically. "Why? You wanna be a lawyer? Tough shit, baby. You don't have the balls for law school—literally."

I growled. "Call me baby again, and I'll shove that imaginary law degree down your throat."

"Don't take her bait, Matt," Harry said, not turning away from the door. "She's an instigator, just like that crazy hippie chick."

As I was about to respond, I spotted a large man dressed in a tan suit slowly ascending the stairs behind Harry and his friend. I fought down a smile. *Great timing, Chief...* I flicked my gaze back to Harry and discreetly tucked my gun into my back waistband. "You know what? This all stinks. I'm calling the police," I said.

Matt scowled, slipped his hand behind his back, and flicked out a stiletto. "You talk too much," he muttered.

I froze, my gaze zeroing in on the blade. "Interesting method of practicing law," I said, about to reach for my gun again.

Chief Lewis approached the men from behind. He lunged at Matt and grabbed his wrist, forcing the man to drop the knife. "That's because he ain't no legit lawyer," the chief said, frowning.

Matt yelped and sank to his knees. "Ow! Ow! Let me go! You're gonna break my hand!"

Chief Lewis pulled a pair of handcuffs from his jacket pocket and secured Matt's arms behind him. "You're gonna wish it was broken when I get done with you."

Harry stared open-mouthed. "Wh-What are you doing? Who the fuck are you? Let go of him!" He abandoned the door and cocked his fist back, about to give the chief a good shiner.

Chief Lewis, despite his hefty size, dodged the wild blow then wrapped him up in a standing armlock that had Harry whimpering like a baby. Keeping Harry secured in his nearly arm-breaking move, Chief Lewis whipped out his badge from his coat pocket and shoved it in the other man's face. "I'm the chief of police at the Fifty-Fourth Precinct, and you and your friend are under arrest."

"Oh shit..." Harry hissed.

"You're knee-deep in it, Lawton," the chief said.

I sighed in relief. "I'll call the station." I rushed back to my office and dialed the Fifty-Fourth Precinct. Afterward, I returned to the hallway, where the two white-faced con men were cowering on their knees while Chief Lewis finished reading them their rights. "They're on their way," I told the chief.

"Good. While we wait, I want to have a word with the business owner." Chief Lewis approached Crazy Bob's door and knocked. "Hey. You inside. This is the police. Mind coming out so I can ask you a few questions?"

I moved closer to the chief. *Finally, I might be able to get a glimpse of Bob now,* I thought, making sure I would have a good view. After a few moments, however, no one answered the door. I listened carefully for typewriter sounds but heard none.

I sighed. "Well, howd'ya like that?" I grumbled. "All that trouble, and he ain't even there."

"Seems that way," Chief Lewis said, turning back to the two men. "You fools are in luck. You get to take a first-class trip down to the station. We'll let the prosecutor decide what to do with you next."

Harry blinked. "Wh-What! But we didn't do nothing! This is crazy!"

"Let's see," Chief Lewis began. "Assault, harassment, attempted breaking and entering…"

"Don't forget loitering, fraud, and disturbing the peace," I added with a firm nod.

"Hey, i-it was a joke, th-that's all," Harry stammered.

"Tell that to the judge," the chief said.

We waited in the hallway until two officers arrived and picked up Harry and Matt.

After the two con men were escorted away, I returned to my apartment. "Come in, Chief," I said, opening the door. "I have a lot to tell you."

CHAPTER 15

Almost an hour of emotions had gone by when I finished telling Chief Lewis about every detail of the disturbing incident at the massage parlor.

"Christ..." Chief Lewis muttered, slowly rising from the wooden school chair in front of my desk. He rubbed a hand over his face and paced around the room, his expression pale.

I growled. "I wasn't expecting to encounter something so despicable. I figured you'd want to know about this."

"Yeah..." An agonizing silence filled the room for several long moments. "You know the hardest part about this job? Me caring too damned much."

"I know the feeling," I murmured, averting my gaze.

"Some cops eventually get immune to this shit because they've seen it so many times. I've been on the force for over twenty years, and even now, my stomach still turns."

"That's because you're a decent human being. Decent people should never get immune to this."

He stopped pacing and looked at me. "My wife and I could never have children of our own. I'll be damned if I ever become immune to people hurting a child. You're the closest thing I have to a daughter. If any man ever lay a hand on you, I swear I'll tear him apart with my bare hands."

I smiled. "Don't worry. I can handle myself. I was the top student in self-defense at the academy, remember?"

The corner of his mouth twitched. "Yeah. You were a bad little thing. Anyway, you're family in my book. And no one fucks with my family."

I smiled, and my eyes stung a little. "Thanks, Chief. That means a lot. I couldn't ask for a better person to be a part of my family."

"Heh. Who knows? Maybe your dad and I were long-lost brothers in another life." He sighed and turned away from the desk. "Anyway, I can't say that I'm surprised about all this. I remember, a couple years back, we did a big child prostitution bust up in Yonkers. Fucking perverts infest this city worse than the rats."

"The rats are cleaner than these dirtbags," I said. "I don't know how big this operation is, but I intend to find out."

"No, Tootsie. This is a police matter now. It might even be hovering near federal territory, depending on how far this operation has spread."

"Wait. I made a promise to that girl that I would get her out of there. There may be other kids. I want to find more proof, more evidence before you send in the boys in blue."

"Look. This ain't some two-bit lost-and-found job. These kinds of people don't just have weapons. They have connections. Power."

And you wouldn't have known anything until I told you. I frowned. "Fine, Chief. Do it your way."

He narrowed his eyes. "Rita, I mean it. Stay away from that parlor, understand?"

I chewed my bottom lip. He never used my real name unless he meant serious business. And I couldn't blame him. But the urge to help that little girl was strong. She was probably being tormented right then as we spoke. I'd made a promise to her that I intended to keep, no matter what. A lot was at stake, including my own life. But I would do whatever it took to see Sherry set free from that nightmare.

"Loud and clear," I replied. "You won't see me there. I trust the police to do their job." *And I'll be doing mine.* "I have other business to take care of elsewhere, anyway."

He nodded curtly. "Good. I'm glad you're finally being rational for a change."

"I just want to see them all brought to justice."

"Oh, don't worry, they will be."

"By the way..." I retrieved the manila envelope containing the *National Esquire* photos from my desk and handed it to Chief Lewis. "Try running some fingerprint checks on these photos. You may be able to identify possible suspects who may be connected with Felix Audrey and his operation." *And I can hopefully confirm who the mysterious drop-off guy was.*

Chief Lewis swiped up the envelope and peeked inside. "Aren't these the photos from—"

"The front page of the *National Esquire*, yeah," I finished.

"Gotcha. I'll get the boys started on it ASAP." He closed the envelope. "Damn, I can't believe this operation has been going on right under our noses for who knows how long."

"You can't blame yourself. There are probably many others we don't know about... yet. But we will. And they will be dealt with one by one. These sickos can't get away with their crimes forever."

His face dulled. "That's the worst thing about it. This happens all too often. Every day is too late for the victims."

"Hey, you're doing the best you can. You and your boys are stretched thin these days. I heard rumors floating around about the city possibly enacting a hiring freeze on the entire NYPD. That true?"

"God, I hope not..."

"Not like there's any money left to go around, anyway. Say, did you ever get a chance to check on those telephone logs from last Friday?"

"Yeah. Brian, one of my rookies, took care of it. The only number that came in during that time last Friday was from a pay phone on Ninety-First Street in Queens."

I perked up. *Ninety-First Street? That's where the parlor is.* I couldn't remember if I'd seen a pay phone anywhere around there. "Okay, thanks a bunch, Chief." I glanced at the clock over the front door. *One fifteen. I should probably pay Diego a visit before Chief Lewis sends out his cavalry.* "I, uh... need to head downtown to take care of something for a client."

He nodded. "And I need to get back to the office. Thanks for the tip. I'll let Captain Peterson know so he can get a search warrant for that parlor."

Time was of the essence. No telling what Mr. Audrey would do to Sherry if he discovered cops swarming the place. I had to get her out before that happened. The front door wasn't going to be an option, but maybe I could find another way in. Then I remembered something Luis had mentioned the other night about his uncle and the strange sounds underground. Maybe there was something to that. Time to pay a visit to Thrifty World.

The bus dropped me off in Jackson Heights around three fifteen that afternoon. A trip that should've only taken thirty minutes ended up taking two hours due to lunchtime traffic and road-construction delays. Thank goodness I didn't take a cab. It would've cost me a fortune, with all the idling.

The neighborhood looked much different during the day. The sidewalk bustled with passersby, some lugging bags of groceries, others shouldering sacks of laundry, and others simply walking along with somber looks, as if they'd already had enough of the day. My nose twitched from the mouthwatering beef and pork aromas wafting from a Colombian restaurant across the street. The entrance was wide open, and the small hole-in-the-wall place was packed with late-lunchtime patrons.

The massage parlor was also open. Without the glow of the lamplights in the windows, the building's exterior appeared a bit more inviting in the daylight. My stomach turned. *Sherry...* I hauled my attention back to the thrift shop. The steel security gate and window coverings were rolled away, and a blue-and-white Open sign hung prominently against the glass of the entrance.

Entering Thrifty World was like walking through a time machine. The front of the store was full of circular clothes racks stuffed haphazardly with a mix of T-shirts, faded jeans, men's slacks, and little girls' ruffled dresses. Another rack was full of gaudy, old-fashioned zoot suits, frilly house dresses, and other eyesores several decades out of style. Beyond the clothing section were a few shelved aisles of shoes, handbags, scarves, old children's toys, kitchenware, and a bunch of odd trinkets and gadgets that would've been better off in an antique shop. One corner of the store housed a bookshelf full of spine-cracked paperbacks and dusty, jacketless hardbacks. Two long tables were set up in an open area, displaying a small television, an old gramophone, a couple of typewriters, and a vintage radio with a knob missing.

An aged Puerto Rican man appeared from behind a velvet curtain beyond the front counter. He was average height and had a solid build like he'd spent some time in the gym. A pair of black tortoiseshell glasses was nestled atop his balding grey hair. Lifting his chin and narrowing his eyes, he scrutinized me for several moments. "*Hola*. What can I do for you, *jovencita*?" he said in a rich Spanish accent.

I approached the counter, a glass display case containing all sorts of watches, some old and some new. "Hi. I'm just looking around. Are you Diego?" I asked.

He stiffened then reset his glasses on his nose and studied me again. "*Sí*. Who are you?"

"The name's Tootsie. I'm a private detective and a friend of your nephew, Luis, who works at Gatestar Media. He suggested I come talk to you."

His body slowly relaxed, but he maintained his wary gaze. "Luis sent you? Why? Are you with the police? I did nothing."

I gave him a reassuring smile. "Relax. I'm not with the police. Luis and I were talking the other night, and he mentioned you had some noisy neighbors. I thought maybe I could check it out and possibly help you with your little problem."

Diego frowned. "*Sí*. I don't know what's going on over there, but it drives me crazy."

"What does the noise sound like?"

He shrugged. "Little thumps."

"You sure it's not rats?"

"I hope not. I hate rats."

I whipped out my notebook from my trench coat pocket and jotted down some notes. "How long have you been in this building?" I asked.

"Seventeen years," he replied.

"And how long has the massage parlor next door been there?"

Diego wrinkled his nose. "Ehh... maybe five years. First was a bookstore there, then empty for a long time. Now those noisy people moved in, but it ain't none of my business what goes on over there."

I continued writing. "Understandable. Mind if I take a look around? Maybe I can find some clues about the mysterious noise. Y'know, holes in the walls, secret doors, that sort of thing."

He frowned a moment then gave a slight nod. "Okay, but only 'cause you're helping my nephew. Look, but don't touch nothing. *Tu rompes, tu compras*—you break, you buy."

"I dig." I turned away from the counter and traversed the shop, scanning the walls and ceiling for clues. I snaked through the aisles of clothing, trinkets, and junk. All the while, I could feel Diego's hawk gaze on me. Ignoring him, I checked the back room, which looked like it was used for storage.

The front door opened, and an old woman walked in, all smiles. She eyed Diego and waved. "*Hola*, Diego. *¿Cómo estás?*"

Diego lost interest in me and greeted his new customer. I tuned out their conversation, which was completely in Spanish, and finished my search in the back room. I checked every inch of the room but didn't notice anything out of the ordinary. Judging by some of the old architecture, the building had been around for the last forty or fifty years. Such an old building was bound to have noises galore.

On my return to the main shop area, my foot sank about an inch on an uneven section of the grungy, thin carpet. I started and looked down behind me. Part of the floor had buckled slightly and gave a hollow creak when I lifted my foot. *Hmm...*

Diego rang up the old lady for a couple of pieces of vintage jewelry and waved goodbye. After she left, he joined me in the back room. "Well, Detective? Did you find anything?"

"Maybe..." I studied the carpet curiously then knelt and pressed my hand on the indentation. "When did you put this carpet down?"

His forehead wrinkled. "Ain't mine. It came with the place. *¿Por qué preguntas?*"

I located a tiny piece of the carpet sticking up and tugged on it. "There's something under here."

"*Ay!* Stop! You're messing up the floor!"

I pulled harder and soon heard a faint tear. "Chill out. I'll pay for the damages if I have to."

"B-But... ah..." he stammered.

I tore away the strip of carpet, which revealed a couple of thin wood panels nailed haphazardly to the rest of the wooden floor, attempting to hide a hole that looked just big enough for an adult to fit through. "Now, what do we have here?"

Diego blinked. "*¡Dios Mio!*"

"My thoughts exactly." I tried yanking on the nailed-down pieces of wood, but they didn't budge. The nails were rusted, and the wood looked several decades old. "This hole was definitely here for a while. Got a hammer?" I asked Diego.

He hesitated then rushed to a dresser in the storage area and pulled out a small toolbox. He retrieved a hammer and handed it to me. "What are you going to do?"

"I'm going to find the source of that noise." I took the hammer and began wedging up the nails from the boards.

"You think it's coming from down there?"

"Seems obvious, but I need to be sure." I pulled up the first nail, which slipped and fell into the hole. I heard a faint ping a few seconds later. *Hmm... Doesn't sound like it's a very deep hole.*

Diego clasped and unclasped his hands. "*Ay.* All this time. A big, giant hole in my floor! No wonder rent was so cheap." He swore under his breath in Spanish.

"Who knows if the landlord knew? This carpet looks really old, and it doesn't look like it's been disturbed in a very long time." I removed the rest of the nails and slid away the wood panels. The hole appeared slightly smaller than a manhole. I reached into my trench coat pocket and pulled out my thin silver pen flashlight.

"How could he not know?" Diego said. "Why else would he charge less for this place?"

"Maybe he was desperate for a tenant." I clicked the penlight on and shone it around the jagged hole. "This doesn't look like it was dug up with any machinery." I knelt at the edge of the hole and pointed the light into the blackness. It was just bright enough for me to see the bottom of the hole, which was a solid concrete floor about six feet down. The hole continued into what looked like a narrow tunnel supported with masonry and timber.

Diego looked at me wide-eyed. "Y-You're not going to go down there, are you?"

"You want that noise stopped, don't you? Now, listen closely. I want you to go outside and lock up your store. In case whatever is down there is dangerous, at least you will be safe, and you won't put any of your customers in harm's way."

He hesitated then nodded. "O-Okay... but what about you, Detective?"

"I'll be okay. Just let me handle it," I said then peered back into the pit. Some small iron rungs were affixed to the concrete wall, similar to manhole sewer ladders. I carefully reached a hand out to one of the bars to test its sturdiness. The flimsy old metal jiggled and broke off the wall. It fell to the bottom of the hole with a loud, echoing clang. Wincing, I listened for other sounds but heard none. I shuddered to think of what I might find down there. I didn't care much about the rats, but the cockroaches... ugh. I *hated* cockroaches.

"You're a brave lady, Ms. Tootsie. I hope there's no trouble down there." Diego's lips thinned. "Should I call the police?"

"No, not yet. Leave the police to me. Now, go."

Diego nodded again and quickly turned and rushed out of the shop. The front door clicked several times as he activated the two locks.

Once he was gone, I retrieved a wooden stepladder that was propped in a corner of the storage area then returned to the hole. Peering into the darkness, I sighed. *Here goes nothing.* I'd packed my .38 before I left my apartment earlier, so I wasn't completely defenseless. I retrieved the gun from its holster in my trench coat and secured it in the waistband of my jeans. Then I took off the coat and hat and tossed them atop a pile of junk in a corner.

Whether or not the hole was significant was still unclear, but if I were a criminal, I would find it a perfect place to hide. Judging by the age of the carpet, the wood, and the nails, it might've served that very purpose for gangsters back in the twenties and thirties. *Maybe I'll find some bodies of dead gangsters.*

My discovery might end up solving a lot of police cases that had run cold over the years.

Only one way to find out.

CHAPTER 16

With the wooden stepladder in hand, I slid down into the hole in the floor of Diego's thrift shop and landed with a quiet thump on the rocky concrete. The cold, dry air carried the stench of rat piss. I unfolded the ladder and positioned it beneath the edge of the hole so that I could climb back out.

I assessed the tunnel, which was wide and tall enough for a large adult to fit through. The tunnel, constructed of old masonry and timber, seemed to have held up over the years. Its purpose? Most likely smuggling, probably during Prohibition. Where the tunnel led, however, was still a mystery. Old splintered timber supported the walls and ceiling, which were cracked in some places. Still, it looked sturdy enough to walk through.

My pen flashlight was just bright enough for me to see ahead. Hugging one wall and listening for sounds, I slowly crept deeper into the tunnel. Small concrete pebbles crunched under my boots, echoing off the stone and drawing out the sounds of the squeaks and skitters of the numerous vermin living down here.

The ceiling was low, about six feet. My nose twitched at the odor of mildew, aged wood, and something else. It was a pungent smell, yet I could also detect a faint flowery scent as well. Ahead, my flashlight shined on the remnants of broken, splintered wood littering the ground and covered in hundreds of rat droppings.

Rats, I can deal with, I thought, hoping they would be the worst of my problems while I was down here. Beyond the debris were some wooden milkcrate-sized containers stacked near a timber-framed passage. The frame housed a large wooden barricade, which looked more like a makeshift door of several wood planks nailed together over an opening. I ran my flashlight over the crates, noting the wood's rough, splintered texture. The lids were open, revealing nothing inside. I moved one of the crates aside, uncovering a large, brown, mangy rat. I started then sneered at the rodent. The rat looked back at me with its dark, beady eyes then slinked away from the glow of my flashlight, seeking refuge behind another crate. On one corner of the crate's lid was a tiny image of a purple five-petal flower, branded into the wood. *Purple flower...* I blinked, recalling my conversation with Sherry. *Could this be...?*

I memorized the flower image before continuing my search. Stopping at the barricaded doorframe, I listened for sounds beyond but heard none. I took a step and heard skittering to my left. Startled, I whipped the flashlight around, revealing a massive, dark-brown cockroach on the wall. I shuddered, the flashlight wavering in my hand. The disgusting super-sized roach crawled out of sight behind one of the crates. *Ugh... no...* One would think that someone like me, who'd lived in this city all my life, would be used to those evil, fiendish creatures. But no. Not since that fateful day back in fourth grade when Roy had dropped a giant live cockroach down the back of my dress as one of his stupid pranks. From that moment on, I had been forever traumatized.

I quietly knocked on the makeshift "door." It sounded hollow. I shined the light along the planks. Like the crates, the wood was rough and splintered and didn't appear very old.

A glow of light shone through the tiny spaces between the planks. I pressed my face closer and peered through one of the spaces. The area beyond was a large finished basement. More wooden crates were stacked to the ceiling.

Two sets of heavy footsteps thumped in the distance and drew closer. My throat tightened, and I shut off my flashlight. *What's going on out there?* I wondered, not taking my eyes off the room. The light winked from the space between the door as two men walked past my line of sight.

"Put it over there," a man said in a gruff voice. He sounded like he was standing right next to the door, but I couldn't see him. "That one's goin' with Cedrick tomorrow."

I blinked. *Is that... Frank?* A chill ran up my spine as I recalled my first encounter with him and the sinister way he'd looked at me. The fact that Frank was here only confirmed that this tunnel led straight into the hornet's nest.

"I'm tellin' ya, that sunnovabitch needa lay low and not be goin' nowhere," another man grumbled. His voice sounded farther away.

"Hey, you know who to talk to if you gotta problem," Frank said. "Now, grab another box from storage so I can pack the rest of this shit up."

Uh-oh. I withdrew my .38 and backed away from the door.

"Yeah, yeah," the other man said. "I still don't know why th' fuck is he sendin' Cedrick, anyway. I got more contacts 'round Boston than that clown."

"Look, I ain't the one who gives the orders," Frank said. "Now shut up and get me a box."

A shadow eclipsed the light, and the door shook slightly.

I had no time to get away from these guys without being spotted. I panicked and squeezed into a small crevice between some crates stacked against the wall of the narrow passage and crouched. I held my breath while silently praying I wouldn't be found.

The door opened. Light from the basement poured into the passage. One of the men's footsteps thundered in my direction. His long, wide shadow stretched toward the end of the tunnel. One of the stacks of crates near me jostled then stopped.

"Hey, Frank, what's that over there?" the man said.

A layer of sweat formed under my arms and beaded along my forehead. *Oh no, they found me.* I let out a silent breath.

"What're you talkin' about?" Frank's voice boomed, then his shadow eclipsed the door.

"I see somethin' ahead. Gimme that," the other man said.

A flashlight flicked on. The light shone on the crates a moment then farther down the passageway. The two men filed in a single line, slightly crouched, and inched along. They squeezed past the crates, one of the men jarring the stack with his hip. I sucked in a breath, feeling the heat of the two men's closeness.

"There's a light," Frank muttered. "Shit. Is that a hole in the ceiling?" As he passed, he pulled out a gun concealed in a holster under the back of his shirt.

"Looks like it," Frank's friend said, retrieving his holstered gun at his waist. He was tall and hefty, built like a wrestler. "Ain't that the shop next door?"

Darn it. I'm trapped. Thank goodness Diego was gone, in case those two goons decided to investigate. But that was my only means of escape because I sensed nothing good waited for me the other way. *But Sherry was somewhere in there.* I remembered her saying that she stayed in the basement. Maybe she was somewhere in that room. If I could only get her out through that tunnel somehow...

My thoughts were disrupted when I spotted something large moving in my periphery. I shifted my gaze. A full-sized cockroach crawled down the wall and onto my shoulder, mere inches from my face. I paled and bit into the sleeve of my turtleneck shirt, holding in a scream. The monster's long antennae jittered in my direction, then it skittered off my shoulder. It crawled onto the wall, squeezed its fat body into a tiny crack in the rock, and disappeared. My anxiety remained, knowing that disgusting creature was still alive. I willed myself to refocus on my situation.

Once the two men had gone completely past, I sidled out from my hiding place, silently cocked my gun, and backed up toward the basement entrance.

The men reached the end of the passageway, where light from Diego's shop was pouring in from above. Frank and Hefty stepped into the light and discovered the stepladder.

"Someone's down here," Frank said to his friend.

I continued quietly backing away toward the basement entrance, then my right heel hit one of the crates in the middle of the walkway. I stumbled and fell backward, my heart dropping into my gut. My lower back crashed onto the edge of the crate with a loud, echoing thump, inflicting sharp pain but breaking my fall before the back of my head could hit the concrete ground.

The two men turned toward me.

"I'll get that nosy bitch," Hefty said then shouldered his way through the narrow passage like an angry football player.

Ignoring the pain in my back, I scrambled back to my feet and rushed toward the light of the open entrance to the basement. Hefty's footsteps thundered behind me.

The basement was lit by a single dingy bulb set into the low popcorn ceiling. The large finished basement extended into another dark area in the far opposite corner of the room. At the edge of the ring of light was a wooden staircase leading up into darkness. A sliver of light appeared at the top of the stairs, from a door that was left partially open.

More stacked crates filled the basement. Unlike the ones in the passage, these were sealed and looked like they were ready to be shipped off somewhere. The strong smell of fresh pine overtook the passage's fetid stench. Noting more of those purple flower symbols on the crates' lids, I guessed what was most likely contained in those boxes.

Hefty's footsteps drew nearer. I tried to push the makeshift door closed, but it got stuck on one of its wooden planks, which dragged on the floor. I abandoned the door and zipped toward the stairs. Hefty entered the basement. As I reached for the wooden banister, a strong force yanked me back by the back of my shirt and tossed me to the ground. My body shook as fear and adrenaline coursed through my veins. A gun cocked. I stared at two polished brown shoes standing inches away. My gaze traveled up from the man's dark-brown bell-bottom slacks to his red-and-white-striped polo shirt, which clung to his muscular chest and arms tighter than a corset. I stared at his hard, ruddy face and his raging brown eyes. He looked to be in his thirties, maybe slightly older.

He pointed his Colt .45 at me, and his finger slowly moved over the trigger. "End of the line, bitch."

CHAPTER 17

"Don't shoot!" I spat, my mouth going desert dry. Slowly, I raised my hands in surrender. The basement's cool air whisked over my exposed arms. My .38 dangled on my right index finger.

The hefty-sized henchman growled like an angry bear with a messy, dark-brown mop top, hulking, sweat-soaked arms, and a .45 in his greasy hands. My mind spun. Maybe I should've listened to Chief Lewis and let the police handle it. I'd definitely bitten off more than I could chew. Somehow, I had to get out of here alive.

The cold steel of Hefty's gun pressed against my temple. "Drop the gun," he barked.

I took a deep breath, inhaling his wet-dog stench, and did as he ordered. As soon as my .38 hit the ground, he kicked it away, sending it skittering across the concrete floor.

"Now, bitch," he continued, smirking darkly. "I'm gonna blow your fucking brains out."

Think fast, I thought. This wasn't the first time I had a gun to my head. These types of thugs knew only one language, and fortunately, all my years of rough-and-tumble in the streets had made me fluent.

"Then do it," I dared him. "I ain't come down here to be shootin' the bull with some jive turkey."

"Shut up!" he snapped.

Frank emerged from the hidden passageway at the far end of the basement. His gun was still in his hand as he approached. "Hey, what's she doing here?"

Oh, great. "Hey, Frank. Nice seeing you again."

Hefty looked at his friend. "You know this broad?"

"Yeah, she stopped by last night." He pinned his cold gaze on me. "Answer my question."

I took a deep breath and shrugged. "I was *checking out* the place next door—y'know, while the ol' man was out to lunch—seein' how much bread I can get for some o' that junk, you dig? Anyway, I saw this hole in the floor of his shop, so I decided to do a little searching for treasure."

"Bull," Hefty said through gritted teeth. "You're dead, bitch."

I held my breath and squeezed my eyes shut.

"Wait," Frank said.

I felt the cold barrel of the gun slide away from my temple and slowly opened one eye. Frank had his hand over Hefty's gun and pointed it down and away from me.

Hefty growled at his comrade. "What the hell?"

"Look, I don't know what you're waitin' for," I said. "If you ain't gonna kill me, then let me go so I can get my bread. At least one of us'll be productive tonight."

"Shut the fuck up!" Hefty snapped at me.

I smiled crookedly. "I've dealt with suckers like you. All talk. Think you're so high and mighty. Takin' me as some schoolyard punk. My last victim did, too, and he learned the hard way. His body's probably finally made it to the bottom of the Hudson by now."

Frank narrowed his eyes. "A girl like you with a gun? Naw. I don't peg you as the killing type. Just like I don't peg you as someone who likes getting serviced by little girls."

Hefty's gaze shot to Frank. "The fuck?"

"Hey, I got my vices, just like you got yours. Don't judge me. As for killing, well, I don't normally brag about my accomplishments, but seeing as your friend here is about to put me six feet under..." I gave a head tilt toward Hefty.

"C'mon, man, lemme ice her." Hefty growled. His hand shook as he fought against his friend's pacifying grip on the weapon.

"Hey, chill," Frank said, slowly releasing his hand from atop the gun. He looked me over with his wolfish hazel gaze and cracked a dark smile. "You like the dark life, huh? One o' them bad girls?" He looked back at his friend and continued in a low volume, "She's got spunk. More than the rest of these mindless broads around here. Besides, look at 'er. She's barely pushing twenty. Mr. Audrey will be interested, know what I'm sayin'?"

My ears perked. *Mister Audrey...* I tightened my jaw. I wasn't dead yet, and it seemed my youthful appearance might just get me off the hook. I swore, if I made it out of here alive, I'd never complain again the next time someone mistook my age.

Hefty scrunched his nose. "Fuck that. She's seen too much. I say we shut her up for good."

"Look, either kill me or let me go," I interjected. "Ain't nothing down here worth jackin,' so I'm gonna grab what I can from the old man's shop and sell it for a little bread so I can get a one-way bus ticket to LA and out of this dump."

Hefty backhanded me across my right cheek. My head jerked to the side, and a stinging, fiery pain ran up the side of my face. My eyes watered, and I squeezed them shut and yanked back the pained tears with all my might.

"Shut the fuck up, girl!" Hefty barked. "You ain't goin' nowhere!"

I swallowed back the pain and slowly opened my eyes. I dared to look Hefty straight on, with deep-seated fury. I had to stay strong and keep up my charade, to try to catch them in a mistake I could quickly use against them. *Hmm... they already made the first mistake about how old I was.* I held my chin up high. "Hey, I just turned nineteen two months ago. I ain't no 'girl.' I'm all woman, and don'tcha forget it, buster."

Hefty raised the butt of his gun as if he was about to hit me across the face with it.

I pursed my lips, keeping my eyes locked on the weapon. My whole body tensed in anticipation.

"Leave her alone," Frank said to his friend. "Y'know, the boss'll probably give us both a raise outta this. He likes the dark meat."

Hefty scowled, his nostrils flaring, and he lowered the gun. "Fine," he muttered. "You better be right."

"I know I'm right," Frank said.

I snorted. "You two ain't worth a nickel. Fine. Take me to your beloved boss. I'll give 'im a piece of my mind."

Before I could say anything else, Frank swept behind me. His slimy hands grasped my shoulders. I stiffened. The stench of stale cigars and whiskey burned my nostrils. I had no easy escape.

These two were already riled up. Fighting back would likely buy me a ticket to an early grave.

Hefty aimed his gun at me. "If this bitch don't shut the fuck up..."

"Put it away," Frank told his friend. Then his hot breath brushed against my cheek, and I cringed. "Let's see what else you're packin' before we go," he purred.

Rough hands frisked me from top to bottom, back to front. Grimacing, I kept my hands up and resisted the urge to drop-kick the guy. It would've been foolish to try, anyway. Hefty was getting trigger-happy. *I have to do this. For Sherry,* I thought.

"I don't got nothing," I said.

Frank smirked. "Oh, you got plenty." One hand slid down, and he squeezed my left butt cheek.

I grunted, clenching my fists, ready to knock him out, but Hefty sneered at me, and I stayed my hand.

Frank grabbed the back of my arm. "Look, baby. There ain't no opportunities in California. If it's just bread you want, Mr. Audrey's gotcha covered."

Baby... I sneered, tempted to try my luck and give him a good shiner, but my rational side reeled in those urges.

Frank nodded at his friend. "Watch her a moment. I need to get something." Then he disappeared into another dark section of the basement through a door with a small window.

Faint light glowed from the porthole, cutting through the darkness. The door closed, releasing a whiff of the larger room beyond. I inhaled a familiar, pleasant flowery scent as I peered through the window from a distance. I spotted a young nude woman with her head down, wearing a surgical mask and standing at a glass table, which was covered with various packaging materials, mechanical scales, and other apparatuses that looked like they'd been taken from a mad scientist's laboratory. A dark-skinned man wearing a short trench coat over a green collared shirt slowly paced back and forth. A gun in his hand, he watched the woman.

The woman's body was bruised and battered, and her makeup-caked face held a blank, emotionless expression, like a mindless robot, as if she'd given up on life. Her hands moved automatically as she sorted, measured, and packed a white substance into tiny packets.

Another woman walked over to the male guard and handed him a small packet. She, too, was nude and wearing a surgical mask over her made-up face. And her body also had bruises. The man looked at the packet a moment, glared back at her, then smacked her in the side of the head with the butt of his gun. She crumpled, but he yanked her back onto her feet and shoved her away, out of my line of sight. He stabbed a finger at her, yelling something I couldn't hear, then went back to his guard-dog mode, watching what was going on at the rest of the table.

I chewed my bottom lip, trying to maintain a neutral expression in front of Hefty. But deep inside, I was overwhelmed and furious. I'd busted only a couple of tiny amateur drug operations during my eight years as a shamus. The rest of them were left up to the cops. The boys in blue never did let me have any fun going on drug stings while I was on the force. They'd just expected me and the rest of my fellow female employees to have their coffee brewing when they got back.

This time, I was smack-dab in the middle of a drug operation like peanut butter and jelly.

Frank exited through the doors, sending out another whiff from the room. As the door closed, the woman looked up in his direction, though her hands didn't stop working. She had large doe eyes that seemed soulless, which sent a chill down my spine. I could sense beyond that look of terror a tiny sliver of fury, my only indication that the woman had not quite yet given up. Then, the man in the green shirt walked by and whacked her in the jaw with the back of his hand. The fear in her eyes overtook the last ounce of her anger. She lowered her head and returned to her work. The man continued his patrolling and walked out of my line of sight.

Frank returned to me and Hefty, grinning deviously and carrying a set of handcuffs. He moved my arms behind me and cinched the cuffs around my wrists. "Let's go," he continued, tugging me up the stairs.

I swallowed hard and gingerly lumbered up the stairs with him, wincing as the metal dug into my wrists from the cuffs' tightness. Reaching the top of the stairs, we went through a door and entered a large, windowless, dimly lit room with red-cedar walls and furniture. The familiar flowery scent was evident up here as well. Ornate gold-framed portraits of butterflies and nature decorated the walls, each topped with a red velvet valance. A warm glow filled the room from ambient lighting along the walls and ceiling.

Frank, his arm locked with mine, pulled me in front of a large executive desk, where an older balding man with white hair sat, chatting on the telephone. The desk was piled high with papers, ledgers, and leather folios.

Frank tossed me down, forcing me onto my knees. Grunting, I reluctantly complied.

The older man looked distinguished, but a sinister cloud surrounded him. He wore a burgundy velvet smoking jacket over a dark-grey two-piece suit. The features of his angular, olive-skinned face were hard and defined, with wrinkles and small pockmarks along his jawline. His dark-brown eyes, edged with faint crow's feet, flicked to me for a moment. Then his forehead wrinkled. "...call you later, Pat," he said, his deep voice dripping with poison. "You better have those numbers for me when I do." Not taking his eyes off me, he hung up the telephone. "What'd you bring me this time, Frank?" he asked his henchman.

Frank grabbed a handful of my hair and yanked my head back, forcing me to look up submissively at the older gentleman at the desk. "Found her snooping around downstairs, Mr. Audrey. Just a nosy li'l broad lookin' for work."

Mr. Audrey. So this is the evil son of a snake. I locked eyes with the older man for a moment, and a chill ran down my spine. His expression was emotionless, unreadable. That meant he was unpredictable, the worst kind of criminal. Sweat beaded in my palms and around my wrists, causing the handcuffs to slide rigidly along my slick skin. I took several deep breaths and regained my composure. I had to keep up the charade as long as I could.

After taking a moment to muster up more courage, I narrowed my eyes at the boss. "Hey, I ain't do nothin.' Geez Louise. Can't a girl earn a little bread?"

"Should we keep 'er around?" Frank asked in a calm voice. "She also happens to like little girls."

"Does she, now?" Mr. Audrey reached for a cigar case on his desk. He opened it up and pulled out an extra-thick stogie. Afterward, he retrieved a closed, silver-handled switchblade from atop the desk. "Hmm... now that is interesting," he finally replied, flicking open the blade and edging out one end of his unlit cigar. "Who are you, girl?" he asked me.

"My name is Rosa. Rosa Timms," I spat without hesitation. My eyes were locked on the blade, watching its every move as Mr. Audrey finished preparing his cigar.

"How'd you get down there, Rosa?" he asked, lighting it with a gold-plated lighter. Sitting back in his chair, he idly puffed away on the cigar. The tobacco's acrid stench quelled the pleasant flowery smell from the basement.

"How else? I snuck into the old man's secondhand shop next door. I was just gonna grab the cash out the register and leave. Then I found this hole in the floor in the back of his shop, so I thought maybe he was stashing something good down there."

"A hole? Interesting…" Mr. Audrey gave his cigar another puff.

"We'll take care of that hole, sir," Frank said. He gave a quick glance at Hefty.

"You do that. I trust there were no witnesses?" Mr. Audrey said.

"No. None," Hefty said. He stepped forward and dropped my items on the desk. "She had a gun on her."

I sighed in relief internally. I would never have forgiven myself if anything happened to Diego or any of his unsuspecting customers.

Mr. Audrey examined the gun and sighed. "I'm sure Little Miss Rosa here can be groomed into a valuable commodity. But I have some other business to take care of first. Go put her somewhere. I'll deal with her later."

I blinked. "You givin' me a job? What am I gonna do? When do I start?"

Mr. Audrey's gaze hardened. "You start when I tell you. If you're going to work for me, then you best learn your place, girl."

I opened my mouth to reply but was cut off by a sudden knock on the door leading out of the room.

"The press passes are done, sir," a woman said from beyond in a muffled voice.

I clenched my jaw. *No, that can't be!*

Mr. Audrey dismissed us with a wave of his hand. "Get the girl out of here," he said to his henchmen then called, "Come in, Cindy."

"Yes, sir," Frank said. He yanked me by the handcuffs. I stumbled backward alongside him. Hefty zipped toward the doorway leading down to the basement. Meanwhile, Mr. Audrey remained at his desk, casually examining my gun while he enjoyed the rest of his cigar.

We passed Cindy on the way out. She gave me a quick once-over and furrowed her brow. I got a good, long look at her. She looked just like the picture in Allison's office, mushroom hairdo and all. She was actually quite pretty up close in person, like maybe she'd done a little modeling in a previous life. Her short, skin-tight cherry-red dress showed off her curves.

Frank lugged me down a short hallway with three closed doors. Affixed on the wall next to one of the doors was a small sign that read Lobby. The sign was lit up with a red light. The door opened, and a young, curvaceous woman strolled in. She was dressed in a short, ruffled, red-and-black petticoat, and a matching corset top. Her jet-black hair was done up in pigtails. She furrowed her brow curiously at me.

"Hey, Claire. Done for the day?" Frank crooned.

Claire wrinkled her nose at him. "Yeah. I ate something that didn't agree with me. I cancelled the rest of my appointments today. I'm getting some rest." She nodded at me. "Got yourself a new playmate?" she asked him.

"Nah. This one belongs to the boss," Frank replied. "Give me five minutes. I'll come join you."

Ugh. I'm going to be sick, I thought, half listening to the banter. My gaze flicked to the half-opened lobby door, which Claire held open while she talked. A beaded curtain hung from the doorway. Beyond the door was Kimberly, whose back was turned as she spoke with a female customer at the front desk. Beyond the desk in the sitting area was Sherry, dressed in a cute black-and-white maid's uniform as she dusted the furniture with a feather duster.

Claire frowned. "No, Frank. I don't wanna see no one tonight."

"Of course you do." Frank smirked. "I'll make you feel better. You can count on it."

"No."

Narrowing his eyes, Frank pointed his finger at her. "You don't say that word to me," he said through clenched teeth.

Claire pursed her lips. She let go of the lobby door and stormed down the hall to Mr. Audrey's door without another word.

I continued to watch Sherry as the lobby door began to close. Sherry stopped dusting, turned, and made her way toward the front desk. Her eyes raised in my direction, and for a moment, our gazes locked. Her eyes widened. Then the lobby door closed, shutting off our line of sight.

At least she's still okay, I thought with some relief.

Frank hauled me in front of a door marked Janitorial. He opened the door, and a humid, musty odor wafted out from the dark room. He yanked on a long, white string hanging from the ceiling. A dingy, yellowish light bulb buzzed awake. The room was merely a tiny, six-foot-deep closet containing a wooden shelf of various cleaning supplies, and a broom and a mop leaned against one of the cracked yellow-tiled walls. A white porcelain service sink was mounted on the back wall.

Frank shoved me onto the grungy, smooth concrete floor. "Welcome to the Waldorf Astoria," he quipped. "Don't bother calling for room service. Stay quiet, and the boss might be inclined to give you a job around here."

My cheek touched the cold floor and I shivered. I glared up at him. "Can I at least get out of these handcuffs?" I asked.

Smirking, he shut off the light. "Be a good girl." Then he closed the door, shutting me away in blackness.

I waited a few minutes for my eyes to adjust. I soon noticed the faint light of the hallway beyond coming under the door. All was quiet. Sighing, I drew my knees to my chest. I'd been in tight jams before, but this one was turning out to be tighter than a pickle-jar lid. My own life wasn't the only one on the line. As I thought about all the things I'd seen and heard, my gut ached for the numerous, nameless others I hadn't encountered. This entire nightmarish prison was full of victims.

CHAPTER 18

My heart was racing. I was trapped in this dark, stuffy janitor's closet like a rat. The fear—the nightmare—was becoming a reality. The fear of the unknown. The fear of not being in control. The situation was beyond anything I could ever remember, even during my time on the force.

I just want to get out of here. That little voice in the back of my head screamed for freedom, for safety.

But what about Sherry? She was the reason I'd come here, risking my life. My efforts couldn't be for nothing. *Sherry's counting on me. I can't fail.*

My eyes burned as a mix of emotions toyed with my flustered mind. *Now I know how solitary confinement feels.* The helplessness sparked every nerve in my body. I was miraculously still alive, but I'd seen the heart of their operation, so who knew how long that would last?

Focus, Tootsie, I told myself. *Dick Tracy's been in worse situations. What would he do at a time like this?* I smiled slightly, the thought of my childhood hero easing away some of the fear.

I'd lost track of time. Did minutes pass? Hours? My shoulders ached from my wrists being cuffed behind my back for so long. Numbness tingled down my arms. The steady dim light under the door indicated no one was outside. No sounds came from beyond the door, either, so I assumed I was alone. I had seen the exit door to the lobby on my way to this closet, so all I had to do was escape and get to it.

Grunting, I pushed myself up onto my knees. Then I straightened and rolled my shoulders wide and back. That gave my arms more length so that I could lean slightly forward and arch my back. Slowly, I inched my arms around my butt then to my thighs. I stumbled a bit forward but quickly regained my balance and threaded my legs through my arms. I worked my hands forward. Gritting my teeth against the pull of my shoulder joints, I stepped over my cuffed wrists. Then, at last, my arms were in front of me. My aching shoulders thanked me for it.

The outline of a supply shelf next to me showed in the light from under the door. I felt around for something small and skinny, like a paperclip, a pin, or a firm metal wire but found nothing. My ears perked at the faint sounds of hurried footsteps approaching. The light under the door flickered. I held my breath and sidled along the wall to the side of the door. A shadow stopped in front of it. The handle jiggled, then all was silent, but the shadow didn't move.

I pursed my lips. It couldn't have been one of my captors, who would've had a key. This was somebody else. Remaining silent, I watched the shadow, listened, and waited.

"Miss Rosa! Are you in there?" a young girl's voice whispered.

My heart swelled with relief. *Sherry*. Smiling, I inched closer to the door and knelt. "Sherry?" I whispered back.

"Yeah. Why did Mr. Frankie put you in there?"

"Don't ask. I just need to get out of here. Do you have a paper clip or bobby pin?"

A brief moment of silence passed. "Um, I don't have a paper clip, but..." The shadow moved slightly.

A door creaked open in the distance, followed by the thump of footsteps. "Hey, girl! Get away from there!" Frank barked.

The shadow jerked. Something small pinged against the door. "Ah! S-Sorry, Mr. Frankie. I, um... I just needed to get the mop."

The footsteps pounded closer. "Did Miss Kim tell you to come back here?"

"N-No, but... sh-she was talking, and I didn't want to bother her, so I—"

A loud slap came from behind the door. Sherry yelped. The shadow grew larger, and the door thumped and shook. A tiny black bobby pin slid under the door.

Frank's voice lowered. "You know what Mr. Audrey does to bad little girls like you."

"P-Please, don't tell him. Please!"

"Shut up!"

Sherry whimpered.

After a pause, Frank ordered, "Leave. Now."

His voice lowered more, and I couldn't make out all the words—something about punishment. Whatever he said didn't sound good because Sherry blubbered a reply in a fearful tone.

I gritted my teeth. *I can't let anything else happen to her tonight.* I had to think of a way to get us both out of here.

The shadow disappeared, and Sherry's sobs echoed down the hall.

I swiped up the bobby pin and returned to my original spot on the floor with my knees drawn to my chest. I slid the pin into the lock on the handcuffs and began fiddling with it. *Almost got it.* Just as I was about to hit the lock's sweet spot, Frank inched closer to the door. Hissing, I withdrew the bobby pin from the cuffs and slid it into my hair.

With a click, the door unlocked then swung open.

Squinting, I stared up at Frank's streamlined silhouette as light from the hallway cut through the darkness of this janitor's closet.

Frank yanked on the light cord, filling the closet with its obnoxious yellowish glow. He looked at me a moment, and then frowned under his moustache. "Already being a bad girl, I see," he said.

After a moment, I realized he must've noticed my arms were in front of me instead of behind. I scowled. "Stuff it, Frank."

He rumbled with sinister laughter, grabbed my face, and forced my chin up so that I looked at him in the eyes. "Your feisty little punk ass needs to be taken down a notch," he muttered.

I swallowed, training my gaze on him. His hand reeked of tobacco, laced with something tangy, musky, and sour, like bodily fluids of the female kind. My throat stung with bile that inched farther up from my stomach.

He leaned his face closer, his hot, alcohol-tinged breath making my nose hairs curl. "I should punish you myself," he continued.

I sneered then spat in his face.

Growling, he pulled back, wiping his face. He looked back at me, his dark eyes full of fury. Then he delivered a solid blast of a punch to my midsection, knocking the wind out of me. "Bitch. You're mine, now."

I doubled over, gasping for air. Before I could fully recover, my left arm throbbed as Frank yanked me out of the janitor's closet. With my wrists still handcuffed, I walked beside Frank down the narrow hallway and toward the door leading out into the lobby. The pain in my midsection was still throbbing, but I was once again aware of my surroundings. The sign next to the lobby door was lit up green. *Hmm... wasn't it red last time?*

We went through the door and entered the lobby area, which was currently empty of customers. Kimberly, the hostess, sat at the front counter, her head down, busily scribbling something in a thick open book. As we approached the counter, she looked up.

"Gimme the Egypt key," he said.

"Really, Frank?" she said. "These rooms are supposed to be for paying customers, not your random fuck-a-thons. My girls need to work, not play around with you."

Frank grunted. "Just shut up and do your damn job," he snapped. "Hurry up with that fucking key before a customer comes in."

She wrinkled her nose sourly then turned and plucked a decorative blue-and-gold key from the pegboard behind her. She slid the key across the counter to Frank. "You're going to have to answer to Mr. Audrey if my girls can't perform," she warned.

Frank swiped the key. "This one ain't yours... yet," he said.

"Oh?"

He grabbed the back of my hair in his iron grip, tilted my head back, and forced me to look at her. "Hey, Rosa, say hi to your future boss."

I winced.

Kimberly's eyebrows rose. "What's she doing back here?"

"What can I say? Can't get enough of this place," I quipped.

Frank smirked at Kimberly. "You said you liked repeat customers, didn't you?"

"Hmph. She's the only woman who has ever come here asking for the BG. All my girls prefer adults, not kids. I ain't touching that one with a ten-foot pole, Frank. She ain't workin' here, ever."

"Mr. Audrey will decide that," Frank said.

Growling, she clenched and unclenched her fists. "Leave, Frank!"

"Don't worry, Kim, baby. I'll get to you next." He lugged me toward the stairs before she had a chance to say anything else. "C'mon, sweetheart," he muttered to me.

Kimberly sneered. "I hope all your little fuck sessions make your dick fall off, you son of a bitch!" she said. Then she sighed and returned to the counter.

Frank chuckled mockingly in response.

As we headed upstairs, I calmed my nerves and gathered my bearings. We walked down the familiar hallway of closed doors with brass-framed nameplates. We stopped outside one of the doors at the front of the building. The brass nameplate next to it read Egypt. The door had two keyholes, one on top of the other.

Frank stuck the key in the bottom hole, unlocked the door, and shoved me inside. "In you go, sweetheart."

I grunted and stumbled to the floor on my knees. A sharp pain in my midsection returned briefly. The room was small, with a gold-and-royal-blue color scheme. A king-sized canopy bed decorated like a royal throne sat against a wall. A matching velvet curtain covered the window, which looked out onto

Thirty-First Avenue's early-evening traffic. Wallpaper with repeating images of faux hieroglyphics and Egyptian symbols covered the walls. Cheap-looking brass statues of cats and naked female Egyptian-looking goddesses decorated the top of a teak armoire, and a large vase imprinted with an image of King Tut accentuated one corner of the room. A small blue-and-gold lamp sat atop the night table, providing the room's only dim light.

Frank shut the door behind himself and locked it. He stepped away from the door, leaving the key inserted, and approached me.

As I struggled to stand up, Frank grabbed me and flung me onto the gold-and-royal-blue bedding. I landed face-up with a soft bounce.

The situation is getting worse. I was free of that dark closet but about to fall victim to something far more despicable. Frank was strong, and he had a gun. *Wait... is that my gun?* Getting away from him was not going to be easy, but I had to try. Some way, somehow, I had to try. Frank hated a defiant woman, and the pain still lingering in my midsection was a constant reminder.

An idea suddenly struck me. I would play this pervert at his own sick game, which could help me escape. Maybe I could even help Sherry too. It just might work. It *had* to work.

Frank pulled out the gun—a snub-nosed Colt .38—from his waistband and set it on the night table, strategically far enough away from my reach.

"You were gonna shoot me with my own gun?" I asked, hiding my disgust.

"Maybe. It's my gun now. It was a present from the boss, for me turning you in." He flashed a crooked grin. "I like your spunk, but I got no problem messin' up your pretty little face if you try to fuck with me."

I looked at the gun blankly then returned my attention to his face. "I don't think your boss would like that."

"He wouldn't like it more if one of his girls turned on him. He has us around to keep all you bitches in line." He began undoing the buttons of his dress shirt and continued, "Now, my dear Cleopatra, where should I start?"

I grimaced. "Cleopatra? Really? Who do you think I am, Elizabeth Taylor?"

"Okay, then. How about Bastet? 'Cause you're as feisty as a cat." He finished unbuttoning his shirt, revealing a dark, hairy chest beneath. He wasn't very muscular, compared to his hefty thug friend from earlier, but the way he'd grabbed me, I could tell he was much stronger than he looked. Frank wouldn't hesitate to ice me if I got a little too out of hand with him. Technically, since I wasn't employed by Mr. Audrey yet, I was fair game for a bullet. With my wrists still cuffed, I'd never be able to grab the gun on the night table before he did. *Geez Louise... I've really gotten myself into a fine mess.*

Frank tossed the shirt to the floor, kicked off his shoes, and started undoing and pulling off my boots.

Ugh. This guy was a ticking time bomb. He seemed to be in the moment, but he was also unstable, dangerous. I had to keep him talking to buy time, but I also had to be careful with my words. "Hey, Frank," I murmured. "Before you, uh... start, I'm curious. Do you only like having fun with only one girl?"

Frank arched an eyebrow. "'One'? Bitch, I've had seven at once before."

"Seven?" I whistled. "Impressive. Now *that's* what I call a party. You freaky devil, you."

He chuckled darkly. "The ladies don't call me Freaky Frankie for nothin'."

I tried my hardest to maintain a straight face. *How pathetic.* "I was thinking. That lollipop, Sherry. I want her to join us. Hearing her voice brought back so many great memories. I miss that life, Frankie."

"What life was that, sweetheart?" he asked. He took off my socks, exposing my bare feet, and began giving them a gentle massage. It probably would've felt good if Frank hadn't been the one doing it. Heaven only knew my poor dogs were in desperate need of a good rubdown—but never from the likes of that evil man. Every place on my feet that he touched felt like spine-tingling ice-cold needles.

"Look, I may be nineteen, but I know all about lollipops. I lived that life, Frankie. It was wild. Dynamite. Lollies are fun, and they know how to get down—in more ways than one." I winked.

His moustache twitched. "What do you want, baby?"

Baby... strike one. "I wanna have some real fun. You, me, and Little Miss Lolly."

He released my feet and looked at me intently. "Oh?"

"Yeah," I said, relieved his touch was gone. "And you know what? The more I think about it, the more you're right. There ain't nothing worthwhile for me in California. Not when I have access to a fresh lollipop right here. I wouldn't mind working for your boss if it means I can have her anytime I want."

"She's Mr. Audrey's property."

I smirked deviously. "And?"

His eyes widened a moment, then his expression morphed into a sinister smirk.

I ignored the disgusted feeling in my gut. I couldn't believe I was playing this sick game. And I couldn't believe the plan had a possibility of working. I just needed a way out of these cuffs.

Once I got free, I was going to break Frank's ribs and castrate him. We were alone and far away from Mr. Audrey's office, so nobody would hear him scream.

"Hey," I continued, "if I'm gonna be working here soon, then I think it's only fitting we do a little private precelebration, right?"

He moistened his lips. "Yeah... you need to be broken in."

And I'm gonna break your face in when I get free. My plan was set. I would get Sherry out of here, as promised. But so many other victims were trapped here and also needed my help.

"I hope you don't expect me to service Mr. Audrey," I said. "To be honest, he's too... mature for my tastes. I like an older man who's still very much in his prime and has the endurance of a racehorse. Can you dig it?"

"Hmm..." His smile stretched a little. "You're speakin' my language, baby."

My left eye twitched. *Strike two.*

He looked thoughtful a moment. "You, me, and Sherry, huh?"

A raging flame flared in my belly. "That's right. So? What are we waiting for? Are we gonna get this party started, or what?"

He crawled into bed and hovered on top of me on all fours. He stank of sweat and musky old sex. "Can you handle me? All of me?" he murmured, his breath reeking of stale cigarettes.

I wrinkled my nose, attempting to hide my disgust. "I feel kinda cramped. I need more room."

"Yeah, you're gonna need a whole lotta room to stretch out for me, baby."

"Do I have to do this in cuffs?" I asked.

His smile turned crooked. His eyelids fluttered slightly as he regarded me with a half-aroused, half-amused expression. "Nice try, sweetheart," he said.

"How do you expect me to do anything when my arms feel like they're about to fall off?"

His smile turned coyer. "You wanna be comfy? Okay, sweetheart. I'll make you comfy." He moved off me, grabbed his discarded shirt from the floor, and pulled a tiny silver handcuff key from the breast pocket. A small spark of hope filled my chest. Then he mounted me, bearing down his weight, keeping me pinned. Frank shifted me to the side, away from the night table, and undid the handcuffs.

Relief briefly spread through my arms and wrists. *I'm free!* I wanted to fight him, but he currently had leverage and would rip me apart if I showed any resistance. No, I had to feed into his confidence, feed into his vice until he was too doped up on lust to realize anything. But I also had to protect myself at all costs. *He has strength, but I have wits. I will defeat him. For Sherry. For all the other victims cooped up in this place. This demon must pay.*

Frank bore his weight down, pinning my arms and trapping my legs. He felt like a boulder on top of me, and I gasped for air. He forced my arms above my head, threaded the handcuffs behind one of the bars of the headboard, and secured my wrists again. Afterward, he returned the key to his shirt pocket and tossed the shirt back on the floor. "Now, where were we?" He crawled back on top of me. His dark eyes gleamed sadistically like those of a wolf assessing his prey.

I shuddered and turned my head away. In that moment, I saw Sherry in my mind. *Is this the sort of thing she has to deal with every day?* The way she'd looked at me from the lobby earlier, I could tell that was probably true. Her eyes were full of sadness, yet I'd sensed a small spark of hope in them.

"Damn, I can smell your fear. You're turning me on," he murmured. He ran his hands down the sides of my ribs to my waist, then his fingers moved under my shirt. He flashed a devious grin under his moustache.

I shivered, his cold, rough hands touching my skin as if someone had dropped ice cubes on my stomach. "Wait, Frankie! How do you expect me to get in the mood when your hands feel like Antarctica?" I squirmed, my body jerking, as I tried to move away from the source of the sudden chill.

His dark smile broadened. "Oh, you want me to warm you up?" His hands moved from under my shirt and over my belt buckle.

I hissed. *Keep him talking.* "Aren't you forgetting something?"

"And what am I forgetting, baby?" He began undoing my belt, slow and steady, while he locked his gaze on mine.

Strike three. My heart raced. I quelled the panic spreading through me. "The lollipop. I want the lollipop in on this. She'll help make this moment a whole lot better, for you and for me. I'm getting hot just thinking about a threesome with her. C'mon, Frankie, baby. Go get her, so we can *really* have some fun."

His devious smirk broadened. "Okay, sweetheart. Keep your panties on. We'll have a little fun. I can tell that you wanna fuck me so bad."

I pictured grabbing my gun and blowing a hole in his ugly face. Then smashing his head and his jewels to a bloody pulp with a lead pipe. Sick dirtbags like him didn't deserve to propagate. "Oh, you have *no* idea," I crooned.

Frank crawled out of bed, swiped up his shirt, and slipped it back on. "Stay," he said to me as he fumbled with the buttons.

I smiled sweetly. "You got the key, Frankie. I ain't going nowhere." I emphasized the point by shaking my cuffed wrists against the headboard.

"Damn right." He finished buttoning his shirt, tucked it haphazardly into his pants, slipped on his shoes, then retrieved the gun from the floor. He tucked it back in his waistband.

He went out the door and locked it.

CHAPTER 19

I was alone in this bedroom. The sounds of Frank's hurried footsteps drew farther from the door as he rushed off to retrieve Sherry.

At last. My one and only opportunity. I tilted my head back far enough for my fingers to reach my hair. I pulled out the bobby pin, bent it a little, and fiddled with one of the locks on the cuffs. Thankfully, Frank was so caught up in his arousal that he'd neglected to activate the double-locking mechanism, which made lockpicking much easier.

My hands shook as I tried to focus on hitting the sweet spots in the locks. *Sherry's counting on me,* I reminded myself, the thought turning those nerves of fear into a blaze of anger that fueled my courage. After a few minutes of finagling, the first lock clicked. *One down.* I repeated the same motion on the other lock. At last. *Sweet freedom!* I tossed the handcuffs to the floor. Then I hopped out of bed, secured my belt, put on my boots, and fixed the rest of my clothes. Frank's stench covered me like a bad dream, a constant reminder of what had almost happened in this nightmarish place.

Faint footsteps thumped up the stairs and drew closer. I looked around frantically for something, *anything*, to use as a weapon. The footsteps stopped at the door, and the lock jiggled. I snatched a medium-sized bronze cat statue from atop the armoire. It had quite a bit of weight to it—at least five pounds. Holding the statue by the cat's long neck, I stood beside the door and waited.

The knob turned, and the door swung open, stopping just shy of my face. Sherry, still dressed in her maid uniform, stumbled inside and face-planted on the floor with a high-pitched yelp. Frank appeared behind her and shut the door.

I raised the statue.

"I'm back, my foxy chocolate goddess." He turned to the bed and started. "What the—"

Gripping the statue with two hands, I smashed it with all my might into the back of his head. "That's for calling me *baby*," I muttered.

He grunted and stumbled forward, toward the night table. He teetered, turned slightly, and glared at me. "Bitch!" He reached behind himself for the gun in his waistband.

Gritting my teeth, I swung again, the cat statue's streamlined body making a direct hit from his temple all the way down to his jawline. His head whipped to the side, blood and spittle flying out of his mouth. He spun and crashed face-first onto the lamp, shattering it into a million blue-and-yellow pieces.

"That's for Sherry," I said.

Sherry screamed then crouched in a fetal position, clapped both hands over her ears, and squeezed her eyes shut.

I waited a beat. Frank didn't move, but I could see the faint rising and lowering of his shoulders. I grabbed the gun from his waistband and tossed the cat statue, now dented and bloody, onto the bed.

"Don't kill me! Don't kill me!" Sherry blubbered.

"Relax, Sherry. It's me, remember?" I told the girl while I aimed my gun with both hands at Frank. I eased away from him and toward Sherry.

She hacked and sniffled then slowly opened her eyes. She looked up at me, and her mouth fell open. "R-Rosa!"

"That's right. Now, get up. We're blowing this joint."

She blinked. "We are?"

"Yup. We're going to get you that bakery you always dreamed of having. You thought I forgot, didn't you?" I kept my aim on Frank, waiting a few more beats to see if he would get back up. He didn't. Convinced that he was truly out cold, I finally lowered the gun and secured it in the waistband of my jeans. Afterward, I went to the door, locked it, and rushed to the window.

"N-No, I can't leave," Sherry stammered. "They'll kill me. Mr. Audrey has r-really b-big and mean dogs."

"Dogs?" I arched an eyebrow at her. I sure hadn't seen, heard, or smelled any dogs around. "Where are these dogs? Have you seen them?"

She placed a finger to her lips and looked thoughtful for a moment. "I, um... no, I haven't seen them, but... Mr. Audrey said he had dogs."

"You believe everything Mr. Audrey says?"

"Well... yeah. He's nice. He always says I'm his favorite. He would never lie to me."

I scowled. "Well, Sherry. Just once, I think he's lying to you. And what kind of man is he that he won't even let 'his favorite' have her own bakery that she has always dreamed of having? He sounds like a very mean man who only likes to shatter the dreams of young girls like you." I opened the window and poked my head out. The drop from the second floor was a small one, and the red awning a few feet down looked sturdy enough for me to slide down to safety.

Sherry looked back at Frank's unconscious body and chewed her bottom lip. "Is... is Mr. Frankie... d-dead?"

Part of me wished he was. But I wasn't going to let him take the easy way out. I would make sure he relived every nightmare he'd caused me and every other female, ten times over, while he rotted for the rest of his miserable life in a prison cell. "No. Just hurt really badly," I replied to her. "Now, come on."

Her attention remained on Frank, and she slowly walked toward him.

I blinked. "Sherry. What are you doing? Get away from him. He's dangerous!"

"He's always been mean to me," she muttered. "Always yelling and hurting me. I wish he was dead."

"Sherry..."

She retrieved the cat statue from the bed then held it up over her head. "I hate him, Rosa. I hate him!"

"Wait!" I barked. "Don't kill him. He's going to pay for his crimes in a cold, dark prison."

Scowling, she lowered the statue and tossed it back onto the bed. Then she balled her fists, let out a frustrated cry, and delivered a swift kick in his ribs. His unconscious body jostled slightly.

My heart swelled at her brave gesture. Smiling slightly, I approached her and gently pulled her away. "Come on. Let's go. It's time to be free."

Her expression went blank, and she said nothing.

I led her to the window. "I'll go first, then you follow. Do you trust me?"

She pursed her lips, looking at me long and hard, then slowly nodded.

I scooted out onto the window's narrow brick ledge. The sun had already set, leaving the sky a deep shade of orange. The sidewalk was devoid of people, and several cars were parallel parked along the curb. Sitting between a few nearby cars under the amber glow of a streetlight was a blue police cruiser. Relief spread through me. *Thank goodness!* But then a slight feeling of dread niggled in my gut. What if the cop worked at the Fifty-Fourth Precinct? Chief Lewis had probably told every officer to keep an eye out for me. I wouldn't hear the end of it if he got word of my disobeying his orders. I would have to face the music sooner or later. For the moment, getting Sherry out of here safely was my top priority.

I returned my attention to the girl. "Here I go!" I eased myself off the ledge and landed on the awning, which gave a light creak. Then I slid down the awning and landed safely on the ground. Two mature women walking by stopped, shot me an odd look, then hurried on their way. Standing on the sidewalk in front of the massage parlor, I looked up at the second-story window, where Sherry watched with hesitation.

I waved my arms and called, "I'm okay! It's easy! You do it!"

Sherry crawled out of the window then looked back into the room once more.

"Come on!" I said.

She slid off the ledge, tumbled awkwardly onto the awning, and rolled down it like a runaway avalanche, with the momentum sending her flying right toward me. She screeched.

My arms wide, I stood ready to catch her, bracing myself for a potentially painful impact. She slammed into me. My arms wrapped around her, and I stumbled backward. We both went tumbling and landed in a pile of garbage bags stacked at the curb.

"Ugh…" I stood up and gingerly brushed myself off. Strangely, the smell of rotten eggs and fish was far more refreshing than Frank's perverted stench. I helped Sherry to her feet. "Are you okay?"

She nodded then looked warily at the second-story window. "Th-They're all gonna be so mad at me…"

"Don't worry about them. You're free now. I'm getting you someplace safe." I pointed at the police cruiser nearby. "Look. There's a policeman. This place is gonna be swarming with more of 'em in no time. The rest of the girls in there will be safe too."

She fell silent and nodded again.

Taking her hand, I ran to the cruiser. A uniformed officer was in the driver's seat, his head down, writing on some papers secured to a metal clipboard.

I rapped on the window. "Officer! Emergency!"

The man looked up. He was stocky, appeared to be in his early thirties, and sported a short brown moustache with matching sideburns. I caught a glimpse of his name badge— O'Connell. To my relief, the gold pin insignia on his blue shirt collar was not the Fifty-Fourth Precinct.

The officer regarded me and Sherry with curious blue eyes then rolled down the window. The hisses and murmurs of the police radio filtered out. "You're a little too early for Halloween," he said, arching an eyebrow at Sherry's maid outfit.

I gestured to Sherry. "This child's in danger," I explained. I pointed at the massage parlor. "There's a major drug ring going on in there. Women are being exploited. We barely escaped with our lives."

He looked long and hard at Sherry then did a double take, as if realizing something. He regarded me with raised eyebrows. "Yeah?"

I nodded. "Officer, will you please take us to the nearest precinct?"

He looked back at the dashboard's police radio and turned the knob, lowering the volume. "Yeah, sure. Get in the back," he said to us.

I opened the back door for Sherry. She scrambled inside, and I followed, closing the door behind me. I let out a deep sigh of relief.

"Hang tight, girls. The radio's busted, so I'll need to call the station," Officer O'Connell said, looking at us in the rearview mirror. Then he got out of the car and walked ahead to a telephone booth on the corner.

I exhaled a deep sigh. "We're almost there, Sherry. The police will take care of these bad guys. You can count on it."

Sherry hugged herself, regarding me with her ghost-white face. "I'm scared, Rosa."

I patted her shoulder reassuringly. "Hey, it's all right. Remember that other secret I said I had for you but couldn't tell you until after I got you out of that place? Well, here it is: my name's not really Rosa. It's Tootsie. I'm a detective."

Her eyes widened, and her jaw fell open. "Wow," she whispered.

I looked ahead at Officer O'Connell, still in the phone booth on the corner. He glanced in my direction a moment then turned his back, huddling closer to the telephone. A sinking feeling formed in my gut. *Telephone booth... near the massage parlor... I* recalled Chief Lewis's findings and gasped. *Of course!* That must've been the same booth Frank used to call Allison. I glanced at the radio, its buttons and knobs fully lit. *Wait a minute. That radio looks like it's working fine to me.*

"What about the rest of my friends? Will they be okay too?" Sherry asked, interrupting my thoughts.

I pursed my lips, only half listening to her question. *Something's not right.* "Sherry... we need to get out of here."

She blinked. "Huh?"

I looked out the cruiser's back window. The door to the massage parlor opened, and three men walked out and headed straight for us.

CHAPTER 20

A trap.

I watched in the police cruiser's rearview window as three rough-looking men poured out from the massage parlor's entrance like a pack of wolves. I recognized Hefty among them, the hot-tempered thug I'd run into with Frank in the basement.

Gasping, I reached across Sherry and cranked the window down. "We're in trouble. Get out of the car. Now!"

She hesitated, whimpering, and quickly climbed out the window. She hit the ground, stumbled, and caught herself. I climbed out right behind her then grabbed my gun from my waistband and cocked it.

"Run to that next street and turn down the first alley," I ordered, pointing ahead toward Ninety-First Street. "Run like your life depends on it."

"But, Tootsie, what about—"

"I'll be right behind you. Promise. Now, go!"

The men were walking quickly toward the cruiser. The tall and lanky one scanned the area while he discreetly reached behind himself, most likely for a weapon. The shorter one followed Hefty, who led the charge with his quick strides.

Sherry took off running across the street. I took aim at Hefty and fired. He stopped in his tracks and ducked behind a car that was parallel parked behind the cruiser. Officer O'Connell abandoned the telephone booth on the corner and charged toward us, clawing at the holster on his hip.

That was one gun too many, so I took off. I was halfway across the street when the blinding glare of headlights washed over me. The blare of the car's horn drowned out Hefty's and O'Connell's shouting. I jumped out of the way and hit the pavement, rolling. The car, a red sports coupe, screeched past me, swerved, and fishtailed, sideswiping a car parked in front of the cruiser. The driver attempted to regain control, but another fast-approaching car—a green station wagon—slammed into the back of the coupe, sending it veering off the road and coming to a crashing stop against a lamppost. Glass shattered. Inside the coupe, a baby started to shriek.

My breath hitched. *No...* Screams and shouts from nearby passersby echoed in my ears. I sprang back to my feet and kept running, silently praying that all the people in the cars were okay. I hit the sidewalk on the other side of the street just seconds before a bus zoomed by. Sherry was there ahead of me, running down the street like a scared rabbit. She disappeared around the corner of a run-down brick duplex, and I picked up my pace, sprinting as though I was running the hundred-meter dash.

Tires squealed behind me. A set of headlights headed in my direction, way too fast to be just passing through.

I whipped around the corner and into the alley, a narrow, crooked driveway that extended into the back of the duplexes. Sherry was waiting around the bend. I gave her a confident grin and reached out to her.

"Told ya I'd be right behind you," I said. "Now, take my hand and don't let go, no matter what."

Her small, cold fingers touched mine and squeezed tight. I snaked through the narrow path, finally reaching a dead end occupied by a stripped '56 Chevy, long abandoned. A tall, rotted wooden fence blocked the alley from the road, and graffiti covered everything.

The sounds of car doors slamming made my stomach lurch. I peered over my shoulder. Two human-shaped shadows—one of them wearing a Panama hat—made impossibly long and thin by a streetlight, rippled across the asphalt toward the driveway's entrance. Even with the shadows distorted, I could make out the shapes of guns in the shadows' hands.

One of the fence's planks hung crookedly by a single rusty nail, leaving a gap just large enough for a small person to fit through. I let go of Sherry's hand and checked my gun. *Five rounds left.*

"Go through there and get behind something," I ordered, making a head gesture toward the gap.

She did so without hesitating. I tugged at the flimsy wood, trying to make the gap a little bigger, but the stubborn nail was holding it down good. *Time for Plan B.* I took a step back.

"Hi-yah!" I grunted, smashing my steel-toed boot through the wood with a hard, fast, Jim Kelly–style sidekick. The plank disintegrated into a million wooden splinters that went flying like tiny daggers.

Just as I was about to go through the hole, the men—Hefty, Lanky, and Mr. Panama—rounded the corner. Mr. Panama raised his weapon. I quickly tumbled the rest of the way through the gap and ducked. A bullet speared the wood a foot above my head. I waited a beat. Footsteps thumped closer. Still crouched, I peeked through the gap and fired at my closest target. Mr. Panama recoiled, dropping his gun as he collapsed. Hefty and Lanky leapt away and took cover behind a line of metal garbage cans set against the fence.

I grabbed Sherry's hand again and pulled her to her feet. "C'mon," I said between gasps. "We have… to call the… police. The *real* police."

Sherry fell silent and regarded me with those fearful doe eyes again. "Okay," she whispered, and squeezed my hand tight.

The orange-hued sky went a faint, deep purple as nighttime approached. Things were going to get much more complicated and dangerous once it was completely dark.

We cut through another driveway between two more narrow brick duplex homes and reached another street. I squinted at the sign at the corner and made out the writing—Ninety-Second Street. I grimaced. We were only a block away from that parlor. Skinny, colonial-style row homes lined the other side of the street like a mouthful of bad teeth, complete with a blackened gap where one home had burned down.

"There's a police car!" Sherry pulled at my hand and pointed.

I looked in her direction. A car had turned the corner and was headed our way. As it drew closer, I spotted the car's rooftop siren lights. My skin prickled with goosebumps.

"I have a hunch that's not a good cop," I said and hurried across the street toward the ruined row home.

A spotlight flared to life on the car's side and swept the street with its brilliant beam. The hungry light licked at our feet then lit us up fully. The car sped up.

My heart thrummed, and a fiery pain burned in my chest.

Tires screeched, then a door slammed. "Hey!" O'Connell called, his hard-soled shoes clacking against the concrete.

"Keep running," I told Sherry, not looking back. I released her hand.

She sped alongside me, gasping. We reached the lot, which seemed to have been used as a dumping ground, and dodged old tires, scraps of metal, debris, and other garbage strewn about. A group of young boys and girls hanging out under one of the empty doorframes watched us.

"Police! Stop!" O'Connell yelled again.

I dared to look over my shoulder. He was several hundred feet away but gaining ground fast. The garbage in the lot wasn't much of an obstacle for him. I wouldn't put it past the crooked cop to take a shot at us, either.

"Go! Go! Run!" the kids called, cheering at us.

Sherry and I emerged in a small access road, which ran behind another residential area of row homes. Ahead, I spotted a busy main street. A wave of relief began to ease my anxious nerves.

"Try to keep up with me, Sherry," I said. "Or do you need to hold my hand again?"

She panted. "No... I... I just need a break."

"No breaks. He's coming!" I grabbed her hand, and off we went again.

We zipped by passersby who didn't seem fazed by us being chased by a cop. Ahead, an older man, unshaven and wearing tattered clothes, lumbered in our direction. A dirty, unkempt Dalmatian trotted beside him. The dog looked at us and barked.

Sherry whimpered and squeezed my hand. "Tootsie, that dog looks mean..."

I gritted my teeth, looking at the man, and wondered if he was one of Mr. Audrey's goons. I kept my gun ready, just in case, but also remained mindful of the dog. "Help!" I said to the stranger. "That man is about to shoot us!" I had no intention of stopping, in case this stranger wasn't on the level, but I hoped he might slow O'Connell down.

The stranger halted and watched us a moment, his wrinkled face rigid. The dog let out deeper barks then lowered its body, as though biding its time to lunge at us. My stomach did flip-flops. *Keep... running...*

"Bah, quiet, Butch. Y'know better than to bark at women," the stranger muttered to the dog as we zipped by. He gave the animal a firm nudge in the ribs with his knee.

We neared the end of the street. Cars whooshed back and forth on the main road.

"Outta my way!" O'Connell's voice snapped behind us.

The stranger jumped out of O'Connell's path as the officer sped past. Butch the Dalmatian barked furiously.

I looked ahead again, my legs feeling like jelly, but my adrenaline was too pumped to stop.

"Stop, Butch! Damn it, get back here!" the stranger yelled.

I looked back again. Butch the Dalmatian gave chase to officer O'Connell, who was gaining ground on us quickly. Butch lunged at the officer from behind, tackling him to the ground.

"Ahh!" O'Connell yelled.

The stranger caught up to them and tried to pull the dog off the officer. "Get off him, Butch!"

Butch latched his jaws onto O'Connell's gun hand, while O'Connell whacked the dog repeatedly in the head with his fist.

"Get this fucking mutt off me!" he cried.

"Hey, stop hitting him, you son of a bitch!" the stranger said.

With O'Connell preoccupied, Sherry and I drew farther and farther away from the confrontation. Reaching the main street, I scanned for the nearest corner. We were on Thirty-Second Avenue. Beyond the street sign and across a massive construction lot, the dingy awning of a bodega glowed in the distance. *Finally, someplace with a telephone!* At that point, I didn't care if Chief Lewis was going to chew my head off for defying him.

Two shots rang out far behind us. A man yelled, and a dog gave a high-pitched squeal. A new burst of adrenaline rushed through my veins.

"Let's go," I told Sherry. "We're almost there."

We hightailed it across the street, weaving and dodging oncoming traffic and ignoring the occasional shouts and curses from angry drivers. The bodega sat between a Laundromat and a nail salon near the corner of Thirty-Second Avenue and Junction Boulevard. I flung open the door and yanked Sherry inside then stopped dead in my tracks.

A uniformed police officer stood at the counter, holding a wrapped submarine sandwich while he chatted with the female store clerk in Spanish. I swallowed, eyeing the officer's badge— Sanchez. *Is he a good cop or a bad cop?* I wondered.

The door slammed shut behind me, and I jumped.

"Help!" Sherry cried.

The officer and clerk stopped talking and looked at us.

"*¿Qué es?*" the woman asked.

"What is this, a costume party?" Officer Sanchez quipped, eyeing Sherry's maid uniform.

I settled my wary gaze on him. "No. There's a man claiming to be a cop chasing us. I think he shot someone just now, an innocent bystander," I said.

Sanchez's eyebrows shot up. He set the wrapped sandwich on the counter and walked over. "Who is this man? Where is he now?" he asked, adjusting his hat.

I turned and peered outside through the glass door. O'Connell was nowhere to be seen, but I knew he was still out there somewhere.

"His badge said O'Connell," I explained. "We ran into him outside the massage parlor on Thirty-First Avenue."

Sanchez's look of concern turned to disgust. "O'Connell?" One corner of his lip curled. *"Mierda..."*

I blinked. *Okay, so maybe this guy isn't in cahoots with O'Connell.* "Do you know him?"

"Sí, he's my sergeant," he spat. "You said he shot someone?"

I nodded. "Yes. I need to make a call." I flicked my attention to the clerk. "I don't have my wallet. Is there a telephone somewhere in here?"

She furrowed her brow, and Sanchez relayed my request to her in Spanish. "Ah," she replied, nodding to me. *"Sí, por ahí. En la espalda."* She pointed toward a door in the back with a sign that read Employees Only.

"Gracias," I said and quickly led Sherry toward the door. Inside was a tiny area used as a break room and storage. A harvest-gold wall telephone was on the far wall. After a thorough scan of the room, I told Sherry, "I'm going to call for help. Keep your ears open for O'Connell, okay?"

Sherry chewed her bottom lip. "What if he finds us?"

"He's not gonna find us. I'll make sure of that. You just have to trust me, all right?"

She gave a slow nod then pressed her ear to the door.

I checked my watch. Seven thirty—still early. Chief Lewis was most likely still at the office. I picked up the receiver and dialed the chief's personal office number.

"Robert Lewis speaking," he answered.

"Chief! It's Tootsie! Emergency! Ten thirteen! Send everyone you got!" I blurted, only to realize I'd inadvertently spat out police codes. Some old habits never died, it seemed.

"Damn it, Tootsie! Where are you?" Chief Lewis asked.

I gave him my location and tried to fill him in as much as I could, as quickly as I could, but I couldn't explain everything in only a few minutes.

Sherry gasped, her face lighting up in shock. "Tootsie, I hear a man out there," she told me in a loud whisper. "There's shouting."

I gripped the receiver. "Chief, I gotta go. O'Connell is here."

"We're gonna have some words later, Rita," he said, annoyed. "Stay safe and out of sight. The boys are already on their way to the parlor."

"Noted." I hung up before he could say any more. He was furious, but right now, I didn't care. If it meant keeping Sherry safe, I would gladly face the music. Beyond the door was the muffled shout of a woman, followed by her yelling some obscenities in Spanish.

"I told you no one came in here," Sanchez said in an angry voice.

"Don't bullshit me, Sanchez. I'll have your badge stripped. Now, move out of the fucking way!" O'Connell barked.

Sherry backed away from the door and ran to me.

"It's time to go," I told her. "We'll take the back door."

We scrambled through the back exit and emerged into an alley behind a wooden fence that separated more row homes. We snaked through the maze of fenced-in areas, dodging a toppled birdbath in a ruined garden, flower pots, parked bicycles, and other obstacles as we made our way out onto the main sidewalk.

More cars were parked along the curb. The street sign was too far away for me to make out which it was. But looking ahead, I noticed heavy traffic zipping back and forth, indicating it was a large main road.

"This way," I directed Sherry, who was footsteps behind me.

People walked to and fro along the sidewalk, not paying us any mind. At this point, I was afraid to yell for help. If Mr. Audrey had crooked cops working for him, we had no way of telling who else was undercover. Two cars turned down the street and headed our way. They seemed to be driving at a normal speed, so perhaps they weren't more pursuers. I decided to keep our escape more discreet.

We crossed the street and hopped a low wrought-iron fence that led through another narrow alley running between two row homes. We turned a corner and dead-ended in a tightly enclosed area. The wooden fence partitioning the block of row homes beyond was way too tall to climb.

I'd practically lost all sense of direction. Perhaps finally lying low might be best for a while. We were fugitives, and Mr. Audrey's thugs seemed relentless.

Sherry bent over and sucked air. "I'm so tired of running, Tootsie. Can we just hide for now?"

I did a quick sweep of the area, ensuring it would be safe enough for a rest. We seemed to be alone. The cream-colored row home before us had two small angel statues flanking the barred back door. A hanging plant swayed gently from the awning. I slipped my gun back into my waistband and approached the back door. As I suspected, it was locked. I knocked a few times, but no one answered.

I leaned back against the fence and slid to the ground with an exhausted sigh. "Okay," I finally said. "I don't think anyone saw us leave out the bodega's back door, so we might be safe for now."

Sherry sank down next to me and hugged her knees to her chest. "I'm scared, Tootsie. I don't want to go back..."

Smiling reassuringly, I wrapped my arm around her. "You're not going back."

She fell silent for a moment, biting her bottom lip. "What about Claire? Francine? All my big sisters. Will they be okay too?"

I swallowed a lump in my throat. The disturbing memories of that drug operation stung my mind. *So many of them.* "We're going to save them all," I said, though I wasn't entirely sure how.

A car—a brown Cutlass—creeped around the bend and stopped, blocking our only exit. I perked up and reached behind myself for my weapon.

The passenger's door slowly opened.

I shoved Sherry behind me, whipped out my gun, and took aim at the mysterious car.

A man stepped out of the passenger's side with his hands raised in surrender. My heart stopped. I stared back at the man, at his hefty frame, and widened my eyes.

We were trapped, and this time, we had no escape.

CHAPTER 21

Frank's friend, Hefty.

A nervous lump formed in my throat. I wasn't sure what this guy was planning as he stood outside the passenger-side door of the brown Cutlass with his hands in the air. I kept my gun trained on his center mass.

"Oh no, it's Mr. Martin!" Sherry whimpered, huddling behind me.

"Shh," I hissed at her.

"Hey, put that thing away. I'm only here for the girl," Martin told me. Then he nodded to Sherry. "Hey, Sherry. Get over here. Mr. Audrey wants to see you. He's very upset, y'know."

"No!" Sherry cried. Then she looked at me with doe eyes full of fear.

I scowled at Martin. "Get back in the car and scram!" I ordered.

Martin remained where he stood. "Let's make a deal. You give me the girl, and you won't see us again."

My eyes cut to a movement in the driver's seat of the car. It was too dark to see inside the car, but I sensed Martin was not alone. I cocked my gun. "Not a chance. This is your last warning. Leave, or else."

I heard a car door open. A lanky man in a tan-plaid blazer and a matching newsboy cap slowly rose and looked over the roof of the car toward me.

I quickly trained my gun sights on Lanky's head since only a small part of his chest was visible over the height of the car roof. The situation was getting dangerous for both me and Sherry.

"Stop, or I'll shoot!" I warned, my finger hovering over the trigger.

Lanky stayed still. Out of my periphery, a shadow moved quickly—too fast for me to distinguish—and a brief flash of steel caught my attention. I shoved Sherry out of Martin's line of sight and ducked. A shot rang out. A dog barked in the distance. The head of one of the angel statues next to me shattered, tiny pieces of stone flying everywhere.

I squeezed the trigger of my gun. Martin jumped out of the way, and my bullet speared a hole through the back passenger window of the Cutlass.

Sherry screamed. My heart pounded. *No... is Sherry...?* I wanted to check on her, but I had to stay focused on the immediate threat in front of me. I looked for Martin, but he was gone.

I fumbled with my gun, trying to refocus, but a sharp pain seared my forearm. *Oh no! I've been hit!*

Lanky whipped out his gun from his blazer and aimed at me. "Don't even think about it, bitch."

Gritting my teeth, I tumbled behind the other statue, anticipating another shot, but none came. Remaining crouched, I listened and waited.

Sherry was safely beside me, huddled in a tight ball against the house. Her hands covered her face.

"Stay here, Sherry. Don't move," I muttered to her. Then I slowly peered around the corner.

Both men were gone. My heart raced.

Shadowy movement shifted near the car. I eased back slowly behind the statue, just enough to look out with one eye.

The shadow emerged, slowly rounding the front of the car, revealing Martin's lanky friend. His gun aimed, he inched his way toward me.

Sinking my teeth into my bottom lip, I pointed at his center mass and shot. He managed to fire off a round as he fell backward, but the bullet hit the chimney of one of the nearby row homes. The man hit the ground and didn't get up.

One down. I cocked my gun, readying another round.

Martin's voice growled nearby. "You're dead, bitch. You're fucking dead!"

Footsteps echoed closer. I peered out again but saw no one. Then a shadow loomed over me like the Grim Reaper himself. I felt the unnerving warmth of a sinister presence too near, looking down from above. I looked up, and Martin was right there, his .45 pointed right at me.

I dropped the gun and raised my hands in surrender. Fiery pain surged up my forearm. I glanced at a tear in the fabric of my turtleneck. A small shard of rock, most likely from a ricocheting bullet, had nicked my arm, from which a small trickle of blood oozed.

"I should've killed you back in the basement when I had the chance," Martin told me with a sneer. Then he looked at Sherry. "Come here, Sherry. Now."

Sherry, still huddled into a ball, slowly lowered her hands from her face. She was ghostly white but unharmed. She looked up at Martin.

I had a gun aimed at me and a girl at this man's mercy. It seemed like a no-win situation for me.

Sherry eased onto her feet and walked toward Martin. I glanced back at the gun in his unwavering hand. It was easily within my reach, but at any sudden movement from me, he wouldn't hesitate to pull the trigger. *But what about a distraction?*

With her head lowered, Sherry dragged her feet toward the man. He seemed to be focused on her, but I knew he wasn't keeping me out of his sight. I discreetly slid my foot out in front of her. Her dragging foot caught mine, and she tripped, toppling forward and letting out a yelp.

Martin's weapon hand wavered then relaxed a little. He reached out to her, grabbing her maid's blouse to keep her from face-planting on the concrete.

That momentary distraction was just enough for me to spring into action. Wincing at the stinging pain in my arm, I jerked to one side, away from the gun's line of sight, and grabbed Martin's wrist with one hand and the back of his elbow with the other. I jumped to my feet and gave his wrist a sharp torque down and away, shoving his elbow joint fast and forward beyond its natural placement. The bones from his wrist up to his shoulder cracked like popcorn.

Martin yelled, and the gun fell out of his hand. He released Sherry and held his disabled arm.

The gun was too close to his feet, too close for me to grab without getting grabbed myself, so I kicked the weapon away, far from his reach and mine. Time to fight dirty. I stood in front of Sherry, blocking her like a wall as I prepared to square off with Martin, now enraged.

"Move away, Sherry!" I told the girl.

She whimpered again then rushed to the opposite side of the dead-end alley.

Martin regarded me with fire in his eyes. Gritting his teeth, he let out a throaty growl and rushed me like a runaway freight train. "I'll kill you!"

My heart pumping, adrenaline rushing through my veins, I whipped one leg around in a spinning hook kick. The heel of my boot connected with his temple full force, like a homing missile. His head snapped back and to the side. He wobbled around like a cartoon character for a second then fell backward, crashing into the other angel statue. The back of his head smashed against the statue's concrete base. He slid to the ground and didn't move again.

I waited a moment, unsure if he was alive or dead. When he still didn't get up, I grabbed my gun, tucked it back into my waistband, and ran back to Sherry. "Are you okay?" I asked her.

She looked at me, bug-eyed. "Is... is he dead?"

"I don't know." I frowned then looked over toward the front of the Cutlass, where Lanky lay dead on the bloodstained ground. I swallowed a lump in my throat. *Too many deaths tonight.* I was ready to get as far away from this place as I could. I would rather deal with Chief Lewis's scolding than have to endure another moment in this nightmare.

The Cutlass was still running, our fortunate means of getting out of here quickly. I grimaced. I hadn't driven a car since leaving the force six years ago. I didn't even have a license anymore. I sure hoped I remembered how to drive. "C'mon. Get in the car before more of Mr. Audrey's goons come," I instructed Sherry. "I'm going to drive us to the police station."

She took one look at the dead body in front of the car then rushed into the passenger's seat. I walked around to the driver's side. I was about to hop in when I heard the cacophony of police sirens screaming in the distance.

I smiled.

CHAPTER 22

Funny how remembering how to drive a car felt a lot like remembering how to ride a bicycle. I was surprised how quickly things came back to me. I lost count of the number of full-siren police cars that zoomed past as I returned to the Bronx, headed north on the Major Deegan Expressway. Every precinct in the city must've been closing in on that massage parlor, and I couldn't be more relieved. Mr. Audrey and his gang had nowhere to run.

I pulled up along the curb in front of the Fifty-Fourth Precinct. A few uniformed officers were entering and exiting the front doors. Even at almost nine at night, the place was still lit up inside and looked as busy as ever.

Sherry and I got out of the car, and I escorted her inside. Walking in after so many years brought back memories. The smells of day-old coffee and carbon paper and the musty odor of mildew from the water-stained asbestos ceiling tiles rekindled thoughts of the past, the good days and bad, and the reasons why

I left and didn't look back. Life as a female cop in a man's world meant the system was always rigged against you, and I rarely, if ever, had any opportunities for advancement. I became tired of compromising my pride and dignity just so I could pay the bills.

Chief Lewis made a big mistake thinking he could hold me back from being a police detective just because of his own insecurities. Him getting upset at me for taking care of my own business, which happened to intersect with police business, was his own fault, for not giving me a chance before. I was independent, no longer under his thumb. I knew the law as well as he did. He couldn't arrest me without probable cause, and the work I'd done under the radar for him and his boys practically granted me amnesty.

In other words, he couldn't touch me, and he knew it.

Looking around the office, I noticed only one female officer present, and I could already tell by her cold stare; her curled upper lip; and the stiff, violent stabs she was giving the typewriter keys that she was beyond fed up. Yeah, I remembered that feeling. I shook my head. Some things never changed.

I walked up to the front desk, where the sergeant, a middle-aged Black gentleman, was just ending a call. He wrote something down on a yellow legal pad and looked up at me and Sherry.

His brow furrowed quizzically as his gaze lingered on the kid. "Uh, yes? What can I do for you young ladies?" he asked.

I slapped both hands on the desk and looked eye-to-eye at him. "This is an emergency. I need to speak to Chief Robert Lewis right away."

He gave us both another curious once-over then lifted the telephone receiver again. "Name?"

I cleared my throat and gestured to Sherry. "Her name is Sherry," I said, avoiding talking too much about myself. "She is twelve years old. Please get the chief. It's important."

He nodded slowly and punched in Chief Lewis's office extension. The desk sergeant kept his gaze trained on me as he spoke. "Hey, Chief. Two girls here. One of them's named Sherry... oh, okay... sure thing... that's right... okay." He hung up the telephone and pointed toward a set of stairs at the entrance of a narrow hallway. "Up those stairs, make a left," he instructed.

I took Sherry's hand and led the way. We climbed the narrow staircase to the second floor and turned left down a line of offices in a long hallway. Chief Lewis's office was the last one. I could feel the stares from officers walking by and people sitting in chairs outside a few of the closed doors. I rapped lightly on the frosted glass of Chief Lewis's office. Seconds later, the door flung open, and Chief Lewis stood with his arms crossed over his broad chest, his face dark and stony.

Pursing my lips, I looked up at him in silence. I could already see the wheels turning in his head and feel the heat of his blood boiling.

Chief Lewis flicked his gaze to Sherry, and his expression softened a little. He abandoned the door, returned to his desk, and picked up the phone. "Tell Officer Willard to come to my office," he muttered into the receiver.

I hesitated in stepping into his office. But he'd left the door open, so the invitation was obvious. I took Sherry's hand and stepped inside and guided her to an empty chair in front of his desk. She slowly lowered to the edge of the chair and fidgeted with her hands. Meanwhile, I remained standing, watching, waiting.

Chief Lewis hung up the telephone and scrutinized Sherry. "Hey... Sherry, was it? It's okay. No one's going to hurt you anymore, understand?'"

Sherry gave a timid nod.

The door opened again, and a uniformed Black woman with a flip hairdo walked in. She was middle-aged, average height and size, and her eyes were intense, like she'd seen and experienced a lot in her day. "Yes, Chief? What do you need?" she asked, her voice strong.

"Willard, this is Sherry, one of the vics from tonight's bust. This kid's been through a lot. Take her to the break room for a while. Get her a soda or something."

Officer Willard looked at the girl, and her rigid expression softened. "Sure thing." She reached out for Sherry's hand.

Sherry's gaze bounced from the officer to Chief Lewis then to me. She chewed her bottom lip. "Um..."

Chief Lewis got up, went around the desk, and knelt before Sherry, meeting her eye level. "Hey, young lady. Listen to me. You were very brave tonight. A true hero. You're safe now, okay? The rest of the police are out taking care of those bad guys who hurt you."

Sherry slowly nodded.

He rose and stepped out of the way so that Officer Willard could take Sherry's hand.

Sherry stared at the other woman's hand, hesitated, then looked at me.

I gave her a reassuring smile. "You're in good hands, Sherry. Don't worry. Go on, now."

After Sherry and the officer left, Chief Lewis locked the door and returned to his desk. At last, we were alone.

I slid down in a chair and exhaled. "All right, Chief. Go on, let it out. Yell, scream, whatever," I said with a groan.

He sat back in his chair, crossing his arms, and studying me with narrowed eyes. "I'm more disappointed in you. You lied to me, Rita. You fucking lied. And for what? To needlessly risk your damned life? You don't think the police can do their job?"

I swallowed a lump in my throat and lowered my gaze to my lap. Despite his disappointment, there was shakiness in his voice. Being this close to him, I could hear his fast-beating heart. Tears stung my eyes, and I blinked them away. *Disappointment.* I hated disappointing him as much as I hated disappointing my own father. I'd always known Chief Lewis to be fearless and strong, no matter what. But tonight, that mask was off. Beneath his superhero disguise, he was human like me.

"Of course not. I know you guys are more than capable," I finally said. "By the way, I didn't lie to you. I told you that you wouldn't see me there. And you didn't, did you?"

He growled. "Don't be a smart-ass, Rita."

"Look, I had no intentions of trying to take down an entire organization on my own. I know all this is my fault, but I had my own reasons for going in here."

His eyebrow arched. "Oh yeah? Well, entertain me, then. We have all night."

I sighed again. There was a lot to talk about, and not just my recklessness. I shifted in my seat. I couldn't forget what almost happened, what *could* have happened. The blood, the screams, the deaths... Frank's sadistic smile as he rubbed his ice-cold hands under my shirt... I shuddered. The wound was still fresh.

I looked at my sleeve, where the small rip from the stray ricocheting rock revealed the thin cut on my skin. The trickle of blood had stopped and coagulated around the wound. It stung a little and itched, a constant reminder that irritated my brain worse than my conversations with Beth. I was tired. Hungry. Yet all I felt compelled to do was to sit there and wonder about the night.

"Okay," I finally answered the chief. I flicked my gaze over to his desk clock: 8:20 p.m.

It was almost 11:00 p.m. by the time I finished telling him everything—well, almost everything. I explained why I'd done everything in the first place, from helping Paige and Allison to untangling Joey's blackmail. I told him about Frank, about how he was a sick pervert, and left it at that. I didn't have the heart or stomach to go into that detail. Chief Lewis was already a worrywart, and his face was paler than a ghost's from my story. I didn't need him going on some violent tirade about Frank on my behalf. No, that was one demon I would fight myself. And I would make sure I always won.

I struggled to keep my eyes open, and my body ached from all the adrenaline-fueled running I'd done earlier. But mentally, I felt better after getting all that off my chest.

Chief Lewis closed his eyes and pinched the bridge of his nose as he tried to process everything I'd told him. "So let me get this straight. You went through all this trouble because of some damn tabloid photos?"

I shrugged. "Yeah, I guess that's it. Funny, huh? One thing led to another, and... okay, it might've been a little of my pride too. I didn't want my business to be associated with any sleazy tabloid."

"I get it, but this wasn't the way."

"I know, Chief, and I'm sorry. Really, I am. I hope you know that I would never intend to make you mad or upset, and I don't just do things without a reason. Yes, I was taking a risk, but I had a reason for it, that little girl being one of them."

His jaw clenched. "I'll do everything in my power to make sure each and every one of those bastards pay for what they did to those girls—and to you. Words can't describe how sad and furious I am right now."

I half smiled. "Well, now I know why you were always bent on me never being transferred to vice."

"God, I would have had a heart attack. You almost gave me one tonight. I'm furious that you went behind my back and did this by yourself, sticking your neck out and almost getting it chopped off by those thugs. I can't keep letting you do this. For your safety and my own sanity's sake. You need to leave this shit to the police from now on."

My smile slowly fell. "I didn't mean to get too deep into that operation. Besides, I was captured. It was too risky to get the police involved without endangering all those trapped victims even more."

"I still don't like it. You were almost killed tonight, don't you see? I would've never been able to forgive myself."

"I'm sorry that I worried you. But this is my home, and I'll do whatever it takes—including laying down my life—to make it a better place."

He looked me over long and hard then heaved a deep sigh, clearly in a mental war with himself. "I want you to go straight home now. Get some rest. We'll talk more tomorrow, okay?"

I nodded. "Thanks, Chief. By the way, what's going to happen to Sherry and all those other women?"

"I'm going to have Officer Willard try and contact Sherry's parents or other family members. If that doesn't work, I'll have to end up getting my social services contact involved. As for the other women, we will try our best to contact their family members also. Otherwise, we'll send them to a reputable group home that will help them get back on their feet."

I nodded once and sighed. My gaze fell to the tiny wood grains on the desk as my mind wandered.

"Hey," the chief said, interrupting my thoughts. "It's over now. We got the bastards."

"Yeah…" I slid out of the chair. "Is Sherry going to stay here, then?"

"For now. Sherry will be under Officer Willard's watch until we can locate the girl's family. Officer Willard is a huge asset to this precinct. Still a rookie, but she reminds me a little of you."

"Oh? I hope she has a future here this time, unlike me."

He frowned. "She does. She wants to be a police detective, and I'm not stopping her, even if it may cost me my job. We lost a good person and a valuable asset when you left. I'm not making that mistake again. To hell with politics."

I smiled. That was the Robert Lewis I knew as a kid, the then-officer who listened to his own judgment and morals instead of the patriarchal society. "It'll be a sad day around here when you retire," I said.

He chuckled. "Well, don't worry. I intend to stay here for as long as I can. Maybe this city will return to its senses in a few years."

"Does Officer Willard or anyone else around here know about our… professional partnership?"

The chief shook his head. "No one knows about us, and they never will."

"I sure hope not." I stood and headed for the door. "Oh, hey. Can one of your boys grab my coat and hat? They're in the thrift shop next door to the parlor. All my essentials are in there, including my wallet." I felt strange being without my coat and hat—my uniform—for this long.

He sighed and plopped down behind his desk again. "Yeah, sure, I'll relay a message to Captain Peterson."

I rubbed my chin. "Oh, and also, if any of your boys find those negatives of Joey, can you give them back to me?"

"No can do. It's evidence."

I wrinkled my nose. "Circumstantial evidence, you mean. Those negatives have nothing to do with the drug-and-sex-trafficking ring."

"We'll see what the police detectives have to say about it. In the meantime, those negatives stay where they are."

I rolled my eyes. "Fine, Chief. Whatever you say. Goodnight."

I saw my way out. Chief Lewis was right. I needed to go home and rest. I couldn't keep my eyes open another minute. Yet I dreaded closing my eyes, in fear of what the next day would bring. No doubt, at some point, I would have to retell my story, which meant having to relive that nightmare all over again.

CHAPTER 23

Friday morning. *Where did this week go?* The previous night was a blur, a roller coaster of emotions. I was surprised I'd slept as much as I did. I rolled over on my daybed and faced the window, which glowed with light from the early-morning sky. I winced. My legs ached, as did the rest of my body. *Geez Louise. I'm not even thirty yet, and I feel like a broken-down old lady.*

The telephone rang, jolting me out of my thoughts. Clearing my throat, I grabbed the receiver and sat up. My aching muscles tensed, and I grimaced. "Detective Carter speaking," I said, trying to hide the sleep from my voice. I glimpsed the numbers on the flip-clock radio, which read 8:23.

"Hey, Tootsie! *Oooh-eee,* baby! I gotta say, you're a doll. A real doll! I love you! I love you! I *looove* you, baby!" Newsie chirped.

Cringing, I pulled the receiver away from my ear. "Ugh, it's too early for this, Newsie. What do you want?"

"What do I want? I wanna thank you, that's what I want! Hell, I think I wanna marry you! Whaddya say? Roy don't need to know."

I rolled my eyes. *He's either drunk or high as a kite.* "What are you jiving on about?"

"Haven't you seen the front page of the *Esquire*? It's golden. The paper is flying off the stands faster than all the other newspapers combined. No one gives a shit about today's *City Star Daily*'s front-page spread about some big drug bust last night. Hell, it even trumped the Watergate updates! Today, the people are more concerned about all the kids at risk of being exposed to dangerous, exploding candy. It's beautiful, Tootsie! Absolutely beautiful."

"Candy?" I mumbled. After a moment, I remembered that bogus story I'd fed Newsie the other day. *That actually worked?* "Oh, yeah. Right."

"And guess what?" Newsie continued. "I just got promoted to managing editor! My former receptionist, Marcie, got bumped up to copy editing, and one of my colleagues, Trish, who also helped write this article, is now her assistant."

"Good for you," I said in a lackluster tone.

"Guess I'm gonna need to find a new receptionist now. Ooh! Maybe the boss will let me get Ms. Timms transferred over. *Mmm mmm mmm!* Sweet Rosa Timms."

"I'm hanging up in three seconds."

"Wait, Tootsie! There's more! My boss is on the phone as we speak, talking to the television station WXIP about getting this article featured on *Good Morning, New York with Wes Avery*. I'm gonna be on TV, Tootsie! Can you believe it? It's dynamite, baby!"

I yawned. "Swell."

"Hey, I owe you dinner. Or maybe a movie. How 'bout both? C'mon, baby."

"How about no. And don't call me 'baby.'"

Ridiculous. How had Newsie managed to get all that fame and glory over such a wacky story? Or was the exploding candy phenomenon really confirmed to be true? *No. It's science. Science never lies... right?*

"Goodbye, Newsie." I slammed the receiver back on the cradle before he had a chance to gab on even more.

Fully awake, I slid out of bed and trudged to the bathroom for a quick, hot shower. The night before, when I'd gotten back home, I'd turned into a prune after staying in the tub for too long, trying to scrub away the tears, sweat, and stink of that nightmare. And even now, as I scrubbed and scrubbed, I could still see the mental image of Frank's dirty fingerprints on my skin. I was thankful that he hadn't gotten as far as he'd hoped. And that cut on my arm was healing quickly but still remained.

The thought of quitting my line of work crossed my mind again. I'd gone to the fiery pits and back, all in the name of justice. I'd foolishly put my life on the line. Chief Lewis had every right to be angry at me. Sometimes, I wondered if everything was worth it. But the more I considered throwing in the towel, the more I thought about Sherry and the hundreds of other victims out there that needed to be saved from the corruption in the city. *No, I can't quit. I can't give up. This is my home. I've got to keep fighting, no matter what.*

After I was finally clean—as clean as I was going to be—and dressed, I whipped up some scrambled eggs on the hotplate and toasted a slice of bread. As I migrated to my desk with my breakfast plate and a glass of OJ, the telephone rang again.

Sighing, I picked up the desk receiver. "Hello. Detective Carter speaking," I answered in a much more alert tone.

"Morning, Tootsie. How are you doing?" Chief Lewis asked.

I smiled. "Better, thanks."

"We need to talk."

I gobbled a forkful of scrambled eggs. "Agreed. Let's talk."

"Not on the phone. I'm coming over there in an hour."

I paused midchew, hearing concern in the chief's voice, and my skin prickled with a small bout of anxiety. "S-Sure thing, Chief. By the way, can you pick me up a copy of the *City Star Daily* and the *National Esquire* on your way over?"

He went silent a moment. "The *National Esquire*? What do you want with that rag?"

"Just doing a little, uh… research."

"Right. See you soon."

After ending the call, I quickly finished my breakfast. Since I was stuck here until Chief Lewis came over, I decided it was a good time to make a few important phone calls, starting with Paige Russell. I would fill her in on the details about Joey. The receptionist at Gatestar Media gave me the runaround for almost five minutes but finally transferred my call to Paige's office. To my relief, she answered.

"Good morning, Detective," she said in a sullen tone.

"Hi, Mrs. Russell," I said. "I, uh… thought I'd let you know that—"

"Save it. I already know about one of my employees getting arrested last night. I still can't believe it. It's despicable. Allegations of being an accessory to a drug-and-sex-trafficking organization? Ugh. Makes me sick. My exposé is ruined, also. I was all ready to publish when the police reports started coming in like crazy." She sighed. "I can't believe I missed my opportunity to debut my big story. All those months of hard work gone."

I opened my mouth to reply then closed it and furrowed my brow. *Which one of her employees?* I thought for a moment then remembered the woman I'd seen the other night. *Of course. Cindy. The one who lied about her vacation.* "This employee wouldn't happen to be Cindy, would it?"

Paige growled. "Please do not mention that bitch's name any more. She ruined me."

"I understand. Well, look on the bright side. Maybe it was a good thing you didn't publish that exposé. From what I hear, everyone has been more interested in the exploding candy story that the *National Esquire* published today."

"Oh, for fuck's sake. I hate that damned rag with a passion."

"Let things die down a bit," I suggested. "Once everyone else has moved on to the next thing, you can publish your exposé. I think this is worth revisiting at some point, anyway."

She went silent a moment. "Maybe you're right. I was just hoping to finally catch my big break, make my father proud."

"Even though I never knew the man, I think he'd be proud of you for tackling such a tough subject on your own like this. Your story deserves to be heard. Just give it some time."

"Thank you, Detective."

I gathered my thoughts again about the real reason I'd called Paige. "Have you talked to Joey yet?"

"I saw him late last night when I came home from work. He didn't say much. He seemed distant. I guess he has a lot on his mind."

That's an understatement. "I found out who was blackmailing him and why he was dissuading you from writing that exposé. In spite of all that, he did help me with uncovering what was going on in that massage parlor. But I still think he's a bad husband."

Paige snorted. "Who would want to blackmail my Joey, and why? He's a good man, and he loves me."

I sighed. "Look, I'm not a marriage counselor or anything, so I'll just let the photos speak for themselves."

"Photos? What photos?"

"You'll get them soon enough." I made a mental note to give the confiscated photos back to Allison, hoping she would show them to Paige without a hitch.

We ended the call. Around nine thirty, I decided to take a quick trip downstairs to check my mailbox. As I closed my apartment door behind myself, something bright sparkled from the corner of my eye. I looked next door at Beth's head shop. Dozens of hand-drawn, hand-painted antiwar posterboards and picket signs were leaned up against the wall by her door. A couple of the signs had letters covered in glitter. I arched an eyebrow. *What in the...* Beth sure did have a severe case of that... "anachronistic displacement" thing, or whatever the chief had called it. How and when would she ever be cured of that madness?

Beth's door opened, and a cloud of skunk-smelling cannabis smoke billowed out. She exited, carrying another large, colorfully decorated posterboard under one arm. She wore a white gypsy blouse, abstract-print harem pants, and a pair of brown heeled clogs. Her face was taut. She was planning something, all right. She looked at me, and her expression softened. "Great rising, Tootsie," she said in greeting then leaned the poster against the wall with the others.

"Hey." I gestured at the posters. "What's all this?"

"I'm travelling to Washington DC this weekend to join the war protests. We're marching on the Capitol."

I blinked. "'We'?" *There are actually more crazy people like Beth?*

She tilted her head curiously. "Yes, Tootsie. All of my fellow brothers and sisters will be there. We are making our voices heard loud and clear."

"You mean they don't realize the war is over either?"

"Of course the war is not over, Tootsie. Whatever gave you that idea?"

"Um… you're going all the way down to DC to protest a war that's already ended."

She snorted. "Oh, for Pete's sake. Let's not go over this again. When will you get that ridiculous propaganda out of your head?"

"It's not propaganda."

"Those bastards have brainwashed you so they can keep funding this war. Don't give in to the lies, Tootsie."

I sighed. "Whatever you say. Have a safe trip to DC, I guess." I turned to leave. Talking to Beth always exhausted my brain.

"Wait," Beth called.

I paused and then looked over my shoulder.

"Would you mind helping me make a sign?" she asked.

I furrowed my brow. "Don't you think you have enough signs?"

She frowned. "You're upset I'm going to Washington, aren't you?"

I opened my mouth to reply then closed it and rethought my answer. That was a loaded question.

"Uh… yeah. Yeah, that's right. I am upset. I'm very upset. Why can't you protest closer to home? Like downtown at city hall or something?"

"No, Tootsie. In order to make change, you have to get to the root of the problem. And the root lies in the heart of this nation's capital. I must go there and make my voice heard. Will you at least consider coming with me?"

"Oh, no," I said quickly. "That is, I don't have time. My job's pretty demanding. In fact, I'm about to go on a case right now."

"Oh, all right. Well, I'll leave a blank poster and some craft supplies for you to make a sign, at least. Thank you."

"B-But I didn't agree to—"

"Tootsie. I am so honored and grateful to know such a kind and considerate person like you. You are a true friend." She smiled and went back inside the shop before I could say another word.

I let out a deep sigh, my shoulders slouching, then I rubbed my temples. *Ugh, my head hurts.* I quickly went downstairs to the first floor and made a beeline to my mailbox in the vestibule. I unlocked my box and pulled out the accumulation of mail for that day and the one before. I found a couple of bills, a bunch of junk advertisements, a letter from my parents, and a *Service Merchandise* catalog.

The passing *clip-clop* of high-heeled shoes drew my attention from my mail to the back of a woman in a navy-blue suit carrying a small brown portfolio under her arm. She paused in front of the enclosed black-felt letterboard directory in the lobby then approached the cage elevator. Like most of the elevators around the city, it had been out of commission for I don't know how long, and the repairmen were dragging their feet, with no urgency to fix it. After a few moments of pressing the call buttons with no luck, the mysterious woman sighed and headed up the stairs.

Hmm... I frowned. Her professional attire reminded me of the way Allison was dressed when she first came to see me. I wondered if this woman was another potential client? I hurried up the stairs after her.

The woman reached the top of the stairs of the fourth floor and stood there a moment, staring into the small hallway of doors. I stopped also, one flight shy of her, curious as to which door she would pick. Her head turned, and she looked back for a moment. I sank out of her line of sight and waited. The clip-clopping of her shoes quickened down the hallway. I took another peek and noticed she was gone, so I climbed up the final flight of stairs and stood quietly in the hallway, watching from a distance. The woman had approached Crazy Bob's door. Was she another weirdo coming to harass him?

The woman knocked on the door. It wasn't a pounding like Bob's previous visitors, so that was a good sign. *Maybe she's a friend or family member. Maybe this will be my chance to finally see Bob—all of Bob—in the flesh!*

She waited a moment, knocked again, and leaned in close to the door. "Mr. Doe, it's Maya Stephens from the agency. We talked yesterday," she announced.

I blinked. *Agency? They talked? He speaks?* My mind was swimming with thoughts. *Hmm... so his last name is Doe. Bob Doe. Kinda odd. A little generic, but whatever.*

I heard the rattle of a chain and the flip of the lock. The door creaked open slightly. *This is it.* Maya obviously knew him, and he knew her, so I couldn't wait to see what he looked like and maybe figure out what he was up to in there. Finally, I'd find closure about the mysterious Crazy Bob.

But the door remained half open, and nobody appeared on the other side.

Darn it! I quietly stepped a little closer.

"Good morning, Mr. Doe. May I come in?" Maya asked, craning her neck slightly.

Bob's thick, hairy arm appeared from behind the door. The sleeve of his red-plaid flannel shirt was rolled halfway up his bulging bicep. He made a sweeping gesture with his hand, welcoming her inside.

"Wonderful. Thank you. This will only take a few minutes of your time." Maya started to squeeze through the narrow space.

I blinked. *He's there!* I sprinted toward the door. *Maybe I can take just one little peek—*

As soon as the woman was all the way inside, the door began to close. I stopped short of the door as it slammed just inches away from my face. I caught a whiff of cigarettes and whiskey.

Grumbling, I shook my fist. *Okay, if I can't see him, then maybe I can hear him.* I slowly pressed my ear to the door. All I could hear was bits and pieces of Maya's voice, something about a contract renewal. Bob didn't say anything—or maybe he did, but I couldn't hear it. Maybe he was whispering his replies in her ear. *This is ridiculous.* What kind of secret meeting was going on in there, anyway? I could bust an entire drug ring, but this one man next door seemed to always be two steps ahead of me. *Some detective I am.*

I decided to stick around for a bit. I couldn't miss a moment of this opportunity. I glanced at my apartment door, and a blank posterboard and a basket of craft supplies were leaning against it. I sighed, having already forgotten about the picket sign I'd somehow involuntarily agreed to design for Beth's imaginary protest.

Footsteps echoed up the stairs. I quickly pulled away from Crazy Bob's door. A long-haired shaggy man wearing a tie-dye

Bohemian shirt and holey, dirt-and-grass-stained bell-bottom jeans ascended the steps. He glanced my way then grinned, giving me the shaka sign as he walked past in his pair of old, worn Chuck Taylor sneakers. The odor of freshly smoked cannabis emanated from him.

I didn't have to guess where he was headed. The hippie guy strutted into Beth's head shop, the little bell over her door jingling happily.

Crazy Bob's door opened. I jumped back, leaned against the opposite wall, and began thumbing through my *Service Merchandise* catalog, trying to act casual.

"Thank you, Mr. Doe," Maya said. "I'm very glad that we're continuing this partnership. Next week is going to be out of sight!" She squeezed back through the small space in the door.

As soon as she was outside, the door shut quickly.

I pushed off the wall and caught up with the woman before she headed downstairs. "Um, excuse me," I said. "Can we talk?"

Maya looked at me, her forehead wrinkling curiously. "I'm sorry, but I'm really in a hurry."

"It'll only take a second. My name's Tootsie. My office is right next door to that man you just saw. I'm wondering about him."

Her eyebrow arched. "What do you mean?"

"I mean, I've been in this building for years, and I don't even know who he is."

"Mr. Doe prefers his privacy."

"Is Mr. Doe really his name?"

"My associates and I refer to him as John Doe to protect his privacy."

"Is he... some sort of famous celebrity?" I widened my eyes.

"I cannot divulge that information."

I spotted the portfolio under her arm, which had the initials
B. R. ingrained the lower corner. "What agency are you from?"

"I'm very sorry, Tootsie, but I really must be going. Please
excuse me." She sidled around me.

I opened my mouth to ask another question but finally gave
up as she went down the stairs. Her lips were sealed tighter than
Spandex. *B. R.... what kind of agency is that? It's a possible clue, but
it could literally mean anything.* Whatever was going on in Crazy
Bob's apartment wasn't meant for the world's ears. Still, I
wondered. Was Bob on the level? I would find out what he was
all about if it was the last thing I did.

CHAPTER 24

I can't believe I'm actually doing this, I thought as I sifted excess glitter off the posterboard and funneled it back into its small tubular container. Designing a picket sign for Beth had taken me all of ten minutes—a sign for a war that had been declared over globally for the past month. *Maybe she just never got the memo... whatever.* If she wanted to waste a trip to DC, who was I to stop her? I kept the sign simple: a giant glittering peace symbol. Once I finished, I cleaned up the rest of the craft items from my desk and leaned the sign outside my door for the glue to dry. Afterward, I gave Beth a quick call to stop by and pick up her things.

I slid the thick, dog-eared Manhattan phone book sitting on my desk closer to myself and thumbed through the Yellow Pages section in search of that mysterious B. R. agency. Maya, the woman who'd stopped by Crazy Bob's apartment, was dressed like someone who worked in one of those thirty-story executive buildings, so Manhattan seemed like the obvious place to start my search. As luck would have it, no agency with the name B. R. was listed in the phone book—at least, none in Manhattan. The number of different agencies that had B. R. initials made pinpointing it nearly impossible. Maybe the agency wasn't in Manhattan at all. I would have to search all the phone books from all the boroughs. Calling each business would take me all day, and even then, if they were the silent types, like Maya, they probably wouldn't tell me anything about Crazy Bob.

With a heavy sigh, I shut the Manhattan phone book and slid it aside. I spotted the silhouetted outline of a large man approaching my door. I squinted, trying to discern the visitor between the half-opened door blinds.

The man tried the knob then knocked. "Tootsie, it's me. You there?"

I exhaled. *Chief Lewis.* I rushed to the door and opened it.

The chief, dressed in a hunter-green suit and yellow tie, carried a large Bloomingdale's shopping bag in one hand and a briefcase in the other.

"Hey, Chief," I said. My gaze swiveled to the bag. "You, uh… went shopping?"

"In a manner of speaking," he said. He handed me the bag and let himself in.

I shut and locked the door then peeked inside the bag. My favorite London Fog trench coat was there, along with my green Stetson fedora. At the bottom of the bag was my wallet. I gasped and looked up. "You found them!"

"No, Captain Peterson found them," Chief Lewis said. "The shop owner was very generous in covering your ass when he told the captain that they belonged to one of his customers."

I raised my eyebrows. "Diego?"

"That's right."

"Wow, that was swell of him. He also helped me find that secret tunnel in the floor."

The chief clenched his jaw. "Look. I'm trying to keep you out of this as much as I can, but you're not making it easy."

I cringed at the angry edge in his voice. Things were hot for me right now, and for good reason. But I had no intentions of showing my face around the massage parlor anyway. Too many bad memories haunted that building.

"Don't worry, Chief. I promise you I won't go near there anymore. I'll write up a detailed tip sheet to help you with the investigation."

"You do that, and leave the rest of this case to us, understand?" He gave me a stern look.

I nodded and slid into my chair behind my desk.

Chief Lewis plopped down in the uncomfortable wooden school chair that sat before my desk. Unlike my clients, he didn't seem to mind it. I guessed his rear had grown accustomed to hard chairs from sitting in the one in his office for so long. He opened his briefcase, and his expression softened. "I found these."

"Huh?" I wrinkled my brow.

He pulled out a manila envelope and shook the contents. Then he opened the envelope and retrieved my photos and negatives of Joey. "The man in these photos was identified as Joey Russell of Gatestar Media."

I beamed, relieved that the chief was able to find the negatives. "Great! Where were the negatives?"

"In a safe, along with half a million bucks, stashed away in Felix Audrey's office."

I whistled. "Half a mill! Sounds like a job well done for you guys." I reached out for the envelope.

Chief Lewis shook his head. "No can do, Tootsie. The investigators want to know what connection Joey has with all of this. These photos are officially evidence."

I rolled my eyes. "Like I said before, it's circumstantial. Joey told me he was being blackmailed. I was hired to take those photos, but for an entirely different reason. I had no idea the photos would end up in the hands of a criminal."

"Who hired you?"

I grimaced. I really hated talking about my clients' cases, but this was a police matter, after all. "It was a Gatestar Media employee. She was just trying to get some evidence photos taken of Joey cheating on her boss. Leave her out of this, please, Chief. She's not a part of this mess."

Chief Lewis rubbed his chin. "That depends on the evidence presented. As soon as we get this arrest warrant, we're going to bring Joey in for questioning. I'm sure we'll get something out of him."

"Maybe..." Since Mr. Audrey was locked away, I thought Joey might be more inclined to tell his whole story to the police, especially when the negatives were in their possession. "You guys have the carrot, so dangle it in front of Joey, and he'll tell you everything you want to know."

"Oh, I intend to do just that." He glanced at one of the photos, and his mouth twisted into an amused smirk. "Everyone at the station was cracking up over these. Is that a mole on his ass, or did he forget to wipe?"

I laughed. "Yeah, that's his freaky Cyclops eye on his butt. I thought my camera lens was gonna break."

"By the way, it turned out we were able to match several fingerprints on those photos you gave me to a few of Felix Audrey's men. It was a little difficult because there were so many prints muddled together, but we managed to pinpoint some names."

"That's great, Chief. You guys are really on top of things."

"Hey, when you're dealing with an operation like this, you have to be." He perked up. "Oh, I almost forgot." From his briefcase, he pulled out the two newspapers I'd asked for and handed them to me. "Here."

I took the papers and turned my attention to the front page of the *City Star Daily*. "Massive Underground Prostitution and Drug Operation Foiled!" the headline read. I set the paper on my desk with a sigh.

"Nice headline, eh?" Chief Lewis said. "That operation was a heroin mill using fentanyl."

"*Fentanyl?*" I repeated, widening my eyes. "Geez Louise! That stuff's more lethal than heroin by itself. And to mix the two?"

"That's right," the Chief said. "And the detectives were able to link it back to the string of recent drug overdose deaths around the city. The little packets with the purple flowers on them were the same ones found at every one of those death scenes."

All I could think about in that moment was how many others might have fallen victim to those drugs before I'd stumbled on that operation. "They killed so many people…"

Chief Lewis slapped a hand on the desk, causing me to jump and straighten in my chair. "Hey," he said in a stern tone. "You can't save the world. But mark my word—there will be a special place in hell waiting for those murderers. For now, though, I hope they rot in a cell for the rest of their lives."

"How can we be certain that will happen?"

"If I have any hope left in the justice system, then it's now. There is too much evidence stacked against that operation. We found ledgers, receipts, press passes, even a ticket to a medical convention in Boston this weekend. It was like Christmas in there. It's going to take time, but I think there's a strong case here."

"I see…"

Still, I couldn't shake off a funny feeling in my gut. Something bothered me, but I wasn't sure what it was. Another article on the front page caught my eye: "Harry Lawton, Political Pundit for Future's Century Party, Arrested." That really made me wonder what kind of book Crazy Bob was writing.

At last, I took a look at the *National Esquire*. Newsie's grand article about the exploding candy filled the entire front page. With a sigh, I stuffed the paper in my desk drawer. *Meh, I'll read it later when I'm bored.* I returned my attention to Chief Lewis. "Was there anything else you needed to talk about?"

"Yes," he said, shifting in his chair. He reached into his suit jacket's inner pocket and pulled out an envelope. "This is for you." He slid it across the desk.

Curious, I stared at the envelope a moment with a raised eyebrow. Then I picked it up and slowly opened it. Inside was a check made out to me for a thousand dollars. I gasped, dropping the check. It fluttered back to the desk.

I looked back at him, bewildered. "Chief, this… this must be some mistake."

He shook his head. "It's no mistake. You're owed every penny and more."

"But I don't understand. You didn't hire me."

"You disobeyed me, and for that, I'm furious; however, I still must give credit where it's due. You found their operation, and you escaped. You risked your life and helped us in more ways than you can imagine. You deserve to be paid for your service."

I smiled weakly. "I appreciate it, but…" I stuffed the payment back into the envelope and slid it back to him. "I'm not on your payroll. I can't accept money from you."

He slid it back to me more firmly. "You can, and you will. Consider it a donation if you must. Your work is not going unnoticed. Thanks to you, we rounded up several crooked cops who were involved in this operation, Officer O'Connell being one of them."

I perked up. "O'Connell? You got him too?"

"Yeah. Didn't take long to find him. The bastard had a couple fingers missing, from a dog that attacked him, or so he claimed."

"O'Connell shot a man. I think it was the dog's owner. I guess O'Connell tried to shoot the dog too."

"Yeah, we found the man's body on that little service road just off Thirty-Second Avenue. Bullet right through the heart. The dog was all right. Pretty smart too. He's good at finding bad guys."

I smiled slightly. "The dog's name is Butch, by the way. He attacked O'Connell. I guess Butch sensed he was a crooked cop. That man was trying to save his dog from O'Connell beating on him."

"Unfortunately, he got caught in the crossfire. The paramedics pronounced him dead on their way to the hospital."

I sighed, slumping my shoulders.

"Needless to say, I'm pretty sure O'Connell will end up being charged with murder, not to mention losing his career in the police department."

I felt some relief at that. But the city's law enforcement still needed to be cleaned up a lot more. And I couldn't shake off the man's death. *Was all this my fault?*

"Some good news, though," the chief continued, interrupting my thoughts. "Lieutenant Saro suggested we try Butch out with a police K-9 team or maybe find him a home at one of the fire departments. Who knows?"

I smiled a little. "I think he'll be useful no matter where he goes."

Chief Lewis rose from the chair. "I need to get back to the precinct now."

I got up as well and saw him to the door. "Of course. Thanks for everything, Chief." I paused and sighed. "I'll get that tip sheet written up for you soon."

"Take your time." He stopped in the doorway and looked at me with his concerned gaze. "You take care of yourself, Tootsie. Okay? I mean it."

I gave him a small salute and a reassuring smile. "Don't I always? Catch ya later, Chief."

The bell above Beth's door jingled as the door opened and Beth exited, all smiles. Approaching my apartment, she took one look at Chief Lewis, and her smile quickly fell into a frown. "Oh..." She looked at me. "Tootsie, are you okay? Is this man bothering you?"

Chief Lewis raised his eyebrows.

I cleared my throat. "No, Beth. This man is with the police. He's, uh... helping me locate those evil guys in the suits who came here the other day."

His gaze shifted to me.

"Oh!" Beth's warm expression returned. "Hello. I'm Beth. Nice to meet you. We had G-men in this building, trying to solicit us in joining the war. Can you believe it? It's terrible."

Chief Lewis whipped his head back and forth between me and Beth. "Ah... what?"

I cleared my throat again and changed the subject. "Uh, Beth, I finished your sign, see?" I gestured to the glittering peace sign on the posterboard leaned up against the wall.

Her face brightened more. "Oh my goodness, Tootsie! This is wonderful! Yes! A thousand times yes! This means the world to me! Thank you so much for your help. You have no idea how many people you will save with this!"

"Um, it's just a sign," I said.

Beth carefully picked up the posterboard. "It's not just a sign. It's hope. It's up to us to make a change in the world. You are a bright, shining star, Tootsie! That beacon of light in this dark, scary world!" She rushed back to her apartment with the sign and shut the door.

I exhaled.

Chief Lewis swiveled his gaze to me, his eyebrow arched.

I shook my head at his silent, confused question. "Don't ask," I muttered and closed my office door.

CHAPTER 25

The night of the Ali-Lyle watch party at Roy's bar, I didn't feel much in a celebrating mood. I was thinking about Sherry and all the other victims involved in that big bust. Was Chief Lewis going to be able to help them all? I would hate to see them go back to that life again—especially Sherry, who had those big dreams of being a pastry chef. Despite what those goons had done, Sherry still had her spirit. I hoped the other victims were just as strong.

I decided to give Luis the Janitor a call, to let him know the news about his uncle Diego's shop.

"I'm sorry—it'll probably put a dent in his business for a while," I told Luis. "But that whole building has become a crime scene. I'm hoping your uncle will get some sort of compensation."

Luis sighed. "*Sí*. I hope so, but I'm not holding my breath. First my brother's adoption troubles, now this. *Tío* Diego is gonna be in a bad mood for a while. He hates not being able to work."

"Is there something else he can do in the meantime?"

"I don't know. I'm sure he'll figure out something. He always does. I'm just glad he's okay. *Muchas gracias*, Detective." He sighed again.

My conversation with Luis remained on my mind long after I hung up. I really didn't want to go to Roy's party, but Roy was counting on me to be there. After all, he had helped me out with the case. Showing up at his bar was the least I could do for him.

To my surprise, Sid took the night off to go with me to the watch party. The tough bulldog was a real gentleman, coming by my apartment and picking me up. We took a bus to Queens. It was weird not seeing Sid behind the wheel for a change, though he still wore his favorite brown newsboy cap. He was average height with a stocky build, and he wore a white T-shirt that showed off his big tattooed guns. I'd never felt safer than I did tonight. I sure wished he'd been around before, to deal with Frank and the rest of that gang at the massage parlor.

The bus dropped us off near Kronos Lounge, which sat on the corner of Hempstead Avenue and Springfield Boulevard. We walked the rest of the way.

"Thanks again for coming along, Sid," I said.

He grinned. "Hey, Ali's fightin.' I wouldn't miss that for nothin'!"

We finally reached Kronos Lounge, which was housed in a nondescript, graffiti-covered unit of a run-down building. Cars were parked along the curb on both sides of the street. None of Roy's bouncers were standing outside the bar's entrance, which gave me pause. As we drew near, I began to hear the sounds of music and laughing. I tugged on the entrance's barred metal door. It wasn't locked, so I let myself in.

Roy's friend and one of his bouncers, Mitts, stood at the entrance, looking ahead toward the bar, where a yellow portable television sat on the counter. Roy was fiddling with the foil-topped antennas while two of his gorgeous barmaids walked around, serving drinks. The mostly male crowd converged around the television while they chatted with one another and downed their drinks. Another group of guys played pool in the corner, and six women sat around a tiny table, gabbing on about their day. A short, stout man wove through the crowd, flashing wads of money in his hand as he took bets.

Sid grinned. "Now, this here's my kinda place!"

Mitts whipped his head toward us, his expression briefly shocked, then relaxed. "Oh, hey, Tootsie. You made it." He glanced at Sid. "Wait, isn't that…" He narrowed his eyes a moment then did a double take. "You gotta be kidding me…" His gaze swiveled back to me, and he grimaced. "Seriously, Tootsie? You and the taxi guy?"

Sid growled at Mitts then raised a fist in warning. "Why I oughtta…"

"Whoa! Hold on, Sid." I said, rushing between them and spacing them farther apart.

Sid didn't take his eyes off Mitts. "You think I ain't got no decency, punk?" The Italian bulldog bellowed.

Mitts held his hands up. "Uh… s-sorry, haven't seen you in a while. And it's not often I see Tootsie with another man…"

"Sid's a friend—always has been," I said. "And I'm here to have fun with my friends."

Mitts stepped aside to let us pass but still gave Sid a wary stare. "Right on. Well, uh, make yourselves at home. The fight's gonna start soon."

I nodded to Sid to let him go ahead. While Sid wandered off into the crowd, I stayed behind to chat with Mitts a little more. "I can't believe Roy still has you working tonight," I said.

Mitts laughed. "Yeah, he's a slave driver, ain't he? But naw, I'm off the clock. I don't care so much for the fight. I'm just sticking around to keep the peace."

"Is Newsie here?"

"Naw, he's layin' low. Y'know how he is."

"Yeah." I was a little relieved to know I wouldn't be confronting him tonight. He would most likely talk my ear off.

"Here we go!" Roy announced once he got the television picture clear.

Cheers swept through the bar, and the crowd edged closer to the television.

"Last call! Get 'em in, folks!" the short bookie announced, waving a handful of bills.

"Spot me! Spot me!" Sid called, waving a ten-dollar bill.

The pool players abandoned the table and migrated to the television. I left Mitts and joined the crowd. I squeezed my way through and reached Roy, who was alone at the other end of the bar, fixing himself a drink.

"Hey," I said, sliding onto the last empty stool at the end of the bar.

Roy paused and looked up, and his face brightened like the sunrise. "Tootsie! When did you get here?"

"A little while ago. You were busy fiddling with that television set."

"Hey, I got that baby for a steal at J&R." Roy finished mixing his drink—a rusty nail—then pulled down another empty glass from the holder above the bar. "You're in for a treat tonight. I'll whip you up a Tootsie Roll cocktail for the occasion."

I opened my mouth, about to refuse the drink because I didn't consume alcohol while I was working. But technically, I wasn't working now. I leaned an elbow on the counter and stared idly at the television, where the prefight formalities were going on live at the Las Vegas Convention Center. My mind was racing. Racing about Sherry—*is she okay?* Joey—*has Paige finally come to her senses?* Frank—*how long is he going to be put away? Forever, I hope.* Newsie's unbelievable article—*how can people in this city be so gullible?*

"Hey, you all right?" Roy asked, disrupting my thoughts.

I swiveled my gaze to him as he set the newly created Tootsie Roll cocktail in front of me.

"Yeah," I finally muttered. "Just one of those days."

"Did you finally get your case solved with your precious pictures?" he asked.

I smiled slightly. He had no idea. And for his sake, it was best that he didn't know anything about that—especially the things that had happened to me at the parlor. Roy was annoying sometimes, but in the end, he cared. It was bad enough that Chief Lewis worried about me like an overprotective father. I didn't need Roy to be all up in my business too.

"Yeah, case solved," I said. "Didn't Newsie tell you the good news?"

Roy rolled his eyes. "Only about fifty times today."

"Thankfully, he's not here."

"With this crowd? Never." He held up his drink. "Let's toast."

I slowly picked up my cocktail and scrunched my brow. "To what?"

"To us. To this moment. To the fact that you finally decided to take a damn break for a change. Maybe you're not as married to your job as I thought."

I quirked a smile. "I'm not married to my job, Roy. I'm just... doing my duty as a taxpaying citizen of this city."

"Touché." He clinked his glass with mine and took a sip.

I briefly sipped mine and set the glass down. The cocktail was delicious, but as usual, Roy really laid on the alcohol. I was too much of a lightweight to finish it all. I hated the disorienting feeling of not being in control.

Roy moved from around the counter, pulled up another stool near me, and sat. He was focused more on the television than my presence, and I was perfectly fine with that. I needed to be alone with my thoughts. The cheering in the bar rose as the main event got underway.

About thirty minutes passed. The shouting and screaming around me became white noise as I occasionally drew out of my thoughts and glanced at the fight. Mohammed Ali, who was wearing white trunks, seemed to be dominating Ron Lyle in the red trunks, with his signature butterfly-floating feet and bee-stinging hands.

Even Mitts had gotten a little more interested in the fight. He'd eventually migrated from his secluded spot by the door toward the rest of the crowd.

I traced a finger around the rim of my half-empty cocktail glass. The ice had melted and watered down the alcohol, which made the drink a little more tolerable. *I wonder how Sherry is doing?* I thought, taking a sip. While I was here at the party, that kid was still miserable somewhere. *Will she ever get reunited with her family? Or will she get passed off in the system with the millions of other kids?* I frowned. Then I perked up as an idea came to me. *Of course!* I tapped Roy on the shoulder.

"Wow! Look at that nice left! Bam!" Roy shouted over the cheers of the crowd, not acknowledging me.

The bell rang, signaling the end of the ninth round. I tapped Roy's shoulder again, a little harder.

He turned to me, grinning wide, as if he still hadn't felt my touch. "It's lookin' good so far, Tootsie," he said. "Ali's smokin' it right now!"

"That's nice," I said flatly. "Is your office open? I need to use your telephone."

His smile fell slightly. "Uh, yeah, sure. Everything okay?"

I slid off my stool. "Everything's fine. I'll be right back." I headed toward the back of the bar.

"Hurry up, round ten is about to start soon!" Roy called.

I entered Roy's office and shut the door. My ears were ringing from the muffled noise outside. I picked up the phone and called Chief Lewis. He picked up on the fifth ring.

"Hey, Chief. Not watching the fight tonight?" I said.

"Oh, I got the radio on," he said. "I may be working late again, but I ain't missing Ali. What do you need, Tootsie?"

"Well, I was wondering if there's been any update yet on Sherry."

He sighed. "Yeah, there's been no luck in locating any family. Her mother got stabbed to death in a gang fight a couple years ago. We can't seem to identify or locate her father or any other family member at this point. My friend Sofia, who's a social worker, is going to take her to Child Protective Services."

I idly wove the coiled telephone cord between my fingers. *No parents... no family...* "If she goes to CPS, does that mean she can be adopted?"

There was a brief pause. "It depends. Why?"

I explained my case with Luis, his brother, and their adoption woes. I told him about Sherry's dream of becoming a pastry chef. It seemed like a perfect match. Maybe Luis's family could adopt Sherry if the powers-that-be allowed it. Sherry seemed like a great kid. She deserved to be happy after having endured so much darkness. And she'd finally have a family—a *real* family.

"That's a bit of a stretch, Tootsie, but I'll talk to Sofia and see what can be done," the chief said.

My heart pounded. I knew everything was out of his hands, but for Sherry's sake, I prayed he might be able to pull a few strings.

The floor vibrated. The cries and howls of the bar crowd rose like thunder.

"Uh-oh, sounds like I'm missing some good stuff," I said.

"Damn, yeah. I'll talk to you later. Lyle's getting pummeled right now."

I hung up the phone and left the office. As soon as I opened the door, the crowd noise became deafening. Most of the patrons were cheering, dancing, and celebrating, while others sulked their way toward the exit with their heads lowered. Sid was on the dance floor with a few other patrons, drinks in hand, doing a silly celebratory dance. *Wow, didn't think the old bulldog could get down like that.*

"This round's on me!" Roy announced, holding up glasses sloshing with liquor. Whistles and shouts swept through the crowd. I glanced at the television just in time to see Ali holding his arms up in victory.

Roy spotted me and rushed over, handing me another Tootsie Roll cocktail. "He won! He won! Eleven rounds, baby! TKO! Drink up! Tonight, we celebrate!" he piped.

I pushed the drink away. "No thanks. Glad to hear he won, though."

His eyes dulled slightly. "So I guess it's back to work for you, then?"

I shrugged. "Come tomorrow, yeah."

He set the drink on the counter and looked at me intently. "I really hate that you're a workaholic. I've missed you."

"You've been doing just fine around here without me, Roy," I said, resisting the urge to roll my eyes at his sappy lines.

"Hey, just you being here made this night extra special for me."

"Please, Roy. You were more focused on that fight."

"What if I was? The fact that you came here tonight means all the world to me. Thank you for coming." He slowly leaned his face closer to mine.

I placed my index finger over his lips, stopping him from going any farther. "You're welcome. Good night, Roy." I dropped my hand and headed for the door. Sid was having too much fun, so I decided to let him be and took the bus back to my apartment. Along the way, I thought about my brief chat with the chief.

There was hope for Sherry, hope for a little light in all the darkness of death and despair. Maybe Roy was right. *Tonight just might be a great night after all.*

CHAPTER 26

Twelve days later...

It was late afternoon, almost dinnertime, and I had a meeting with Chief Lewis. He'd picked the time and place. I had only an address somewhere in Mott Haven, no phone number. I didn't understand what the secret was all about, but I went along with it. I just hoped the meeting place had food.

More details about the big drug-and-sex-trafficking bust had continued to emerge. As I'd suspected, Allison's friend, Cindy, was heavily involved in the operation. Turned out she was being paid under the table by Mr. Audrey to get some scandalous photos taken of Joey. Moreover, she was forging press passes for his associates to attend a medical convention in Boston, to expand Mr. Audrey's shady business, no doubt. Poor Allison had been hoodwinked by her sisterly friend all that time. Needless to say, the news of Cindy's arrest hit her hard.

There was some good news, however. Most of the women rescued from the operation had gone straight, found jobs, and were living better lives. The rest weren't so lucky, unfortunately, as they'd returned to their old lives on the streets. And Sherry... well, last I heard, she was still stuck in the system. Apparently, my idea didn't fly with CPS. The outcome hurt every time I thought about that, but like Roy and Chief Lewis always said, I couldn't save the world.

Either way, Sherry was in a much better place than before. If only she could find a family...

I stood from my desk and stretched. I'd been sitting for hours, working on another tip report for Chief Lewis. Sighing, I looked at all the unfinished paperwork spread over the desk. I still had a long way to go in documenting the case. I was ready to be done with that nightmare once and for all. As I gathered the typed papers into a neat pile, one of the papers peeked out. Joey Russell's name caught my eye, and I grinned.

Finally, Paige had come to her senses when Joey had gotten called in by the police for questioning. The scandalous photos were displayed to Joey's detriment and Paige's horror. The truth all came out when Paige explained her exposé on Mr. Audrey to the police and Joey admitted to dissuading his wife because of Mr. Audrey blackmailing him. Paige ended up filing for divorce that day and called me about the news.

"I can't believe my Joey. *My* Joey!" she said.

Part of me wanted to tell her, "I told you so," but I couldn't bring myself to add more salt to her wounds. Instead, I said, "I'm sorry."

"Hmph. That cheating son of a bitch won't get no sympathy from me. Ugh. I can't believe I loved him."

"Hey, we all make mistakes. It sounds like the paper will be bigger and better now that he's gone."

"This paper was never going anywhere."

"That's great to hear, 'cause I need my daily dose of *Dick Tracy* strips, y'know."

She chuckled. "Detective Carter, after what you did, I'm giving you a complimentary lifetime subscription to the *Tri-City Beat*."

I blinked. "R-Really? That's swell of you, Mrs. Russell!"

"Please, call me Paige. I consider you a friend now. Besides, I'll be damned if I have to keep that last name any longer."

We had talked a little more. Paige sounded much more confident and in higher spirits before we ended the call. I was happy for her and everyone else who worked there, including Luis and Allison.

My mind returned to the present. I was going to be late for the meeting with Chief Lewis if I didn't hurry. I yanked open my bottom desk drawer and took twenty dollars from my wallet— more than enough to get me to my meeting, grab a bite to eat afterward, and come back. A glint from my old police badge beneath my wallet and gun caught my eye. It was a constant reminder of why I quit that old life, the reason I became a shamus. I couldn't look back to the past anymore. That case with Mr. Audrey's gang proved that.

You had your run. It's time to retire you for good. I tore my gaze from the badge, slammed the drawer shut, and stuck the money in my pocket. Marching to the front door, I glanced at the coat rack, where my hat and trench coat hung. Since it was just a casual meeting and I wasn't currently working on an active case, I decided to forego my signature uniform. That was usually unheard of for me, but sometimes I liked to surprise myself now and then.

Opening the front door, I spotted a small, rectangular package wrapped in brown paper sitting at my doorstep. My skin crawled with goosebumps as I stared at the suspicious package. *Oh no... I wasn't expecting any packages. I bet this is a "surprise" from one of Mr. Audrey's associates.* Someone was already out to get me. Assuming the worst, I had to get whatever this was out of the building and away from innocent people. But doing the latter was going to be hard in this city. I stared at the simply wrapped package once more. How many times had I read about Dick Tracy encountering suspicious packages in the comics? But this situation was no comic.

Wait... none of Mr. Audrey's goons know that I'm a detective, that I work here... do they? I thought back on my case. No one knew... no one but Allison. And Paige. Maybe Harry Lawton and his friend, too, but Chief Lewis had taken care of them.

I blinked. Maybe this package was from Joey. Maybe he was getting revenge against me for his wife divorcing him. All the paranoia was making my head hurt and my stomach churn. Either way, I had to deal with the package. Finally, I took several deep breaths, bent down, and with both hands, carefully picked it up. It was light, but it had a slight bit of weight to it. It was smooth on the top and bottom, but I could feel small indentations and grooves on the sides. *What is this? A book?* I listened carefully for mechanical sounds but heard nothing. It seemed harmless enough, but after all that'd happened recently, I didn't want to take any chances. I slowly walked down the stairs, keeping the package level and steady. My heart pounded, fast and furious, as I assumed the worst. I reached the third floor without a hitch, but as I hit the second floor landing, a young woman came walking up the stairs toward me while she held her little boy's hand. I grimaced.

No! No! Not here, not now! I swore under my breath as the mother and child walked closer. The woman flashed me a curious gaze. I did an about-face, carefully went back up the stairs to the third floor, and waited. To my relief, the woman walked through a door that read Geoff & Sons Insurance Brokers on the glass. It was the only business on the second floor, along with two vacant units. As soon as the door closed, I hurried back down the stairs. I made it to the lobby in one piece—literally—and rushed out the entrance door.

Outside, I looked around. This wasn't a busy main street, but people were still walking about. I had no safe place to get rid of the package without possibly endangering innocent people—if this package was, indeed, an explosive. I had to assume the worst. I eyed a row of steel garbage cans sitting on the curb. *That will have to do,* I thought, making a beeline for them.

"Outta the way!" a man called.

I halted mere inches from the garbage cans. Out of my periphery, a tall shadow quickly came down the sidewalk at me. I turned my head.

Crash!

Blackness. My back hit the concrete, taking my breath away, and the package flew out of my hands. The heavy weight of another body pressed down on top of me. Groaning, I slowly opened my eyes. A man wearing a tank top and shorts quickly got off me and stood, steadying himself on his roller skates. Scowling at me, he swiped up a blue Mets baseball cap from the ground and slapped it back on his head. "What the hell is wrong with you, lady?" he barked. "Watch where the fuck you're goin'!"

I took a second to regain my bearings then frowned at the stranger. "Hey, you ran into me!" I retorted.

Rolling his eyes, he waved a hand dismissively. "Bah, forget it." He skated past me, muttering under his breath, "Stupid broad..."

I watched him until he was out of sight. Then my mind quickly drew back to my current problem. I gasped. *The package. It's gone!* I looked around frantically and spotted the package in the gutter. Part of the brown paper had been ripped away, revealing the letters *eut* on a glossy surface. I blinked. *So it is a book.* I hopped to my feet and retrieved it from the gutter, which was dry, thankfully. My anxiety subsiding, I carefully tore away the rest of the brown paper. Sure enough, it *was* a book, a dust-jacketed hardcover titled *Maxie Barker, Super Sleuth* in big, bold letters. Beneath the title was the name R. John Doewell and the words *New York Times* Bestselling Author beneath that. I stared at the author's name set against the cover's orange-hued color scheme. *R. John Doewell...* I blinked. *John Doe? Is that...*

Opening the book, I checked the dust jacket's inside flaps for clues. There were no photos of him, unfortunately. The author biography mentioned that he was a former political columnist. His bibliography page contained a list of published political satire works, his most recent titled *Taking the Law out of Future's Century.*

I raised an eyebrow. *Law... Future's Century... Harry Lawton?* So that must've been what Sue-Happy Harry was all up in arms about. Was this Maxine Barker book another one of his political satires? Sure sounded quirky enough. I turned to the copyright page. There, I noted a particular line of interest. R. John Doewell was currently being represented by the Brook and Richter Literary Agency. *Brook and Richter—B. R.* Everything made sense. That woman must've been his literary agent.

Relieved that mystery was finally solved, I flipped through a couple more pages. I paused at the dedication page.

"To the kind girl next door.
Thanks for keeping the vermin away."

I swallowed. Was this really Crazy Bob? *Have I been living next door to a world-famous author all this time?* I rushed back inside and up the stairs to Crazy Bob's door. I knocked several times and called, "Bob? Are you in there? Is this your book? I just wanted to say thanks." I waited a few moments, but nobody answered. With a sigh, I dropped off the book in my apartment and returned downstairs.

Back outside, I walked to the Parkchester subway station and took the train down to the Brook Avenue station in Mott Haven. Though most of the tourist groups were starting to thin, riding the subway around this time was still relatively safe. It was plenty packed with well-dressed people on their way home from work.

Emerging from the underground station, I pulled from my pocket the slip of paper containing the address I'd written down. According to it, the meeting place was a short walk up East 138th Street. I spotted Chief Lewis's red car parked along the curb, and I knew I was close. I looked at the row of businesses nearby: a Dominican bakery, which looked too tiny to seat customers, an electronics store, a salon, and a Puerto Rican restaurant. I tried the latter.

The restaurant's weathered green-and-yellow awning read La Isla Gran Bonita. A neon Open sign flashed in the restaurant's glass window. A construction worker exited. The older, greying gentleman looked at me and tilted his head curiously. "*¿Entrando, jovencita?*" he asked, holding the door open.

Smiling, I stepped inside. "*Sí. Gracias,*" I replied.

He flashed a grin, released the door, and left. I inhaled the mouthwatering mixed scents of spices, garlic, and various types of meat. I loved Puerto Rican food, but I couldn't remember the last time I'd had it. If Chief Lewis was in here, then he'd picked a good spot for a late lunch or early dinner.

I scanned the restaurant's midsize interior, which also had a smaller space in the back. Out of the seven tables in the main area, only two were empty. Behind the tall counter, a family of four scrambled to and from the kitchen. A short, slender waitress rushed out from behind the counter, expertly carrying a tray of plated food with one hand. She power walked over to one of the occupied tables.

Toward the back of the main area, near the corner, was Chief Lewis. He was sitting alone at a two-seater table, nursing a bowl of some kind of chunky soup while he read from an open book set on the table.

"Hey, Chief," I said, sliding into the empty chair across from him.

Keeping his gaze lowered, he dipped his spoon into the mysterious soup and brought it to his lips. "You're late again," he said then slurped.

I arched an eyebrow and glanced at a lighted plastic Marlboro clock hanging over the front entrance door. "Geez Louise. It's only five minutes this time."

"That's five minutes wasted." He finally looked up at me. "I need to be back at the station in an hour, so we'll have to make our meeting quick."

I stared at his soup, and my stomach growled. The young waitress walked by and delivered a plate of a lasagne-looking dish to a nearby table. My mouth watered.

"Okay, let's talk," I said, "but can I order some food first? I'm starving."

"Yeah." Chief Lewis nodded and motioned the waitress over. "You should really try this chicken *mofongo*. It's the best."

I moistened my lips. "Mmm. I love me some *mofongo*."

He dog-eared the page in his book, shut it, and set it aside. I eyed the cover. *Maxie Barker, Super Sleuth*.

"Hey, where'd you get that book?" I asked the chief.

He gave me a puzzled look. "Doubleday Bookstore. Why?"

"Do you always read R. John Doewell's books?"

"Sure. He's a popular political columnist. I like his satire books. This one is his first foray into fiction. It's a thriller. Pretty good. It came out this past Tuesday."

I rubbed my chin. *Tuesday?* Could Crazy Bob have left me a belated present on my doorstep? Maybe the book wasn't from him, after all. *Then who?* "Have you ever met R. John Doewell in person?" I asked.

Chief Lewis shrugged. "Nah. I just like his books. He's got so many. I swear, he must write all day and all night with no sleep. I don't know how he keeps churning 'em out. They're good, though, I'll tell ya what."

That didn't surprise me. Sometimes I would hear Crazy Bob typing away all night long. I'd become accustomed to the noise, just like the rest of New York's never-ending cacophony.

The waitress walked over, carrying a small notepad and pen in one hand and a menu in the other. I studied her up close. She looked like she was barely pushing sixteen. She wore a navy-blue waitress dress over a blue-checkered collared shirt. Her long, dark, wavy hair was tied back in a neat bun. A few freckles peppered her caramel skin around the bridge of her nose and across her soft cheekbones. She smiled cheerily at me, her light-brown eyes glittering like jewels. "*Hola*. Here's a menu for you.

Would you like to hear about the dinner specials?" she said, handing me the trifold paper menu.

I tilted my head, studying her a bit more. Something was familiar about her, but I couldn't quite put my finger on it— something about the eyes, the shape of the face. *Maybe my hungry brain is playing tricks on me.* "No, thanks," I said, politely rejecting the menu. I made a small head gesture toward Chief Lewis's dish. "I'll just have what he's having. And a 7-Up to drink, please."

"You should also try a slice of their coconut cake," Chief Lewis added then gobbled another spoonful of his meal. "I hear it's outta this world."

I smiled and nodded to the waitress. "You heard him."

The waitress scribbled my order on the notepad and tore off the sheet. "Okay, thank you. I'll be right back."

She walked off toward the counter, where she handed the slip of paper to a portly older woman standing behind the cash register. Something niggled in the back of my mind.

"Got some bad news for you, Tootsie," Chief Lewis said in a low volume, interrupting my thoughts.

Sighing, I propped my elbows on the table and rested my palms against my cheeks. "Out with it, Chief."

He slowed his chewing and stared down at his bowl, deep in thought. "The prosecutor said the charges against Cynthia Hempstead couldn't stick."

I blinked. "Cindy? How could that be? She was an accessory to a crime!"

"I agree, but my hands were tied with this one. This case was way too big, way too complicated. Her attorney found some legal loophole that cut her loose."

I gritted my teeth. "I can't believe this."

His gaze flicked back at me. "Look, I'm not thrilled about it either. But it is what it is."

"What about the rest of Mr. Audrey's gang?"

"So far, so good. Their bond has been denied. The evidence is as plain as day. They were directly involved in the operation, and there doesn't seem to be any legal loophole in the world that could save their asses—at least for now. There's still a lot more information that the DA is reviewing."

The waitress soon returned with my bowl of steaming-hot chicken *mofongo* and a bottle of 7-Up, which she popped the top off of. I inhaled the delectable aroma of garlic, chicken, and plantains, and all my anxiety over this case faded away. My stomach growled again, and I picked up my spoon.

"Here comes the cake," Chief Lewis said, cracking a smile.

Quiet footsteps approached, then I heard a gasp.

"Tootsie!" a girl exclaimed.

My body straightened at the familiar voice, and I froze. I looked across the table at Chief Lewis. His smile grew. He was up to something.

I slowly turned my head. There stood Sherry, full of smiles, full of life. She was dressed in the same navy-blue waitress outfit, and her brown hair was tied back into one long braid. The little bit of makeup she wore seemed to be done to hide the ugly scar on her face. But even through the thin layer, I could see the faint outline of that imperfection beneath. Despite that, her eyes glittered with new life, new hope. She was beautiful. She was happy.

"Sherry..." I murmured, staring at her with disbelief. Was this some sort of dream?

Sherry placed the cake plate on the table and gave me a hug. "I'm so happy to see you!"

My muscles stiffened a moment, but then I relaxed and wrapped my arms around her, returning the hug. My eyes watered, and I swallowed the tightness in my throat. "I... I can't believe it. I-I can't believe you're here. Wh-What are you doing here?" I stammered.

Sherry pulled back from the hug and beamed a perfect, pretty smile. "I got a family! This is my big sister, Emilia." She gestured to the older teenaged waitress.

"Ah. Remember how to say it?" Emilia said to her, wagging her finger.

"Oh!" Sherry cleared her throat, looked at the ceiling in brief thought, then said slowly to me, "*Esta es... mi... her-ma-na, Emilia.*"

I opened my mouth then closed it again, speechless. My mind was still spinning, still stuck on the fact that she'd actually gotten a new family. "That... that's pretty good," I said in an absent tone.

Sherry lifted her head proudly. "Thanks! Learning Spanish is fun. Emilia is such a good teacher. I also got a big brother, Angel. He works in the kitchen with my dad. My mom does the money stuff."

"Your idea wasn't so crazy after all," Chief Lewis said, as if he could hear my thoughts. "I talked to Sofia, my contact at CPS, and she was able to work some things out since we were unable to locate Sherry's biological family. I don't know what in the hell she did, but that's why I have her in my corner."

I grinned. That was the best news I'd heard all day. Sherry had a family! A real family! "That's wonderful!" I said, looking back at Sherry and Emilia.

"I'm going to the same school as Emilia too," Sherry added. "It's not far from here."

"Do you like school?" I asked.

Sherry nodded. "Yeah, it's fun. I wish I could take home economics class with Emilia, but I have to wait till high school. But that's okay. I get to make cakes, cookies, and all sorts of baked goods right here at the restaurant. It's so fun, and all the customers love them. Everything keeps selling out!"

"That's great. Well, I told you someday you'd get that bakery, and here you are, doing what you love," I said.

Sherry smiled broadly, the faint image of the scar rearing its ugly outline a bit more prominently beneath the thin layer of makeup. My smile faltered slightly. Even though she was living her dream, the image of her past was still branded on her.

Emilia gently tapped Sherry's shoulder. "C'mon, Sis. We got to go back to work now. Don't you still have those chocolate-chip cookies in the oven?"

Sherry perked up and gasped. "Oh yeah! I better check on them." She gave me a quick wave and said, "Bye, Tootsie!" Then she rushed back behind the counter and into the kitchen. Emilia left our table and approached another, where two patrons had just left, and cleared off the dirty dishes.

My cheeks were hurting from smiling so much. I looked at Chief Lewis. "You did this, Chief? Was this why you wanted to meet here?"

The chief took a sip from his bottle of dark-brown Dr. Pepper, attempting to hide his smile. "Maybe. Or maybe I just felt like having *mofongo*."

I gave him a dubious look. "Out of all the hundreds of Puerto Rican restaurants in this town, you just happened to choose this one?"

His face softened. "You're welcome."

I stared down at my food and fought down a smile. Despite the ups and downs, he still cared.

"Tootsie," the chief continued, "we may not see eye-to-eye on things sometimes, but I know that you are a good person. While I can't fault you for helping to solve this case, I want to remind you how valuable you are to not only me, but to the people of this city. Your passion to help people is strong." He frowned. "Strong enough that you would defy me. You need to curb those impulses, Rita. That sort of behavior is going to be used as a weapon against you one day if you're not careful. You need to slow down."

I casually stirred my spoon around my bowl. "Criminals never slow down." The more bad guys I helped put away, the more vigilant I had to be.

His frown deepened.

He had called me a good person. Maybe in another life I was. Good people deserved to live a better, happier life than me. I wasn't a good person—I lived with the nightmares, regrets, and skeletons of past choices I'd made. Maybe someday, if I ever quit this shamus life, I might know what being a good person is like.

Maybe...

CPSIA information can be obtained
at www.ICGtesting.com
Printed in the USA
BVHW081929201022
649927BV00016B/156/J